WICKED
gentleman

HART HOTELS & SPA

CHRISTY PASTORE

Cover design by Sofie Hartley of Hart & Bailey Design Co.
www.hartandbailey.com

Editing provided by Missy Borucki
missyborucki.com

Proofreading provided by K. Donald

Book formatting provided by Stacey Blake of Champagne Book Design
www.champagnebookdesign.com

WICKED
gentleman

WICKED
gentleman

Stevie

My Fairy Godmother had a wicked sense of humor, of that I was certain.

The first time I met Jackson Hart, I was on all fours with my ass in the air.

At the time of our meet *not* so cute, I didn't know that the handsome man with the most captivating blue eyes was the wealthy, charismatic, and hot as sin hotelier, oh and my new boss.

Well, technically he is my boss's boss. Just skimming the company manual was maybe not the best idea.

But, I digress. Working at Hart Hotels & Spa was a temporary plan.

Now, that plan has changed. Jackson Hart not only wanted me in his bed and in his life, he wanted me working alongside him.

Some offers are too good to pass up.

Jackson

Premium scotch aged to perfection, making money before sunrise, nine holes of golf and interesting conversation. Those are the things most known about me. Toss in a leggy brunette or a stunning redhead at a society event for good measure and there's a story to amuse the public. But, my story goes deeper—to the past that I left behind.

Sooner or later past and present collide. I never dreamed Stevie Brockman would be part of both.

dedication

Nora Bing—this one is for you.

playlist

Wicked Games by The Weeknd

Toothbrush by DNCE

Heathens by Twenty One Pilots

Body Say by Demi Lavato

Freak Me by Campsite Dream

wRoNg by Zayn featuring Kehlani

All I Ask Of You by Josh Groban with Kelly Clarkson

Feel It Still by Portugal. The Man

Now or Never by Halsey

Done For Me by Charlie Puth featuring Kehlani

Gold Dust Woman by Fleetwood Mac

Amanda by Boston

Never Be the Same by Camila Cabello

One Kiss by Calvin Harris with Dua Lipa

All The Stars by Kendrick Lamar with SZA

Meant to Be by Bebe Rexha featuring Florida Georgia Line

Piano Man by Billy Joel

Devil Callin' Me Back by Tim McGraw and Faith Hill

New York Minute by Don Henley

WICKED (adj.):
Naughtily or mischievously playful.

GENTLEMAN (n.):
A man of refinement.

prologue

Three Years Ago

"I AM TRULY SORRY," HE SAID, SMOOTHING HIS BLACK TIE. "IT'S nothing personal, only business."

Everything was collapsing around me, and I couldn't stop it. This was the fourth cancellation in a week. If I couldn't convince him to keep his contract, I would be spending another evening evaluating the financial state of my company and this time there would be no avoiding layoffs. I'd spent everything I had to build this hotel, and I wasn't about to lose it. There had been so much loss in my life recently, I couldn't take it if my business crumbled, reduced to bits of dust just like my personal life.

He cleared his throat, and tapped his finger to my desk. "You see, we don't feel that *your* hotel is the right one for our annual fundraiser."

"John, we've been hosting your events for the last two years. What has changed your mind?"

He stood. "I'm going to give you a bit of friendly advice. Sell your hotel. There is nothing left for you in Miami."

I cocked a brow. "Nothing left for me in Miami? Is this some kind of joke?" And now I was on my feet. My hands curled at my sides.

"Trust me, son, when I say that there is nothing funny about this particular situation." He pulled an envelope from his inside pocket and tossed it onto my desk. "Clear out, Jax, before there's more bloodshed. You're finished in Miami. I wished the circumstances were different, but that's how things are done around here."

He snagged a peppermint candy from the jar on my desk, and then turned on his heel.

"I really like you, kid, and trust me when I tell you that I hate seeing you go out like this, but it's your only option."

I thought about telling him to fuck off as he strode towards the door, instead I took a deep breath. I scooped up the envelope and dug inside for the contents. The letter was signed by the mayor, and the message was quite clear. *I am fucked.*

Annoyed, I sagged into my chair and then pulled the bottle of whiskey from my bottom drawer, where I kept the good stuff. It was the bottle my mother had given me when I opened this place.

I poured a little bit into my tumbler and swirled it around, before taking a long drink. I relished the burn. Pushing to my feet, a hundred thoughts raced in my mind. I stood staring out my window overlooking the ocean. How was it possible that I'd managed to operate one of the most successful hotels in South Beach and now I was being forced to give it all up? For something that was out of my control. My hand shook as I raised the glass to my lips again.

Fuck it.

I'd sell this place, and build a bigger hotel—a resort. I'd have a chain of properties.

I stared at my reflection in the glass, raising a toast to myself despite the fact that I was dying inside. Here's to another new beginning.

CHAPTER

one

Stevie

TO SAY MY DAY WAS LONG WOULD HAVE BEEN AN understatement. Seven hours, twenty-one minutes, and counting, and I was stuck in traffic on Salissa Island Parkway. To make matters worse, the air-conditioning in my car went out about an hour ago. The guy in the Porsche behind me got quite the skin show as I climbed over the center console to crank down the windows in the backseat. I'd ditched my t-shirt a few miles back. I was totally rockin' the pink sports bra and lycra shorts ensemble. Looking back it would have been far easier to have exited the car and rolled them down from the outside.

Hindsight is a cocky little bitch.

In what felt like Satan's asshole, here I sat immobile with all four windows of my Ford Focus rolled down drenched in sweat. It was nearly four o'clock in the afternoon. *Shouldn't there be a mandatory summer rain shower right about now?*

I stared at my reflection in the rearview mirror. What was the point of wearing makeup if it's just going to slide off? Not to mention my hair, which resembled Monica's from the *Friends* episode where they took a trip to Barbados. Where was a hair tie when you needed one?

With the hope that I could at least generate a breeze, I cranked up the fan. Just as we started to move, my favorite Fleetwood Mac song blasted over the speakers. I started singing as loud as I could, and then I turned to my left where Porsche guy grinned. His jet black hair fell over his aviators, and I could see the thick cords of his arm muscles from the grip he had on the steering wheel.

He motioned for me to turn down the radio.

I shook my head, and just kept bopping along.

"That's a great song!"

"Yeah, I know! It's kind of my favorite."

My mother had aptly named me Stevie after her idol, Stevie Nicks. Yep, that was my real name, not even short for Stephanie, like the legendary singer herself. Porsche guy was still staring at me, even as we crawled along the hot asphalt.

"You might rear end someone and scratch that pretty car, if you keep looking in my direction."

"I'm enjoying the view, babe, plus you're entertaining. You have a great singing voice."

I smirked, and rolled my eyes. "You must be tone deaf."

His lane started to move, I watched intently as the sleek black piece of machinery rolled four car lengths ahead. Good. Now I could go back to listening to the radio. *Dammit!* I slammed my hand against the dash. The song was over, but my air kicked on and the cool breeze whipped over my skin. This car was a classic, and by classic I mean piece of crap. But it was my piece of crap. I worked my ass off at the country club to pay for this beauty back in high school.

I was able to roll up my window. I wasn't even worried about the backseat. At this point the air could go out if I drove over a pot hole or pumped my brakes. I steadied myself and by some miracle I was able to reach across to the passenger seat and roll up that window. Apparently, this last year of Hatha yoga was paying off.

Yoga class and graduating college, so far those were the highlights of the year. My mom's health had improved, but then she fell and broke her hip a few weeks ago. She had surgery, but then she suffered some setbacks. I felt bad leaving her, but she demanded I take this job even if it meant moving away from Kennesaw. She wasn't alone, but she might as well have been. My abusive father, the only thing he was good for was providing healthcare and a nice rehabilitation facility.

Beep! Beep!

I looked in my mirror and somehow the man with the Porsche had ended up behind me again. Lifting my hand, I politely waved. This guy, he was wasting his time hitting on me . . . if that was even what he was attempting.

Flirting was a foreign concept to me, at least these days. I hadn't been with anyone since my ex, and that was nearly ten months ago. The only flirting I've done is with my pink vibrator or licking the sugar rimmed glass of the occasional peach margarita.

And I've kind of sworn those off since the last guy who bought me the peachy good cocktail, tried to finger fuck me right there at the bar. *Can you imagine?* In a public space no less.

In between recalling sinfully delicious margaritas and

relishing in the accomplishment of earning my dual degrees in Philosophy and Art History, I realized I was finally nearing my destination.

I eased in between an SUV and a pizza delivery truck. Traffic over the bridge was not looking much better. No matter, I was finally here. I couldn't wait to unpack and settle into my new apartment on Salissa Island. Sunny days are here again, and soon I would start my job at the Maritime Arts & History Museum.

Now. Now was the time to for my new beginning and leaving the bad behind—even if I did have to sit in traffic a little longer.

CHAPTER
Two

Stevie

Several Months Later

WELL, SO MUCH FOR REACHING FOR YOUR DREAMS AND all that crap. Two weeks ago, I got the proverbial pink slip. My assistant curator position at the museum was totally amazing. It was a job many applied for, and imagine my surprise when I'd been selected.

Four months into my job, they lost their biggest donor and I along with a few others, were given two weeks' notice to find new jobs. The person in charge of fundraising had been on medical leave, and I guess no one bothered to pick up the task in her absence. When she returned, the discovery of limited funds called for cut-backs. The good news is that the position would come available again one day and I could reapply. Reapply for the job I already applied for, and earned.

After weeks of searching, and half a dozen interviews later, I finally found something that would pay the bills, with just enough left over to buy a few drinks.

"Hey, bartender," I called, lifting my glass into the air. "I'll have another."

She gave me a smile, her brown eyes twinkling. "You got it, slutina."

I laughed and slid my tumbler towards Krystle, my therapist, and by therapist I mean the best drink slinger at my favorite bar, Quench. It's quite possibly the dumbest name for a bar ever. There's a chalkboard above the liquor wall with a list of names of bars far worse that this one.

It might be a terrible name, but the atmosphere and the people are the best. In fact, since moving here, Krystle has become my closest friend. When she found out I'd lost my job, she told everyone to get the fuck out of the bar and we commiserated over a basket of coconut shrimp and a pitcher of sangria.

Krystle was the best, unlike Tiffany, my best friend from back home in Kennesaw, possibly ex-best friend now. She decided that I was the worst person in the entire world for moving away and having way too much fun without her. During a midnight drunken phone call she decided to lay that bullshit on me. She rambled on about me never calling her, even though I'd left her several text messages and tried to call her on my lunch breaks.

"Cheer up, buttercup," she said, pouring more rum into my glass. "Tomorrow you start your new job and you'll be surrounded by gorgeous, rich, older men. You're bound to score a sugar daddy."

"First of all, can you *not* say things like that? Second, I am sure no man is going to be looking at his golf caddy and thinking, 'man I'd like to trade in my smoking hot wife for this twenty-three year-old loser.'"

She tossed her bar towel at me. "You are *not* a loser. You are going to rock that job, until something better comes along. I believe in you."

"Thanks for the solid vote of confidence."

She splashed some rum and coke into a glass and added a cherry. "That's my job to make your life problems better, blondie."

"I can't believe I have to go back to doing the same job I had in college," I groaned.

Krystle tied her dark hair up into a topknot. "At least you'll be in an environment to meet and connect with people of influence. Before you know it, some CEO will be begging you take a job at his or her company."

As I took another sip, I let Krystle's words sink in. A strange combination of confidence and anxiety twirled through me. I swallowed down the sensation along with the final drops of coconut and lime.

Here's to *another* new beginning.

Just before nine o'clock, I climbed the flight of stairs that led to my apartment. When I reached the top, I stood on the balcony, admiring the view of the moonlight dancing off the ocean. Inhaling deeply, the smell of burnt oil and spicy cabbage raced up my nose. I stared down at the dumpster in the back alley from the Chinese restaurant. That smell was awful. Thank goodness tomorrow was trash day.

Turning on my heel, I pulled open the rickety screen door and then pushed my key into the lock of the weathered wooden door.

The apartment was quiet, which meant Megyn, my roommate, had yet to come home from her shift. Or that she was getting piss drunk with her co-workers again. God I loved Megyn, but that girl couldn't handle her liquor. More than a couple of times, I needed to reel her in by last call or she was bound to ditch her panties to make out with any available guy donning a beard and tattoos in the bathroom.

Who hasn't been shoved up against a dirty bathroom sink and been jack-hammered from behind?

This girl.

My sex life was on life support, and I was coming dangerously close to having the last rites read to my vagina.

After snagging a bottle of water from the fridge, I settled onto the wicker sofa that was much too large for this humble living room. The palm tree pattern was hideous but completely appropriate for Florida. Everywhere I looked I could feel my grandmother's presence, from the sea shell lamp to the crazy collection of old wooden ships that lined her bookshelf. I didn't have the heart to pack any of it away, besides it all added charming character to the space.

I opened my laptop and pulled up my email. After checking out the flash sale at Old Navy, I clicked on the email from my new boss. I scanned the message making sure I had all the details correct.

Dear Miss Brockman,

On behalf of Hart Resort & Spa I'd like to personally welcome you to the team. At Hart Hotels Inc. we are dedicated to providing our guests with the highest level of customer service. Our highly personalized, round the clock service combined with our elegant and luxurious surroundings are admired by many and replicated by none. We offer exceptional quality and our greatest asset is our people. You are now one of those people.

Please arrive at the Hart Resort & Spa Pro-Shop at 7:00 a.m. for your orientation. Lunch will be provided by our catering service. Upon completion of your training, you will receive a $300 club voucher where you will be able to shop our exclusive Hart Designs collection of golf wear.

Sincerely,

Carol Edgerton, Director of Hotel Operations

Hart Hotels Inc.

Nervous, I pulled up the notes app on my phone and typed all the important information. I planned to arrive early, and mapped out my route to Hart Resort. I'd actually driven it three separate times this past week and even planned an alternate route in case of traffic problems.

For good measure, I checked my spam filter in case anything got shuffled over by mistake. Nothing of importance. Just one person asking for $50,000 and a scam for Wal-Mart rewards points. Just click the link to the survey, and you'll automatically earn one-hundred dollars in bonus points. *Right.*

The mention of Wal-Mart made me smile though it reminded me of Gran. When I'd spent a few weeks here with her last summer, the first thing she said we needed to do was hit Wal-Mart and grab some deals. I hated the place, but I'd indulge her because she loved using her coupons, especially when she could double or triple her savings.

One afternoon, as I was packing up the items she'd instructed be donated to the local women's shelter, I'd discovered an envelope with several hundred dollars in Wally World gift cards in her coupon basket. There was no note about what was supposed to be done with them so I called my mom and she told me that Gran would want me to use them to buy groceries and essentials. And that is just what I'd done, but now I was down to my last hundred dollars. This job came in the nick of time, or else I would have been forced to dip into my savings.

That was not happening. Flashbacks to a conversation with my father in high school came flooding back. *You can't balance your finances for shit. You're a stupid little girl. Just one more thing you managed to screw up.*

I snapped my laptop shut, and shoved it under the coffee table. In desperate need of a shower, I made my way to the bathroom. After stripping out of my clothes, I tossed them into the hamper.

I stared at my reflection in the mirror. *You are not stupid.*

Tomorrow was a new day, filled with possibilities to be great.

CHAPTER
Three

Stevie

Hefting my shopping bags into my car, I was fully satisfied with my new work wardrobe. With, orientation and training complete, I was so ready for a drink. Sitting in a conference room for six hours watching videos and taking quizzes left me feeling stir crazy.

I slammed the trunk shut and walked around to the driver's side. I'd just unlocked the door when I heard someone shouting my name.

"Stevie? Hey, Stevie!"

As I turned around, my ex, Cord Robinson stopped short of crashing into me.

"What the shit," I mumbled.

"I thought that was you." He removed his cap and wiped the sweat away with this forearm. "How did you find me here?"

Seriously? Arrogant ass. Of course, he would think I was here for him.

"Cord, I had no idea you were on Salissa Island. I came here for a job."

"Oh, I see. Are you staying here at the hotel?" He seemed genuinely interested, but if he thought he could sweeten me up with small talk he's out of his damn mind.

"No, my grandmother, *Ruby* left her place to me when she passed away just before my graduation."

He flashed his charming smile at me, and then he opened his mouth. "Convenient graduation gift."

I shot him a glare. "Yeah, Gran dying was a super awesome convenience."

His shoulders slumped. "I didn't mean it like that, and I am sorry to hear about your grandma, Ruby was a lovely lady."

"Thank you. I miss her."

I didn't want to be nice to this man. Scanning the parking lot of the resort, I looked for anyone I might have recognized giving me a reason to check out of this conversation. No humans in sight. My eyes flicked to the pelican sitting on the post near the lake. He looked at me and then flew away. Even he didn't have the decency to snatch me up and take me with him. I glanced at my watch hoping that Cord would take the hint.

"Are you hungry? Let's grab some dinner. We could split a pitcher of beer like old times."

Apparently, he didn't get the signal. And why he would ever think I would have dinner with him was beyond me. That was rich.

I laughed in his face. "No, I do not want to have dinner or do anything with you for old times' sake."

He scowled. "Don't be like that, okay?"

"You cannot be serious. There's a reason we broke up and

her name was Cindy," I reminded him.

"*Sandy*," he corrected, folding his arms across his broad chest.

"Oh, of course, excuse me for not knowing the correct name of your side piece."

Cord's remorseful eyes met mine, and for a moment I remembered all the good times we shared. We started dating the summer before my junior year of college. Cord was the Golf Pro at Sweet Water Country Club where I'd worked so many summers. I couldn't believe that Cord Robinson was working at our club. Admittedly, I'd been a little star struck and nearly ran him over with a golf cart one morning. When he jumped out of the way, the coffee he'd been carrying had spilled all down the front of his shirt. I made it up to him by getting him another coffee, and a new shirt.

I never thought I'd be the girl who'd date an older guy. What would a twenty-six year old retired, semi-pro golfer have in common with a soon to be college junior? His passion for golf, and my appreciation of the sport brought us together along with crazy hot, instant chemistry.

Ughh. *No, Stevie.* He's your past, and you need to leave him there. Digging deep I remembered the night I found out he'd cheated on me with Sandy, and how much he'd hurt me. There's the anger I needed to tell him to take a hike.

"Cord, I need to get going, okay?"

"Not even one drink?"

"Nope." I turned away from him, and opened the car door. I dipped my head and slid into the seat.

He took a step forward, catching the top of the door with his hand. "I'm not with Sandy anymore. Turns out she wasn't a faithful girlfriend. So there's your karma if that's what you were looking for."

A smug smile tugged at the corners of my mouth. *Good you deserve that, you cheating dickhead.* Saying nothing I jerked on the door. His fingers uncurled from the metal, allowing me to pull it closed.

Exiting the parking lot, I cranked up the radio. Maneuvering around the main road, I got up to twenty miles per hour and then my car slowed. The radio went silent, and the air conditioning stopped working. I gave it a little more gas. Still nothing. I managed to coast to the back of the hotel parking lot, safely off the road and out of the view of guests. After the car was in park, I removed the key.

It was dead. D-E-A-D. I climbed out and stared blankly. "I have a full tank of gas. I just filled up this morning," I said to no one.

I climbed into the driver's seat turning the key once more. *Nothing. Ughh.* I stood and slammed the door closed.

Looking underneath, the hot pavement stung my hands. "Stupid car."

"Having trouble?" I heard a deep voice say.

With my ass in the air and crouched down on all fours, I must have looked ridiculous. Standing upright it was just my luck to find a pair of gorgeous, intense blue eyes staring back at me. Trouble, I suppose he was the guy Taylor Swift warned us about.

This man was incredibly good-looking. Dressed in a graphite grey suit that looked seriously expensive. My slow reaction gave me a minute to assess the situation, the *situation* being this tall drink of water standing in front of me with the impossibly broad shoulders and a smile . . . well, that smile is where the trouble began.

"What was your first clue, my ass in the air?" I asked, shaking the remnants of earth from my hands.

"Well, the way your ass looks in those shorts, you did grab my attention." His thumb grazed along his chin, a dirty glint shone in those blue eyes. "You want me to take a look?"

"You're wearing a suit, should you be getting your hands dirty?"

"Just hand me the keys and if it comes to that I can show you just how good I am with my hands."

"Key is in the ignition."

"Let's see what the problem seems to be." Sidestepping me, he flashed that killer smile once again.

Did my panties melt and slide down my legs?

He eased into the driver's seat and I watched as his left hand gripped the steering wheel. His fingers tapped against the wheel as he turned the key. Nothing.

He looked up at me. "I assume that you have plenty of gas?"

I nodded. "Yeah, I filled it up this morning."

He ran his thumb along his jawline and stepped out of my car. "I'm going to get my car. I have jumper cables, we can give that a try."

"Okay."

Stammering and speaking only one word? This guy was around me for two minutes, and my tongue was rolling out of my mouth like a cartoon character.

Shaking off my personal embarrassment, I slumped into the driver's seat. My head fell back and I closed my eyes. "Please, just let it be the battery."

I heard the hum of an approaching engine and my eyes snapped open. A sleek black Range Rover parked in front of my puny blue Focus. I wondered what his job at the resort could be. If I was a betting gal, I'd say sales more than likely.

He shrugged out of his jacket, removed his tie, and then rolled up the sleeves of his white dress shirt exposing his holy fucking amazing forearms. *Gahh female Viagra.*

I watched him obsessively as he unzipped the cords from the bag and carefully affixed them to his battery then mine.

"Okay, go ahead get into your seat, and then on my direction turn the key."

I nodded and did what I was instructed. Seconds later, he pointed his finger at me and I couldn't help but smile. I turned the key, but nothing happened.

Fuck you! I bent my forehead to rest on the steering wheel.

I felt his shadow looming over me, and I lifted my head to see him smiling. What the fuck did he have to be so happy about? Oh yeah, he drove a Range Rover. A perfectly nice ride and probably never had car trouble.

"If that's an offer we can work something out, I'm sure of it."

I stared at him confused.

"You said, fuck you—*out loud.*"

I felt the blush creep up my neck and spread to my cheeks.

I chuckled nervously. "Sorry about that. I'm just having a not so great day. Well, actually it was a great day, but then I ran into someone . . ." I snapped my mouth shut.

"Please continue." He smiled again.

"Okay, you have got to stop smiling because I'm having a hard time stopping myself from grinning like an idiot. You make me want to smile, and as you can see, I'm having a rather crap day."

He laughed and walked back around the front of the car. "I

don't know what is wrong with your car. Do you have a company you can call for a tow?"

"No," I answered truthfully. "Do you have any recommendations?"

"Yeah, I might know a guy."

"Might or do?"

He shut the hood of his vehicle and then wiped his hands off onto a towel. This guy was certainly prepared. Probably a Boy Scout when he was younger.

He pulled his cellphone out of his pocket. "Hey, Liza, I need a tow at the hotel. No, a friend of mine, her car is out of commission. Can you send someone over to pick it up?"

Friends? When did we become friends?

He ended the call and I stared at him, my brows raised slightly.

"What?"

"Friends, huh?"

"Well, you did offer to fuck me, so I think that puts us on the fast track to friendship."

"I did *not* offer," I choked out, feeling somewhat shocked and embarrassed by his remark.

He shoved his cell into his back pocket. "The tow truck should be here soon. Can I drop you somewhere?"

"No, that's okay. I can just take the bus."

He eyed me. "I insist, let me save you the trouble of having to wait for the bus."

This guy was quite the salesman. If I were any weaker, I'd probably have bought two timeshares and a month at a villa from him. "You're not going to take no for an answer are you?"

"Nope." He shook his head. "Go get your things. Be sure to grab your garage door opener, too . . . uhmm . . ."

Fantastic, now he was tongue tied. "It's Stevie, and I don't have a garage," I tossed over my shoulder, lifting my tote bag and purse and then kicking the car door closed with my foot.

"Stevie," he repeated, taking the bags from my hands. "Short for?"

"Nope, that's it, just Stevie Nicole Brockman." I had no idea why I felt compelled to divulge my entire name to him.

He smirked, and closed the door. "Good to meet you, Stevie Nicole Brockman."

"You too, uhm?"

"Jax."

Jax. He was beautiful in the way that wicked things were.

Thirty minutes later, I was cruising down the highway on the way to my apartment. In my hands I held a business card and information from the repair shop. My fingers rubbed over the raised lettering. I hoped nothing major was wrong with my car, but with my bad luck I was certain it would be an expensive repair.

My eyes flicked around his car, taking in the beauty of the interior. My navy shorts complimented the burgundy leather seats, and the dash was perfectly shiny and clean. No trace of a rogue French fry or empty water bottles on the floorboard of the backseat. *This* was a grown-up's car.

I started to second guess myself, as I ran my fingers along the white stitching. The only other time I'd been seated in an expensive car was when Dan, Tiffany's date for prom, drove us there in a rented Cadillac. Maybe I should have taken the bus.

At the red light, I looked over at Jax and lingered a bit too long with my stare. It couldn't be helped; he was easy on the eyes. His jawline was covered in a sexy five o'clock shadow, the perfect amount of facial hair.

"I thought I knew everyone who worked at Hart Resort and Spa. But, you're a new face to me." He turned slightly to face me.

"Yeah, I'm a newbie. Caddying for the guests and today was my orientation."

"And how did the training go?"

"It was okay, I guess. I could have done without the hours of videos, though. It's pointless for me to know how to clean up a hazardous spill, or a public restroom. But, I did enjoy the rules for properly cleaning a player's balls." A giggle bubbled up from my throat, but I quickly realized how immature I sounded. Heat crept over my cheeks. My eyes stayed glued to the windshield, afraid to look in his direction. At this point, he had to have been regretting his decision to offer me a ride.

"Yeah," he chuckled. "Caddying and housekeeping training shouldn't overlap."

Okay, so maybe I hadn't fully embarrassed myself. "What about you? Boring desk job?"

"Not always. I do get to travel from time to time."

"My house . . . *apartment* is just up here on the left. You can turn at the light near the Dry Dock Bar and Grill."

He laughed, and I nervously messed with my braided ponytail. There are only a few places in Salissa Island that were perhaps labeled as "run-down" and this area was definitely not as posh as the rest of the island.

"That has to be one of the worst names for a bar," he huffed, and flicked his turn signal.

"Oh yeah, why is that?"

"Well it's a bar, and word 'dry' is in the title."

"That's not so bad. What's in a name anyway?"

"True. I think I just find it ironic."

I snuck another look at him, spying the corner of his mouth turned up. He even had perfect lips, and I wondered what it might be like to kiss him. Wow. *I just took a hard left into Fantasy Island.*

"Speaking of worst names," I began trying to shake the crazy fantasy from my head. "My friend tends bar at Quench. It's my favorite spot. That's where I was going to go after work, but now with my car situation, I shouldn't spend any extra money." I'd done it again, giving up personal information. Rambling was a specialty of mine.

Jax shot a glance my way. "Yep, I've been there, coldest beer on tap in town. I'd love to know their secret."

"The secret to what?"

"How they get their beer to stay so cold."

"Personally, I think it's all in the customer's mind."

He cocked an eyebrow. "Tell me more."

"Quench the coldest beer in town. You tell enough people that and then it's already in their minds, so when they actually take that first sip, they already believe it to be true."

"Preconceived notion." He stated matter of fact. "You have a good mind for marketing, what are you doing caddying?"

I laughed, and knotted my fingers together. "Yeah, well, I'll give you the short version. I lost my assistant curator job at the Maritime Arts & History Museum due to lack of funding. But, I'm going to get it back. I have a good feeling."

"Good attitude, I like your confidence, Stevie. I have a feeling things will be looking up for you."

"Oh, turn right here. It's just up ahead on the left."

"Near The Golden Dragon?"

"Above the restaurant, actually."

He raised an eyebrow. "You live above The Golden Dragon?"

"I know it's not much, but this was my grandmother's place. She left it to me, and I rent out the spare room. It helps to keep up with maintenance and other things." Again, I was offering up personal information to a complete stranger. I needed to learn to keep my mouth shut, before I rambled on about my possible theory that I suspected that Ruby was having a fling with Mr. Lin, the owner of the restaurant.

He pulled into a parking space, and I felt my insides churning. Do I ask him if he'd like some gas money? Do I offer to buy him dinner? Or do I just thank him and say goodbye?

"Let me help you with your bags," he said, pointing to the backseat.

"That's okay," I said weakly, and pulled on the door handle. "I can manage."

I stepped out, and lifted my purse higher onto my shoulder. Jax opened the back door and then handed me my shopping bags along with my tote bag.

"Well, thank you for helping me and for the lift home."

"You're welcome. Have a good night."

"Goodnight, Jax." I turned, and staggered towards the wooden flight of stairs that led to my apartment. Once inside, I flipped on the light and then dropped my bags to the floor. From the kitchen window, I saw the glow from the car's taillights, as he drove back down the alley.

CHAPTER
four

Stevie

L AST NIGHT, I'D RECEIVED A CALL FROM MY MOM, WHO WAS IN wonderful spirits. It was good to hear her sounding so happy. It filled me with an odd mixture of joy and sadness. I was glad she was on the mend, but that meant she'd have to go home and be around my father twenty-four seven. She was being discharged and I looked at the time wondering if he'd actually made it to the facility on time. Mom had told me he agreed to be there bright and early. I seriously had my doubts.

On bare feet I shuffled over to the coffee maker and poured a mug, adding in a pinch of sugar. I rested my hip against the counter before taking my first sip. If only she'd divorce him then this long nightmare could finally be over and I would have her come live here with me.

After taking a seat at the kitchen table, I wrote out a check for the gas company, stuffed it into the envelope, and placed a stamp on it. I popped open my laptop and proceeded to the Mae Net website, where I paid my student loan. *Ouch, that hurt.*

Soon, I would get my job at the museum back or find something even better which would hopefully lead to me buying a beach bungalow. Mom could sit outside, enjoying the warm sunshine and sounds of the ocean. That would be healing therapy for anyone.

Of course, I'd keep this apartment. With some much needed cosmetic updates, I could modernize it and then this place would the perfect seaside rental.

It was all wishful thinking on my part because Mom would never leave the bastard. Hopefully he could stay sober for a few hours, at least long enough to get her home and settled. Second thoughts drove me to think of another solution. Maybe Tiffany could help me out and pick up mom today. That would involve me begging for forgiveness and probably signing away the naming rights to my first born.

Pushing up from my chair, I then walked to the coffee maker for a refill. Dammit. Why didn't Mom let me know sooner? I could have scheduled today as my day off and gone up to Kennesaw myself. Lifting up to my tiptoes, I reached for the box of Pop-Tarts and grabbed the last silver foil packet.

I cradled the phone between my shoulder and my ear, and tore open the wrapper. "Hello, this is Stevie Brockman. Danielle Brockman is my mother. Could you tell me when she is scheduled to leave?"

"Yes, Miss Brockman. She left early this morning."

"That's good. Can you tell me who picked her up?" I asked, before popping a piece of my blueberry goodness into my mouth.

"Her husband."

"Okay, thank you." I ended the call and took another bite of my bad for me breakfast.

Mentally prepping myself, I took a deep breath and then called my mom. I plastered a fake smile on my face. "Hey, Mom, are you settled and glad to be home?"

"Yes, sugar," she answered, her southern accent a bit raspy. "I'm home and everything is fine."

"I am glad to hear that. I would have driven home to pick you up though."

"Stevie, I told you. This is your time to shine. You don't need to fuss over me."

"Dad." I swallowed hard and started coughing. "He . . . helped you . . . get . . ."

Some crumbs must have stuck in my throat. I downed my coffee and came up for air.

"Stevie, are you okay? Take a drink of water."

My mom, always calm, even when I was gasping for breath. "I'm fine," I said through a set of coughs. "Did Dad get your meds from the pharmacy?"

"Yes, I told you everything is just fine. Now, according to my watch, you need to be at work soon. So scoot and have a wonderful day. I love you."

"Thanks, Mom. I'll call again soon. Love you." Hanging up with Mom, I tucked my phone inside my tote bag. I slipped my socks and shoes on and grabbed my keys off the counter. No time to brush my teeth again, I'd do that at work. It was almost ten a.m. and I needed to get to the bus stop.

"Hey, girl." I heard Megyn's voice as she hopped up and onto the counter.

"Morning, I'm off to work. You?"

"I work at four today. Then I am going down to The Keys

with Beau for a long weekend. Sun and fun."

"Ow ow," I chirped, tossing my bag up onto my shoulder. "Things must be getting serious. You've kept this one around longer than a week."

"I'll take that as a compliment," Beau said, appearing from the shadows and tugging his white tee over his mass of blond hair. He kissed Megyn on the forehead and then pulled two mugs from the cabinet.

I winked at Megyn, and she shrugged. My phone rang, it was an unrecognized number.

"Oops, excuse me, I have to take this. You two have fun this weekend." I stepped outside onto the porch, closing the door behind me. The screen door knocked into me, and I fumbled my phone, nearly dropping it. "Hello, this is Stevie Brockman."

"Miss Brockman this is Dawn at Maxwell's Repair. Your car has been repaired, and we're sending someone to deliver it to you. Is your address: 111 South Shore Drive, B?"

"Yes, that is correct. Can you tell me what was wrong?" I held the phone tightly, waiting for the worst.

"The computer chip failed and wasn't able to communicate for your car to start."

I pressed my forehead against the wooden beam of my balcony, salty morning dew and humidity clogging my throat. My heart thumped at the realization this was going to be incredibly expensive. "Can you take a credit card over the phone?"

"The bill has been taken care of, Miss Brockman."

"What? But, how?"

"There's a note on the account, apparently your company took care of everything. That was so nice of them."

"Yes, very nice. Do you have any more information?"

"No, Miss, that's all it says."

"Well, thank you, Dawn. Have a good day."

Puzzled, I sagged into the beach chair on the porch and waited for my car to arrive. Why would Hart Hotels Inc. pay for my car repairs? The only person that knew about my car was Jax and he was just a sales guy. What did he care?

My cheeks heated. *Fucking Cord.* This was probably his way of trying to apologize and get back into my good graces. The sight of my car turning in from the alley put a smile on my face. I'd deal with Cord later. Right now, I had to get to work. Another mental pep talk and I refocused my emotions as I barreled down the stairs.

Smiling, I taped up the picture of Mom and me from my graduation on the inside of my locker. I started to change into one of my new work uniforms. Today, I tossed on a pair of grey shorts with a hot pink sleeveless polo. After doing a quick check of hair and makeup, I shoved my stuff into my locker.

"Hey, Stevie, are you in here?" I heard Abby's sweet voice bouncing off the tile in the locker room. Abby was the lead caddy and a part-time graphic designer for a beverage company.

"Yep. Over here at my locker."

She turned the corner carrying a huge vase filled with an assortment of flowers. I spotted white and pink roses, along with white lilies. I'd known from Gran's funeral that flowers were expensive. This arrangement was at least a hundred dollars.

"Wow, those are gorgeous. Who sent them to you?"

She shook her head. "They're not for me silly. They're yours."

"What?"

"Yep, look at the card, it says Miss Stevie Brockman. Do you have a secret admirer or a new boyfriend?"

I shrugged, afraid to speak. She was right, I did have an admirer and he was a former boyfriend.

She handed me the vase, and my gaze darted around the locker room for a safe place to set the flowers. The computer desk, that looked like a fine place. I pulled the card and pried open the envelope.

Stevie,

Despite your car troubles, and the unnecessary video training, I hope your first week at Hart Resort and Spa was a good one.

–Jax

Wow. That was it. That's all it took for my insides to turn to liquid.

"Girl, you are as pink as the sands of Musha Cay. Who sent you the flowers?"

Was Miss Bubbly still here?

"Oh, this guy I met the other night," I said, folding the note and tucking it into my pocket. "He helped me with my car."

"He helped you out of jam and he's sending you flowers? That seems backwards to me."

"I think he was just being kind."

"Still, you must have made some impression."

"Hardly, I'm sure these are just pity flowers. I was having a seriously tragic day."

She cocked one of her expertly manicured eyebrows. "Whatever you say, hot stuff."

The day went by crazy fast. Despite a ten minute downpour during one of the morning rounds, everything was ahead of schedule. My next assignment was a foursome of "big-wigs" so said our boss. Abby and I stood in the locker room as Carol instructed us to look our best. We re-touched up our makeup, brushed our hair and applied more sunblock.

My mouth gaped at the sight of Cord and Jax entering the clubhouse. *Fuck!* They knew one another. Worse yet, were they friends? And still worse, close enough that they played a round of golf together on a Friday afternoon. No, Cord was the course pro, and Jax was in sales. This was clearly business.

I spun around nearly knocking Abby over in the process. When I glanced over my shoulder at her, she said, "What's going on with you?"

"Can you be quiet, *please*," I pleaded.

"Okay, okay, don't get your undies wedged up your ass."

I wrinkled my nose and pulled her behind the server's station. "So, here's the deal. One is my ex, and the other *is* the guy who sent the flowers."

She clasped her hands together. "That's utterly fantastic."

"You would think that," I groaned, feeling sick to my stomach.

"Suck it up, S. You go out there and do your job, *or* you get fired. Your choice."

She had a point, and I needed the money. "Okay, I'm doing this."

"Which one is your ex? I'll take him."

Neither man had noticed me yet, they were deep in conversation. Slyly, I pointed to Cord, and then we both made a bee line out of the clubhouse. Jax turned to greet another person and I heard Abby gasp.

"Oh my God, *he* sent you the flowers?"

"Yeah, why do you say it like that?"

She shook her head. "How thoroughly did you read the employee handbook?"

"I skimmed it, I've done all this before, you know. I don't care much about Hart Hotels Inc., aside from the rules I need to follow to keep this job until I go back to the museum."

"That man, my clueless friend, is Jackson Hart. Does that name ring any bells?"

"Shut the front fucking door."

"I bet you care a little bit more about Hart Hotels now." She nudged my arm. *"Jackson Hart* sent *you* flowers."

Well, that was absolutely the last thing I expected. We stood just off the putting green, waiting along with the other two caddies. Narrowing my eyes, I saw both Jax and Cord round the corner from the Clubhouse and cross the cart path. I took a deep breath, and Abby squeezed my hand, mouthing the words, *"You got this."*

Desperately doesn't even begin to cover how much I needed this job. And I'll be damned if my personal life was going to interfere. What if I had taken Jax up on his offer the other night? *My offer, according to him.* What would have happened if I'd invited him up and then ripped off all his clothes and had my way with him?

Jax pinned his dreamy blue eyes on me and all I could do was smile. He'd made me smile, *again.* I needed to pull it together. What was it about this guy?

Once more, Abby nudged me. "S, your ex is watching, be careful."

"Right, okay, I'm good," I whispered. "Mister Hart, I'm Stevie your caddy for the day."

"Stevie, yes, good to meet you." His eyes bored into me, and I felt something pass between us.

"Mister Robinson, I'm Abby," she said, hurling her body in front of him. "It's a pleasure to meet someone as talented as you."

Inside, I rolled my eyes. Squaring my shoulders, I put on my charming smile. This round could not end soon enough. Jackson Hart the owner and CEO of Hart Hotels sent me flowers. Damn. What were the chances?

Here goes nothing.

Abby handed me a bottle of water, as we walked towards the clubhouse. The game ended, and neither Jax . . . Jackson, nor Cord had won the round. How was I supposed to address the man?

Across the way, I saw Jax talking to a woman wearing a cute sleeveless top with a black pleated skirt. She was tall, very thin, and her long blonde hair was neatly tied back into a low ponytail. She touched his arm in an intimate way, lingering a little too long.

After we collected our daily tips, we went to the locker room. Somehow I managed to wrestle the hair tie from my tangled sweaty mass of blonde hair, pulling a few strands with it. I peeled out of my clothes and then tossed them into my laundry bag. Scooping up my tote, I made my way towards the showers.

The water was slightly cool at first, as I ducked under the shower head. I let the spray run over me, stinging like icy needles. That was about all I could take before pushing the lever adding more hot water. The steam curled around me. I heard

Abby humming some country tune as she ducked into the stall next to mine.

I stayed in the shower until my skin was red and my fingertips were wilted. Abby had long gone. She was a rinse off and go kind of gal. Clearly, I was hiding out, but I had my reasons, I didn't want Jax to see me when I questioned Cord about my car.

Twenty minutes later, my hair was dried and my makeup reapplied. I shoved my legs into a pair of frayed jean shorts and tossed on a soft white t-shirt. Hurriedly I scooped up all my stuff, including my flowers and power walked to my car.

I spotted Cord hanging out by the Pro Shop taking a drag off a cigarette. Perfect, he was alone. I went over what I knew in my head. Squaring my shoulders, I pulled my sunglasses from the top of my head and covered my eyes. I walked quickly through the parking lot, keeping my focus on the matter at hand. He spotted me, and slow grin spread across his face.

"Cord, I need a word with you."

"Did you have a change of heart about that drink?"

I shook my head. "We are *over*. Can you get that through your head?"

He took a final puff and tossed the butt into the smoker's pole. "Fine, what would you like to discuss? Perhaps you'd like a private lesson. I have superb skills, ya know. I could show you how to handle my club."

Asshat. "Nice, Cord. Real gentlemanly. Did you really think paying for my car repairs would get you in my pants?"

"What car repairs?"

I crossed my arms over my chest. "Stop pretending. You know what you did. After I saw you the other day, my car broke down and I had to get a tow. When it was delivered this morning, the woman at the shop told me that the bill had been taken care of by my company."

"Stevie, baby, I swear I don't know anything about this business with your car."

"Ughh, you're impossible," I huffed.

I was halfway across the parking lot, when I saw *him* wave at me. "Stevie," he called out and jogged up to me. I didn't know what to do about the whole not recognizing him thing, so for the sake of not embarrassing him or myself I decided not to bring it up.

"Hey, *uh* . . . good play today."

"Thanks. You okay?"

"Yeah, I'm all good," I sighed.

"I don't believe you," he said, flashing me that panty melting smile of his.

"Okay, you got me. Thank you for the flowers, by the way."

He shoved his hands into his pockets. "You're welcome. And I'm glad you got your car back in working order."

"Yeah, taking the bus was an adventure in timing."

"I'll bet."

"What can you tell me about the company paying for auto repairs? I know this sounds silly, but the bill was paid and they said the hotel took care of it. Is that like a perk?" I sounded ridiculous, or insane. So much for not making an ass of myself in front of the guy who owned the place.

"I might know something about that." He took my hand in his and gave it a gentle squeeze. "I took care of your bill."

"What?" My brows crinkled, and I snatched my hand back. "Is this your move? What you do to get into women's pants?"

"No, it's not a move. You were having a very bad day, I wanted to do something nice for you," he replied in a soothing tone.

"Flowers are a nice gesture, hell, even cup of coffee or a drink." I tossed my hands in the air, storming off, like a pissed off teenager.

"Stevie, wait!" he called after me. I could hear his shoes tapping on the pavement.

My hands balled into fists, as I turned back, to face him. "I am *not* a charity case, *Mister* Hart."

I waved him off before he caught up to me. He skidded to a halt, and I climbed into my car. In the rearview mirror, he stood there watching as I drove out of the lot.

"Ughh men!" I slammed my hand against the steering wheel. All the way home, my flowers sat in the passenger seat, mocking me.

CHAPTER
five

Jackson

AFTER MY WORKOUT, I TOOK A LONGER SHOWER THAN necessary. I had a ton of work that demanded my attention, but I couldn't focus on any of it because of her—Stevie. All I'd wanted to do was something nice for her, and I went and fucked it all up. I should have known better. The flowers were enough, paying her repair bill that was borderline crazy. Judging by her reaction, I'd definitely crossed the line. Insanity was my only defense.

Stevie wasn't like any of the other women I'd come across, *ever*. I'm aware that men said that kind of crap all the time, but for me it rang true. With this job, I was used to women rubbing up against me during working hours, after meetings, on the course, and social affairs vying for my attention.

Stevie captured my attention, despite being in a shitty predicament she managed to smile, and laugh. I liked her laugh, a lot. Her blue eyes beamed bright every time she laughed. Every time she looked at me with those gorgeous eyes, I found myself being pulled in deeper.

Taking notice of an attractive woman never rattled me, but for some reason this woman did. Maybe I *was* losing it.

She probably took me for a Sugar Daddy and was grossed out. Stevie couldn't have been more than twenty-two, making me nine years older than her. My dick and my brain were in a wrestling match of epic proportions. She was innocence and sin wrapped together and I had the desire to explore every facet of her being.

Scrubbing my hands down my face, I blew out a harsh breath. I walked to the bar and poured a glass of scotch. I recently attended a special tasting dinner at the Ritz Carlton to try a fifty year old Glenlivet Scotch, single-malt at cool $25,000 a bottle. The taste of caramel mixed with a lasting spice and rich leather lingered on my tongue as I relished the slow burn going down.

This scotch was something special, a rarity that most people would never have the opportunity to experience. Rich older men, they managed to keep aged scotch in business. At thirty-one, I was one of them.

Stevie was barely a twenty-something and I couldn't stop envisioning fucking her in every position imaginable. While she was at the point in her life where she felt the sting of losing her first meaningful job, this morning I made enough money to buy a dozen cases of this scotch.

I swirled the liquid in my glass, the color reminded me of her skin—the shade of golden tan. On the golf course today, I couldn't help but study her body. Her legs were toned and sculpted to perfection. During the course of the afternoon, I'd become an expert on her ass. I studied it harder than my golf game. Every time she adjusted her ponytail, I had the urge to wrap it around my fist, yanking her back so that I could kiss my way up the delicate slope of her neck. In my mind, I'd already bent Stevie over my desk and fucked her half a dozen times. I wanted to see her skin tinged pink, under my skilled touch.

I took another drink, and my thoughts shifted to her lips. That pink pout said one thing: "Come here, I need to kiss you." I'd never seen such perfect kissable lips on a woman in my life.

Thinking about defiling this woman was going to drive me to alcoholism.

CHAPTER

six

Stevie

SATURDAY MORNING ARRIVED AND BROUGHT A TORRENTIAL downpour along. My drive to Amelia City was absolutely agonizing. I had about ten minutes to snap out of my foul mood before I arrived at the cemetery. Since moving here, this was my ritual. Grab coffee. Pick up a bouquet of flowers from the grocery. Spend an hour at my gran's grave.

It had stopped raining just as I made it to Amelia City. I turned into the lot and parked under my favorite tree. Slipping off my pink Hunter wellies, I traded them for my flip flops. Bouquet and coffee in hand, I walked along the path to her grave.

"Hey, Gran, it's me, Stevie," I announced, bending to replace the flowers from last week with a fresh bundle of peach colored roses.

I pulled out a cloth, and dusted off her headstone, wiping it free of grass and raindrops. The bench I normally sat on was still wet, so I stood as I prayed silently.

"Okay, Gran, this week has been an epic cluster . . . disaster." I recounted my week, telling her the highlights and lowlights, including my run in with Cord and how Jax had paid for my car repairs.

Utterly sexy, Jackson Hart and his stupid perfect face. *Why do I even care?* I shouldn't care, but I do. Obviously, I had enjoyed the time we'd spent together the evening my car decided to clunk out on me. And, caddying for him wasn't a total awkward nightmare, especially since there were quite a few hand grazes and I loved being on the receiving end of that charming smile.

This is dumb. I had spent all of five hours with the guy and I hadn't been able to stop thinking about him. *Focus, Stevie,* I'd reminded myself.

"Megyn is good, looks like she might keep the new guy around for a while. Oh, and Krystle says hello. She's working on that cocktail for the bar, Ruby's Rum Runner. It will probably have blood orange and blackberries, like I mentioned last time."

Out of the corner of my eye, I saw a family walking down the path to my right. The woman was crying, and her daughter told her that it was okay to cry.

I used to cry a lot when I first started visiting Gran, but somewhere along the way I was able to find peace. It broke my heart that she'd died alone. We'd received the call that Gran had been rushed to the hospital, she collapsed outside the bank. But, by the time we arrived she'd passed away.

I pulled a book from my handbag. Gran had a stash of Nora Roberts and Jackie Collins books in her closet. Lots of notes in the margins, which made me laugh. We started with *Chances*, since I'd never read it. Now we were on *Hollywood Wives*.

"Let's see," I began, and turned to the page I'd

bookmarked. "Okay, so we're now on chapter ten." I began reading, and took a seat on the now dry bench.

An hour later, I was back in my car, and headed to Salissa Island. Instead of going straight home, I decided to stop at one of my favorite places.

The hot air whipped around me when I hopped out of the car. As I climbed the stairs, the smell of caramel from the popcorn shop next door twirled up my nose. I smiled remembering the first time Gran brought me here and we indulged in caramel chocolate popcorn. On super-hot days we'd skip the popcorn and go for ice cream instead.

Baker's Art Gallery, it was the biggest on the island. I turned the knob on the tall French doors and passed through the drawing room. A large piano sat in the corner near the fireplace tiled with stained glass.

For a Saturday afternoon, the gallery was unusually empty. My feet carried me up to the second floor, where all the maritime art was housed. During our trips here, Gran would create a story about the paintings for our amusement.

Unable to let my brain relax, I couldn't help but think about the other day with Jax, and how upset I'd been when he admitted he paid for my car repairs. It hurt, because I liked him. He was charming, polite, a little pervy, but in a non-threatening way. Then again, did he think he would get laid by paying my bill? There were far better ways to get into my pants. *Oh my God, why am I thinking about this?*

Once I'd had a chance to cool down, I would figure out a way to get the money back to him.

Leaning against one of the wood columns, I studied the picture, which was an impressionistic scene of beachgoers shielding themselves from the rain. The bright pops of red and green balanced perfectly against the muted grey and blue-green sky.

And now, I was back to thinking about Jax's blue eyes. I let out an exasperated sigh, covering my face in my hands.

"Is this seat taken?"

Seriously? It was his voice. *The* voice. My fingers curled against my palm, nails biting into my skin to make sure that I was awake. Sure enough there stood Jackson Hart, wearing a pair of dark denim jeans and a grey V-neck t-shirt that clung to his muscles. *Good Lord.*

"I'm not sitting."

He shrugged. "I know, but it seemed like the thing to say."

"What are you doing here? You want to buy me a painting or something?" I smirked, gesturing towards the wall.

He smiled. "Would that get you to forgive me?"

I was totally helpless against this man, it's not my fault he was so damn good-looking. He's to blame for being utterly charming. *Dammit, I'm annoyed with myself.*

"Nope." I shook my head. "Tell me, why are you here? Are you stalking me now?"

"Stalking women isn't in my repertoire. I'm here on official business, I swear."

"What official business?"

"I own this building."

"You own the building?" I stood staring at him with my mouth agape. "Next, you'll tell me that you own the entire island."

"Would it be possible if we just started over, Stevie?" he asked pointedly.

I stared at him, unable to form words. A strange combination of nerves, excitement and fear raced up my spine making a pit stop in my stomach.

Finally, he spoke up outstretching his hand. "Hi, I'm Jackson Hart, but you can call me Jax or Jay whatever you like." A wide grin spread across his face, and his eyes lit up. That's when everything flipped upside down.

When my eyes popped open, there was Jax. I felt his hand on the side of my face. There was a slight buzzing sound, and I couldn't hear what he was saying to me.

"Stevie, hey, there you are."

"What . . . what happened?"

"You fainted. Well, at least I *think* you did."

"Fainted?"

Jesus Christ. That's fucking cliché.

I wiggled free from his hold, shaking my head trying to pull myself together.

"Hey, take it easy," he said, holding onto my arms.

My legs wobbled beneath me as I tried to bring my body upright. I probably looked like that baby giraffe after it was born. Well, if this wasn't the corniest thing that could have happened.

As if things couldn't get more embarrassing, my stomach rumbled, loudly.

"Have you had anything to eat today?" he asked, his eyes filled with concern.

My cheeks heated. "No, just a large coffee."

"Breakfast is the most important meal of the day," he reminded. "Did you have dinner last night?"

What was with all the questions? This guy had no right to

chastise me about my eating habits. I didn't have to stand here and take this from him.

I spun around and ran smack into the wooden column I had been leaning on earlier.

"Shit!" I yelped in pain.

Damn this was worse than the time I ran straight into the sliding glass door at my parents' house.

Strong hands gripped my arms. "Okay, easy there, Megan the klutz."

"Whoa," I replied, rubbing what I could only feel would be a definite bump on my forehead. "How do you know about that book?"

He helped me to sit on the bench in the hallway. "I have a younger sister, and she's into reading vintage YA, as she calls it. She also likes reading self-help books."

I laughed. "Yeah, my mom bought me a bunch of those teen dramas and I loved that one too. Self-help books are so ten years ago."

"Hey, are you making fun of my sister?"

My fingers danced over my forehead. *Shit.* "No, let's blame it on the head injury."

"Are you okay?" he asked, bending to look at me.

"You mean, besides being in pain and mortified. I'm all good."

"Come on, I'm driving."

"Where are we going? What about my car?"

After pulling me to my feet, he took my hand, and led me down to the first floor. "I'll take care of it. Sit here while I make a phone call."

He took out his phone and then swiped the screen. "Hey, Mitch, I need you to pick up a blue Ford Focus from the Baker

Art Gallery. I'll text you the delivery address. And I need you to drop off the keys at The Villa."

The Villa, was that a restaurant on the island? My stomach rumbled again.

After Jackson ended the call, he dropped his phone into his back pocket, giving me a reason to admire his ass in those jeans. *Well done, DNA Gods.*

"Hand me your keys."

"I'm always handing you my keys." I dropped them into his hand. Fire danced across my fingertips. Wow, it did happen, like in the romance books.

I sat staring at him, watching as he gave the receptionist specific instructions. She hung on his every word, all while batting her eyelashes.

He walked back towards me, almost with a bounce in his step.

"Let's get out of here," he said, taking my hand in his and leading me out the door. I glanced around, looking for his Range Rover, but I didn't see it. To my left there was a motorcycle and a shiny silver Mercedes convertible sports car.

He unlocked the door and held it open for me. Nervous knots formed in my stomach once more, or maybe I was just hungry. In less than a week, I'd been inside two luxury vehicles, both owned by a man who at present had me conjuring very dirty thoughts in my head. His fingers curled tightly around the steering wheel and I wanted to know what they would feel like inside me.

Yep, I went there. Megyn would be so proud. I was certain Krystle would be too. I had yet to tell her about the sexy man of my dreams.

"Is the temperature okay?"

"All good. New ride?" I asked, stroking the soft leather my ass was seated on.

"No, I've had this for a few months, but I do love having options."

"Right, so how many vehicles do you have?"

"Just the two, but I also have a yacht and a jet."

"Of course you do."

"The jet belongs to the company, but I could always take it out for a spin. Maybe you'd like to go up sometime?"

"I bet you say that to all the girls you date." I froze realizing what I had suggested.

"Not quite," he replied, grasping my hand and running the pad of his thumb over my knuckles. "Besides my sister, the only females I've traveled with were business associates."

His touch was warm, and I got the feeling that he was trying to ease my nerves. That was a nice feeling. Actually it was more than nice, it felt wonderful.

"How do you feel about Asian seafood?" he asked, removing his hand to shift gears.

"I've never had it," I replied softly. "I'm actually a creature of habit. If I'm not cooking, I'm getting takeout from the Chinese restaurant or eating burgers and fries at Quench."

"Would you rather do that, or are you feeling adventurous?" He turned to face me and wiggled his eyebrows.

"I think I'm up for the challenge," I replied, suddenly feeling not so out of my comfort zone. Who was I kidding though; I was on a maybe date with a gorgeous man who had a private jet at his disposal. I was definitely no longer in Kansas.

CHAPTER
seven

Stevie

JACKSON TOOK ME TO THE HOKAIDO GRILL, IT WAS THE FANCIEST restaurant I think I'd ever been to in my life. We were seated at a large table near the bar, with a prime view of the ocean. This place oozed elegance, and the chic décor had a cool cultural vibe. It made me want to travel to the Far East. A place I'd never thought much of before.

I've never been out of the country, but I hoped to travel one day. My bucket list was long, it included several shipwrecked sites and some small islands, I hoped my first stop could be somewhere near the Bermuda Triangle.

A woman with curly red hair appeared before us, setting a basket of bread on the table. "Good afternoon, Mister Hart, and welcome back. Here is the wine list, and can I get you your usual?"

So this was a place he frequented often. "I'll skip the scotch today, but let's start with bottle of the house Riesling and because we're being adventurous a bottle of the Clos du Caillou Châteauneuf-du-Pape."

"Very good, sir."

"Thank you, Catelyn."

That wine sounded expensive, and I've had Riesling before. Megyn bought a bottle the night she moved in and we stayed up talking and getting to know one another. We met at a "yoga on the beach" class, and we'd get coffee a few times a week. Her lease at her old place was up, and I told her that I had a room for rent. The rest was history.

"You good?" he asked, pulling me back to the moment. "How's your forehead?"

"I'm good. It's okay, no icepack needed." Right on cue my stomach rumbled. *I'm going to start packing granola bars in my purse.*

He pushed the basket of bread towards me. "Eat, before you pass out on me again."

"You're so bossy. You're not like one of those domineering alpha males are you?" I tore off a corner of the bread and popped it into my mouth.

His brow scrunched. "Domineering, I'm not sure, I've never thought about it. Aren't all men Alphas?"

I shrugged. Feeling more at ease, I opted to throw out my earlier plan of not addressing his identity. "Okay, Mister Jackson Hart, why didn't you tell me who you really were the day we met? I can't believe I didn't even make the connection. Abby told me who you were."

"I guess in that moment, I felt like I wasn't the boss. People tend to change their demeanor when they find out I'm the CEO. It was nice just being—Jax, not Mister Hart."

"I can't relate, but I can imagine that for a man of your

stature, it's kind of like being a celebrity—on twenty-four seven."

He nodded. "Yeah, it's a lot like that."

"Well then, I guess I'll be calling you Jax."

His lips curled into that sexy grin. "Good."

Catelyn returned with the wine, and one of the other servers had carried over an extra set of glasses. After Jax poured the Clos du Caillou Châteauneuf-du-Pape, I took a sip and nearly had an orgasm from just one taste. Had I moaned? By the look on Jax's face, I had no idea. I looked around the restaurant there wasn't a soul in sight. Actually, it was completely empty.

"This is an excellent wine," I said, twirling the stem of the glass between my thumb and index finger. The only reason I knew it was good was because it didn't taste like sweet fruit juice. It had layers of flavor, nothing like the sweet swill of the bottles from the corner market I'd had before.

"Eat some more bread, or you'll be drunk before we order."

"Okay, fine," I huffed. "Just so you know I'll be paying you back the money for fixing my car."

"Would you let it go and accept the fact that someone did something nice for you?" His tone was firm but not angry.

"I'm not letting it go." I pointed my wine glass in his direction. "I will pay you back."

"Let's not worry about that right now, how about we have some fun, okay? Besides, I'd like to enjoy a meal with the beautiful woman sitting across from me."

"Surely you must be talking about someone else in here."

He smiled, a smile so bright, I could see the creases around his blue eyes. He's going to have to stop looking at me like that or just stop being so damn gorgeous altogether.

"Okay," I said, before polishing off the last bite of my

bread. "Tell me about yourself."

"What would you like to know?"

Catelyn was back, and refilling our water glasses, before I had the chance to ask Jax a question.

"Would you care to order, Mister Hart?"

He eyed the menu, scanning the single printed card stock. This was the kind of place where the menu changed daily. He was so confident and self-assured, it would be fair to say that he rarely felt nervous or out of place. The certainty of his demeanor made me want to try a bit harder, be a better person and overcome some of my anxiety and fears.

"We're feeling adventurous. First, we'll start with the Lava Shrimp, and the Chef's Seared Ahi Tuna." He looked towards me and I nodded. "And for our entrée, we'll share the Thai Scallops and Shrimp."

And just like that Jax became the first man to ever order a meal for me. The "unadventurous me" would have no doubt been outraged at the thought of a man trying to steal my voice, my womanly power. *Maybe I am drunk.*

"Let's talk about the hippo in the room."

His brows lifted. "Hippo?"

"Yeah, everyone says elephant I changed it to hippo. Besides elephants are gentle creatures and hippos are mean. I feel like the issue of the hippo in the room would need to be addressed rather quickly."

That earned me quite the laugh from Jax. "You're a rule breaker. I like that. So what is this hippo in the room that needs addressing?"

"You're Jackson Hart, and I'm a caddy who works at your hotel. Why would you want to buy me lunch . . . dinner . . . *linner?*"

The afternoon sun had situated itself perfectly in front of our view. I swirled my water glass, the reflection splashed prisms of color across white tablecloth. Signaling Catelyn, he politely asked for her to adjust the shades, and then she disappeared. His gaze met mine once more.

"Asking you to lunch or dinner isn't about job titles. It's about two people sharing good food and some very *excellent* wine. All of that aside, I like you, and I think you kinda like me."

"You're pretty sure of yourself."

"I'd like to think so. But, I'll tell you a secret, I didn't use to be."

Our moment was broken by Catelyn returning with our appetizers. After draping my cloth napkin across my lap, I scooped some of the shrimp onto my plate. I wasn't shy, and I was certainly hungry. Jax picked up his chopsticks and popped a piece of shrimp into his mouth. I wasn't so good with those things. And I had the perfect opportunity to learn since I was pretty much a regular at The Golden Dragon.

"Lack of confidence, how did you fix that?"

"I guess the best way to describe it would be as a step-by-step process. I asked questions. Over time most conversations became easier, and I spoke up. Before I knew it, people started to ask me questions. I positioned myself as a leader, and just adapted from there."

"You make it sound so simple."

"I think with anything in life you have to make a decision and just go for what you want." Leaning closer, he pinned me with those dreamy blue eyes. "When I see something of value, I won't settle for anything less than what I've set my mind on."

Stunned by his words, I stopped chewing and swallowed

the piece of shrimp. It was a miracle I didn't choke. Picking up my water glass, I brought it to my lips and took a long drink. That sentence was laced with some innuendo.

"Do you always get what you want?" I couldn't help jabbing at the suggestive remark.

"No, sometimes I have to work for it."

I took another drink. Still my brain searched for something to say. What could I say? Since we met you've been on my mind, constantly. That would make me sound crazy, possibly a bit foolish.

I set my glass down, and then Jax took my hand in his, lacing our fingers together. He brought my hand to his lips, dropping a few kisses to my knuckles. "You're beautiful."

"I'm not beautiful," I whispered, pulling my hand from his grip.

"A woman should always take a compliment," he pointed out. "Take the compliment, Stevie."

My hands began to sweat, and I swallowed hard. "Thank you for saying that I'm beautiful."

He said nothing, giving me a slow sexy smile. Our food arrived, putting an end to that perfect moment.

Apparently, the chef had been trying some new recipes, and he wanted us to try a few samples. We dipped pieces of food into various sauces and I tried to work the chopsticks but my fingers were not that coordinated. Jax took my hand in his, spreading and positioning my fingers, but it was of no use.

Abandoning my chopsticks, Jax scooped up a Thai shrimp cake and dipped into the sweet chili sauce with his. "Open your mouth," he prompted. "You gotta try this."

My mouth closed over the chopsticks and Jax's eyes flicked to mine. The warmth of his gaze slid over me as the flavors danced on my tongue. The pad of his thumb swept the corner of my mouth and he licked the sauce from his skin. How I wished that were my tongue on him.

Our gazes lingered on one another as we sampled the myriad of flavors. I wasn't sure if the electricity fizzling through me was from the spices or from the way he was looking at me. Before I could give my feelings more thought, Jax dipped a piece of tuna into soy sauce, bringing it to my mouth.

"Oh my goodness," I chirped, covering my mouth with my napkin. "That's so good."

Usually I don't do so well with spicy foods, most things are too hot, but that was perfect.

I'd barely eaten any of my entrée before another small plate arrived to the table. Catelyn said it was cucumber bites topped with avocado and spiced tuna.

"Yum," I moaned, taking a second bite.

Smiling he asked, "Good, yeah?"

I nodded, and watched as his mouth bit into the crisp cucumber. His Adam's apple bobbed in his throat and I had the strangest fantasy of running my tongue over his neck kissing my way up to his mouth.

Snap out of it.

Dinner went smoothly, everything was delicious. Even though we tried so many things, I didn't feel stuffed. I would never forget the smell and all the savory spices. Mostly, I would never forget that Jax told me that I was beautiful.

After our meal, he suggested a walk on the beach. I kicked off my flip flops and dug my toes into the warm sand. Jax wrapped his arm around my shoulders, pulling me close, allowing me to inhale his masculine scent of fresh clean soap and a lavender musk.

"Endless colors of blue and green. Not a bad view."

"It's pretty damn incredible," he admitted. "The sea match-es the color of your eyes, just gorgeous."

I pushed back so that I could look up at him. "More lines." I teased.

He grasped my hand and then scooped up my flip flops. "A compliment. What did I tell you about compliments?"

My eyes dropped to the sand. "Accept them."

"Very good."

We trekked along the warm sand until we reached the shoreline. Jax still had his shoes on, so we didn't get too far into the water. The beach was practically empty aside from a few families and an intense game of beach volleyball.

"Have you always lived here, on Salissa Island?"

"No, I was born in Montana and then the summer be-fore my sophomore year of high school, we moved to Fort Lauderdale."

"Was it hard leaving your friends behind?"

He nodded and blew out a deep breath. "It was at first, I kind of isolated myself. I was pissed that we had to leave and I'd just made the varsity football team. The team roster at my new school was already filled so I had to sit out a season and I that made me even angrier."

"That's tough." Looking up at him, I smiled and squeezed his hand. "Did you end up making the team the next year?"

"I didn't even bother trying out. By that time I'd discovered swimming, surfing and beach volleyball," he replied, turning to face me. "It seems that I was meant to be near the water." Smiling, he took our joined hands and pointed towards the ocean. In the distance I could see the storm clouds approaching and the wind kicked up fanning my hair across my face.

"I love the water," I replied, tucking my hair behind my ear. "Although I'll admit I am a little nervous about the ocean."

He cocked a brow. "Sharks or Jellyfish?"

"Both, but I think it's mostly the trepidation that comes from not being able to see what's swimming around me in the darker waters."

"I'd protect you from the big bad fish and seaweed," he teased, pulling me closer.

Those tingles resurfaced, or maybe they had been this whole time. "Is that so?"

He stopped dead in his tracks, and turned to face me. "Absolutely, scout's honor."

Stepping closer, he tossed my flip flops onto the sand. We were so close. Close enough that I couldn't help it when my eyes darted to his mouth.

My heart was beating a million miles a minute, in anticipation of his lips against my own. His hands glided along the sides of my neck and then pushed into my hair. Shifting his weight, his thigh pressed against me, as one hand snaked around my waist pulling me closer.

I drew in a breath, as my body pressed tightly against his. I could feel the hardness of his muscles through his t-shirt. With a mind of their own, my hands dug into the muscles of his back.

Cradling my cheek in his palm, his lips brushed against mine. The pad of his thumb stroked softly against my cheek. All at once my skin tingled and burned.

Closing my eyes, all I could feel was Jax. My lips parted, and his tongue swept against mine, teasing me.

I melted into him, and he kissed me hard, filling my

mouth stroking all the right spots. My hands roamed up his back, finding their way into his hair. Want and need surged through me, on a moan elicited from somewhere deep inside his chest. I opened my mouth wider, asking for more, perhaps I was begging.

Jax's hands tangled in my hair, and every bit of me ached for him. He had the lips of the devil. And with one kiss, he melted every part of me—setting my soul on fire.

CHAPTER
eight

Stevie

RESTLESS WAS THE WAY I'D SLEPT, OR 'NOT SLEPT,' WITH THE memory of Jax's lips on mine. Sunlight peered through my bedroom window, and eventually the early morning yellow color splashed over the walls. I planted my feet on the rug beside my bed, and stood stretching my arms over my head.

Just past seven thirty, I trekked into the bathroom and brushed my teeth. After washing my face, I threw on my yoga pants and a sports bra. Grabbing my mat and gym bag, I then headed out the door to join the other yogis at the beach.

As much as I tried, my mind kept wandering to thoughts of him. After we left the restaurant, Jax took me to get my keys at "The Villa," which was just the nickname he used for the hotel. Some kind of inside joke I assumed. Jax gave me a quick tour of his office, which was a suite in itself, minus a bed. Just after seven, he dropped me off at home, but not without kissing me once more. I contemplated going to the bar to visit Krystle and telling her about my amazing day with Jax, but instead I changed into my pajamas and settled in for the remainder of the evening with a book.

After shaking the sand from my mat, I rolled it up and shoved it into my bag. Checking the time on my phone, I realized that I missed a call from Abby. I swiped the screen to play the voicemail.

"Hey, girl, I have an emergency with my sister. Her husband is out of town and I'm taking her to the doctor, she's having labor pains. Can you cover my shift today from nine to three? I'll trade you for your Friday shift. Call or text me."

I texted her back and let her know I would be happy to cover for her. After stopping to grab a coffee, I headed home to shower and change.

The day flew by in a blur of heat and humidity. Along with the other three caddies, I spent the morning caddying a foursome, raking the bunkers and replacing divots.

By the time three o'clock rolled around, we were still on the course. A group of businessmen had been taking their sweet time. Finally, they offered to let my group play through. After collecting my tips and grabbing a bottle of water, I went to the locker room to shower and change.

Pulling my phone out of my locker to check my messages, I spotted a text from Abby.

My sister has been put on bed rest for the remainder of her pregnancy. How was the day? Thank you again for helping me out.

Me: The day was great. No need to worry about a thing. Tell your sister to get some rest.

I wondered if Abby's sister had an e-reader. Maybe, I could get her a gift card and she could download some books to read while she's on bed rest. I shoved my clothes into my locker and scooped up my tote.

I turned on the water and let the warm spray cascade over my skin. For a brief moment, I allowed myself to think about Jax as I ducked my head under the shower head. *What was he doing today?* I grabbed my lavender shower gel and poured a generous amount onto the puffy pink mesh sponge. *Did he think of me?* Scrubbing over my arms and stomach, thoughts of Jax standing here with me surfaced. *What would his hands feel like on my wet skin?*

When my fingers looked like prunes, I rinsed the conditioner out of my hair. Voices of laughter echoed through the room. I recognized one of the bartenders from the Cabana Grill. She tossed me a smile, and kept talking to the woman I didn't recognize as they changed into their uniforms.

After changing into my favorite pair of cropped denim jeans and a floral print tank and blowing my hair dry, I packed up all my stuff and then walked out to my car. As I crossed the parking lot, my cellphone rang, nearly scaring me half to death. The caller ID said, Jax.

I don't remember exchanging numbers with him.

"Hello, Jax," I answered, unlocking my car.

"Hello there," he greeted me, and in some odd way the cadence of his voice was soothing. "How was your day?"

Balancing the phone between my chin and shoulder, I climbed into my car and tossed my tote bag on the passenger seat. "Good, I just finished work, and I'm headed to my apartment."

I heard the rustling of papers over the phone. "I didn't know you had to work today."

"Well, Abby's sister went into false labor or something and

she asked me to trade shifts."

"What day do you have off now?"

"Friday."

"Perfect. I'd like to take you on a date. I'll pick you up, say around four?"

"Okay, that sounds nice. What should I wear?"

"Whatever you want, but pack a swimsuit."

"Sounds mysterious."

He laughed. "Just let me surprise you."

"Fine, I suppose I can allow that. See you then."

"Until Friday, have a good week."

I ended the call and shoved my phone into the cup holder. As I drove out of the parking lot, I wondered what glorious date Jax had cooked up. Hearing from him made me smile. It was the highlight of my day, and him asking me out was the cherry on top.

After I unpacked from work, I threw my work clothes into the wash. Staring into the fridge nothing looked appetizing, and I didn't feel like having another carton of lo mein. Grabbing my phone off the counter, I swiped the screen and sent a quick text to Krystle.

Me: Are you working?

Krystle: Always. Come have a drink. It's dead in here.

Me: Be there shortly.

I twisted the handle and locked the door to my apartment. Practically skipping down the steps, I raced to my car and headed towards Quench. Krystle was going to get an earful. She'd be surprised, since I usually have nothing to share, at least not anything exciting, but Jax and our mini date and now another date Friday was definitely gossip worthy.

With a quick flick of my turn signal, I pulled into the parking lot and parked in my regular space near the front door. I peered through the window eyeing Krystle leaning against the bar with her arms crossed watching the evening news. The bells chimed as I pulled on the brass handle of the heavy wooden door.

"My favorite bitch!" she called out and lined up two shot glasses.

"What's up, chickadee?" I took a seat in my chair near the beer taps.

"Slow as fuck tonight and I could use the tips to fix my laptop." She slid a glass of tequila in front of me. "Cheers."

"Bottoms up."

We downed our shots and I handed her my glass.

"You alright there, S?" She smiled crooked as she looked my way.

"All good, and the reason is because your girl was just asked out on a second date by a very hot guy."

She took two tumblers from the rack and filled mine with rum and then added in Diet Coke.

"Really? I didn't know that you were seeing anyone. Dish *now*."

"Well, I had some car trouble at work and this hot guy appeared before me. He had my car towed, and then he sent me flowers. I had complained a little bit about my training when he dropped me off at home, but then I was at that art gallery Gran used to take me too and he was there. Turns out he owns the building." I smirked, before popping the cherry from my drink into my mouth.

Her eyebrow arched. "Hold on, you mean to tell me that some rich guy just happened to be at your place of work and then happened to be at the very art gallery you go to once a month?"

"I never said he was rich."

"Girl, he was golfing or doing God knows what at the Hart Resort and you said he owns the building where Baker's is housed. That screams rich."

Probably shouldn't mention the two cars, the jet or the yacht.

"Judging much?"

She laughed. "I'm not trying to be like that. Tell me more."

"We got to talking and then one thing led to another and we ended up having a late lunch at Hokaido Grill."

A shocked laugh ripped from her throat. "Wow, *fancy*. What's this guy's deal?"

My nose wrinkled up. "How do you mean?"

The sound of laughter rang out in the bar, and four men entered. "I'm telling you, boys, this place has the coldest beer in town."

"Be right back. Keep your ass in that chair." She pointed at me as she rounded the bar.

After taking a very large gulp, I stirred my drink and stole another cherry from the condiments tray. Propping my elbow on the bar, I rested my chin in my hand. My cheeks heated, and my belly was warm. I really needed to eat.

Krystle appeared and filled four icy mugs with the latest pale ale from the local brewery.

She grinned. "These guys, I'll get them to stay until close."

"Yeah, you will."

Her eyes narrowed. "So did you fuck him yet?"

Her question didn't catch me off guard. That was Krystle, no filter. "Yep, right there in the bathroom, at the restaurant."

She took all four mugs in her hands. "No, you didn't."

I shrugged, and tossed her a wink. "I'll give you the details when you come back."

The guys cheered upon the arrival of their beers. Chris, the guy who ran the kitchen, appeared. Krystle breezed past him, and he took a step forward.

"Do they want any food?"

"I think they're discussing appetizers. I'll let you know."

He smiled, and wound the dish towel he was carrying around his wrist. His gaze flicked to me. "You need anything to eat?"

"I'll take the coconut chicken fingers basket with honey mustard on the side."

"I'll get that started for you, Stevie."

"Thanks, Chris."

The guys at the four top called Krystle over once more. I heard someone say, "Let's get that flatbread pizza, hot wings, and nachos."

I laughed. I knew Krystle would have those orders upgraded to burgers in an instant.

My phone pinged with a text.

Mom: *Just wanted to say hello. I hope you had a good week.*

Me: *It was a good week. I'm hanging with Krystle at the bar. Call you soon.*

Mom: *I'll call you. Love you.*

Me: *Okay. Love you too.*

I sat my phone on the bar, next to my purse. Krystle

bounced up to the computer and rang in the order. By the way she was typing I could tell it was a much larger order than the appetizers. She pulled some bottles from the fridge and popped off the caps. Away she went again, delivering more drinks.

"Okay, now tell me more about your guy." She smirked, wiping her hands on the bar towel. "What's his name?"

"Jax. He's an executive at the hotel. Actually, he's the owner."

She stared at me eyes wide. "Are you saying the guy is Jackson Hart?"

"Yep, that is what I am saying."

Krystle leaned on the bar. "You lying little slut."

I held my hands up in mock surrender. "I swear. I'm not lying. Jackson—Jax, is *the* guy."

Krystle rang the bar bell. "Hot damn, girl! Half-price pints and well drinks for the next hour."

I shook my head and laughed. I peered over my shoulder hearing the cheers. One of the guys held up his hand and signaled for another round.

Chris appeared from the back with my food order in hand. He placed the basket in front of me and instantly my mouth watered. Krystle grabbed a plate and a silverware roll. I dipped a fry into the honey mustard sauce, and popped it into my mouth.

"So where is *Jax* taking you on your hot date?"

"I don't know. He said he wanted it to be a surprise, but he did tell me to bring a swimsuit."

She smiled and leaned against the bar. "It sounds like someone wants to get you all wet and maybe, if you're lucky, in more ways than one."

I threw a cocktail napkin at her. "You're disgusting."

She shrugged. "A man that fucking hot, he makes panties wet with just a smile."

Yeah, she was right about that, but I wasn't going to give her the satisfaction of confirming.

CHAPTER
nine

Stevie

THE GLORIOUS SMELL OF COFFEE PULLED ME FROM MY SLEEP. I looked at my phone for the time, it was half past eight. No morning yoga for me today.

With my arms stretched over my head, I made my way to the kitchen.

"Morning, sunshine," Megyn greeted me and slid a mug my way as I walked by the table.

"Hey, how was your weekend away?"

"It was pretty great, I wanted to stay longer but work calls."

"Well, it's good to have you back, and I'm glad you had a nice weekend." I slid into the seat across from her and cradled my mug. "What time did you get in?"

"Around eleven, you were sound asleep."

"Yeah, I was pretty tired. I ended up working yesterday, and then I went to Quench to see Krystle." My index finger traced imaginary circles on the smooth tabletop.

"You haven't stopped smiling since you walked out here."

My brows shot up. "What?"

She settled back into the chair, eyeing me over her mug. "Who put that permanent grin on your face?"

There was no denying it, I *was* happy. Mom was home, work was going well, for the most part, and then there was Jax.

"What, a girl can't just wake up smiling because she's just happy to be alive?"

She laughed, her beautiful green eyes twinkling. "Did the mice and birds from *Cinderella* sing to you this morning, too?"

"You know it."

My phone buzzed, it was a message from Carol warning me of a severe weather alert. I looked around the course. In the distance I saw one foursome packing up their bags.

"Mister and Missus Brandt, I've just received word that there is a thunderstorm headed our way. We're instructed to evacuate the course as soon as possible."

"Thank you, dear," she answered, while adjusting her sunglasses. "I believe we'll play this last hole and then we can go inside."

I looked at Abby and she shrugged. We continued along the course, hefting their bags over the hill towards the ninth hole.

They both shot a four on the last hole. This one was at least going to be a six for her and at best a four for him. Neither one of them were all that great. And they made it clear that they didn't want to hear any helpful advice we could offer.

Mrs. Brandt's ball landed just off the green. However, I was having a hard time finding Mr. Brandt's. Thunder rumbled in the distance.

"Go on, honey, you take your shots while this one helps me find my ball."

Abby's hand flew to her mouth and Mrs. Brandt side-eyed her.

"I think a bug flew into my mouth," she coughed, and made a sour face.

Mrs. Brandt yanked the club from Abby's grip. From the corner of my eye, I saw Mr. Brandt drop a ball onto the ground approximately one hundred fifty four yards give or take from the green. "Here it is. Here's my ball!"

"That's great, Mister Brandt," I called out, clapping my hands together. "You have a pretty good shot from there. I bet you can make it in three strokes with ease."

After hefting his bag onto my shoulder, I walked towards him. I placed his bag in front of him, and he gripped each club finally settling on the seven iron.

Totally the wrong choice, but I wasn't going to correct him. I stood with my hands behind my back, watching Mrs. Brandt swing and miss. "That doesn't count, young lady, you hear me?"

Abby through her hands up in mock surrender. "It's fine, ma'am. Take your time."

Mr. Brandt stood beside me, one hand on his hip and the other resting on top of his club. "I'm sorry about my wife. She can be very difficult."

I smiled at him. "I think she's lovely."

He laughed. "You lie. You should be a sales person, not a golf caddy."

Takes one to know one, you ball dropping cheater. "I don't plan to caddy forever, sir."

The wind kicked up and whipped the flag as Abby fought to hold it still. The storm was coming over the water quickly.

My phone buzzed, and I lifted it from my pocket. Jax's name appeared on the screen with a message: *I need you and Abby off that course, now. Tell the Brandt's I'll buy them dinner at Cranwell's tonight.*

"Uhmm, Mister and Missus Brandt, we've been asked to vacate the course. Because of this weather inconvenience, Jax—*Mister Hart* would like to pay for you dinner tonight at Cranwell's."

In the blink of an eye, Mr. Brandt had his club back in the bag and Mrs. Brandt had tossed hers to Abby.

Golf carts zipped along the cart path, and a few remaining guests along with their caddies hustled to seek shelter. I thought it was cool that the resort had both carts and caddies. Even more, I was surprised at the amount of people that chose caddies over carts.

I sent a quick text back to Jax as we power walked back to the Clubhouse.

Me: How did you know that would get them off the course?

Jax: They're the cheapest rich people I know.

Me: We're headed to the clubhouse now, and the rain isn't far behind us.

Jax: I'll meet you in the main lobby.

Smiling, I shoved my phone back into the pocket of my shorts. Looking up I saw the Brandts had made it inside the clubhouse.

"Hurry up, S," Abby called over her shoulder. She was already past the putting green.

I strapped the bag across my back and hiked up the hill, I

felt the cool splash of rain against my arm. I cut left onto the cart path and up the stairs to the terrace. The rain came with a fury and the wind whipped my visor off my head sending it rolling like a tumbleweed across the bricks. It was a lost cause, and that was my favorite one.

"Stevie in here!" I heard Cord calling as he held the door open.

"Did you see Abby by chance?"

"I'm pretty sure she went to the clubhouse." He lifted the heavy bag out of my grip and set it on the floor. I barely got the door shut, it sounded like rocks crashing over the glass.

"Here," Cord said, handing me a dry towel.

"Thanks." I dried off my arms, and squeezed the water from my ponytail.

"You can stay here until the storm passes."

Cord walked over towards his desk, and started banging away on the keyboard.

"That came in quick, and to make matters worse, the couple we were caddying for wouldn't get off the course." I moved to stand near the display of visors, looking for one like the one I just lost.

"Come here, I want to show you some pictures."

"No thanks, I'm good right here."

"I won't bite you, Stevie. I want to show you my new house."

"Hold your horses. Can't you see I'm shopping?" I found a visor in my size and took it off the wall. "Congrats on the new house."

"Thanks." He clicked on the slide show and the photos began rotating on the screen. On the set of photos that showed the bedroom I felt his hand smooth up my leg. I jumped back, but not before slapping his face.

"Fuck Stevie!" He rubbed at his cheek. "That hurt."

"You don't get to touch me like that, *ever*," I snapped.

"Hey, I was just messing around."

"Fuck you," I spat, and tossed the visor at him.

He took a step towards me. "Don't get all bent out of shape. Are you on your period or something?"

I scowled at him. "Are you fucking serious?" Unsure of why I even bothered, I hefted Mr. Brandt's bag over my shoulder and stormed out into the pouring rain.

Fuck it.

Fuck him.

So what if I got soaked? I needed to shower anyway. My legs carried me as fast as they could down the sidewalk. Once inside the clubhouse, I picked up some towels and then started to wipe off the clubs. I left his bag in his assigned locker stall.

I pulled my phone from my pocket, and I had five text messages: two from Abby and three from Jax. Walking over to the employee locker room, I scrolled the messages.

Abby: Where are you?

Jax: Are you okay?

Abby: I'm in the Cabana Bar drinking with Joe and Kerry.

Jax: I'm in the lobby and I don't see you.

Jax: Going up to my office. Message me when you get this.

I fired off a text to Abby letting her know that I got caught in the Pro-Shop looking at visors. I replied to Jax's text and told him I was about to shower and change.

Jax: You are welcome to use my private shower.

Jax: Glad you're okay. My office is on the twenty-first floor of the clubhouse tower.

My heart pounded against my ribcage.

Being wet and naked in Jax's office?

This was not a good idea. Or was it? Nope. I didn't bother sending a reply. I stripped out of my wet clothes, and then wrapped up in my towel and hurried to the stalls.

That's a new offer from a guy. *"Hey, how about you come take a shower in my office."*

I was so very tempted by his offer, but it felt a lot like reverse walk of shame.

Less shame—instead how about walk of the shameless slut.

CHAPTER
Ten

Stevie

WHAT THE FUCK?

My towel was gone.

"Seriously, not cool." I huffed.

"Looking for this?" Jax's voice boomed out.

I covered myself with the shower curtain and peered out. Jax stood five feet from the shower stall holding my towel in his hands. "Jax, what the hell?"

What was he doing here? And why did he have to look all hot and yummy? He was wearing black dress pants and a white button down shirt with the sleeves pushed up. To make matters worse, his collar was undone—two buttons undone to be exact, showing just a bit dark chest hair.

He laughed. "I told you to come to my office."

"I'd like my towel back please," I demanded, nodding towards the hook. "And, no, you didn't, you said I was welcome to use the shower in your office."

He placed the towel back on the hook, and I motioned for him to turn around. As quick as I could, I snatched the towel. After I made sure the curtain was securely in place, I patted my arms and legs dry.

"Jax, this is the women's locker room, I am sure you're violating at least twenty employee codes of conduct," I informed him, tightening the towel around me.

"Possibly, and I could say I'm the boss the rules don't apply to me, but that line of thinking rests on the corner of douchebag and asshole."

I pulled the curtain back and stepped out of the stall. When his eyes met mine, thoughts of lust swirled inside me, I've looked at Jax before, but this time it was different. I saw the passion and fire dancing in his eyes. Disoriented from the hot shower, I had to be imagining things. I strode past him, and rounded the sinks to get to my locker. "Don't follow me, I need to change."

Mocking surrender, he held up his hands. "I'll stay right here."

"No peeking," I called over my shoulder.

"So I wanted to see you because my sister got me this gift for my birthday earlier this year, and, well, it's about to expire."

My brows pinched together in confusion, as I dabbed the soft cotton against my slick skin.

"What kind of gift would expire?"

"It's a cooking class for two, and if I don't take it now." He cleared his throat. "*Tonight* actually, I lose it."

Clasping the hook of my bra, I shook my head. "What if I already have plans tonight?"

"Hmm, yeah, I was hoping I'd get lucky and this was a night you weren't busy."

The good news for Jax was that the only plans I had were to pick up some takeout, pay bills and then watch some television. The bills could wait until tomorrow morning.

"Okay, I'll go to this cooking class with you. What are we making?"

"The theme is Asian fusion."

I finished getting dressed and then came around to face Jax. "It seems that I am quite the fan of Asian cuisine, so I guess I will save you from having to take this class alone."

"Perfect." He rubbed his hands together, a wicked smile played up his lips. "I'll pick up at your place in two hours?"

"Okay," I said with a smile. "Now *shoo*, don't you have a company to run or something?"

Jax turned to leave, and when I heard the door close I sagged against my locker. I pressed my fist to my mouth to stifle a tiny squeal.

CHAPTER
eleven

Jackson

To say that I was making sane decisions would be a complete lie. I'd gone out of my way to stalk Stevie down in the women's locker room. Apparently, stalking was in my repertoire. I should stay away from this woman, but I couldn't. I'd already asked her out for Friday, but that wasn't soon enough. At present, she was correct in pointing out the employee code of conduct. I was working my way through violating more than half the policies in the handbook.

Thankfully, I didn't have anything about not dating employees drafted. What my employees did with their free time or whom they did it with was none of my concern, as long as they weren't breaking the law or stealing from me, I didn't give a shit.

Stevie Brockman, she ignited something inside me. Those blue eyes of hers reflected innocence, but I wondered if she had a bit of a naughty side. Perhaps she was having the same dirty fantasies about me? I saw the way her gaze had gone a bit hazy when she looked at me earlier. On the other hand, maybe she *was* innocent and looking to explore her deepest desires?

I spent a considerable amount of time thinking about her naked. Seeing her wearing nothing but a towel provoked several shower fantasies. Considering the massive erection I had after leaving the locker room, it was no wonder I ended up jerking off in my own shower. I pictured Stevie on her knees, sucking me deep. My mind went into overdrive as I imagined her pumping my cock and sucking my balls.

Oh the things I can teach her.

Christ. I sounded like a misogynistic pig. The lines had been blurred and I wanted this woman in the worst way. The fact remained that Stevie was an employee and years younger than me.

What was I doing?

What was I thinking?

Playing with fire, and apparently I wanted to see how close I could get to the flames.

I flicked on my turn signal and maneuvered my car down the small alley to her apartment. When I pulled into the parking lot I saw her standing at the bottom of her stairs wearing a floral print dress. The neckline was low, and her necklace fell right above the valley between her breasts. The wind tousled her blonde hair across her face. As she pushed it away, a smile crossed her lips and that's when I remembered why I was doing this—Stevie was beautiful, smart, and a bubbly bright light.

I needed that light.

Things in my life weren't exactly as happy go lucky as I'd led people to believe over the years. I remember it so vividly, when my father left my mother my senior year of college. I came home for Thanksgiving to find my mother sobbing and holding divorce papers in her hand. Jason was in jail and Janessa, my sister, was skiing with one of her sorority sisters in Aspen that holiday weekend.

A year earlier, we'd flown home to Montana to visit family at Thanksgiving and my brother was arrested for possession of marijuana and attempted robbery. He and a few buddies decided to steal from a gas station. By all accounts, that was the beginning of the end for my parents.

I wondered how many other people could pinpoint the exact moment their life took a complete tailspin. Growing up, my dad had been a man I admired and respected. To find out he was nothing but a spineless coward was a tough blow.

I wondered if I somehow inherited his cowardice. Instead of staying in Miami and fighting for my hotel, I ran. I suppose I had no choice given the political circumstances.

Stevie was having a very bad day, a bad few months as she admitted when I met her, yet she still had hope. I liked that about her—a whole lot.

CHAPTER
twelve

Stevie

"How was the rest of your day?" I asked once we were settled into Jax's car.

His hands curled around the steering wheel. I couldn't take my eyes off him. The chambray shirt he wore amplified the blue in his eyes making them twinkle. He was ruggedly handsome with old Hollywood good looks, like James Dean and Clint Eastwood.

"It was uneventful," he answered, before making a three point turn in the parking lot. "You look beautiful by the way. I like your dress."

Heat bloomed in my chest at his words. "Thank you. I found it in downtown Amelia City at a shop near the art gallery."

He turned onto the main road and then flipped on the radio. "What kind of music do you listen to?"

"All kinds. Eighties. Country. Pop. Classic Rock."

"Let me guess, Fleetwood Mac?"

I laughed. "How did you ever guess?"

A smiled tugged the corners of his mouth. "Is that how you got your name?"

"Yeah, my mom is a huge fan. She followed them around the country one year. I think she said she went to like twenty or so shows."

"Wow, that's incredible. How did she afford that?"

"I know that she had money saved up before she left. As she tells me, she made jewelry, bracelets with stars, moon shapes, and lots of fringe and sold them out of her van."

"Sounds like your mom is a bit of a free spirit."

I smiled, and picked a piece of lint off my skirt. The sounds of "Amanda" by Boston blared through the speakers and I let out a small set of giggles.

"What's so funny?"

"A friend of mine used to sing dirty lyrics to this song all the time. All I ever hear are those words. Take you by the thighs and give you a surprise, Amanda."

He laughed a deep laugh that vibrated through the car. "I heard Cord Robinson, the golf pro, singing some dirty lyrics to another song a few weeks ago."

A sledgehammer crashed into my stomach, and I turned my head towards the window. I didn't know what to say. I couldn't keep this from Jax. Cord and I had been over for a while. There were no feelings for him on my part. *None.* Ughh. This was one conversation that made me feel totally awkward. My eyes closed, and I took a deep breath.

"Hey, where'd you go just now?" His deep voice brought my focus back to him.

Wringing my hands together, I looked up at him. "Cord and the friend I mentioned are one in the same. I used to date him."

His mouth pressed into a hardline. He fell silent, obviously lost in his thoughts.

"Is working with Cord going to be an issue?"

I shook my head. "Not for me. As far as I am concerned we are strictly co-workers."

"Good to know," he replied matter of fact.

Before I knew it we had pulled up to the Franklin Culinary School. He parked the car near the front and reached out to open his door.

My eyes watched Jax as he came around the front of the car to open my door. He took my hand in his sending heat fizzling over my skin. After closing the passenger door, he caught me by the shoulder.

"Are you ready to turn up the heat?"

My throat went dry. I'd suddenly lost the ability to speak. He pressed his tall frame against me and I blinked up to see those impossible gorgeous blue eyes searching my face. Just as I was about to respond, his soft lips were on mine. A familiar hum of electricity wound through every inch of my body.

"Jax," I breathed.

His hands came up to frame my face. "I'm just getting warmed up."

No kidding, he was certainly getting *me* warmed up. My legs felt like jelly, and I couldn't even think about the deep ache between my thighs. I had to concentrate really hard to put one foot in front of the other as he led me into the building. With that kiss lingering on my lips and being in such close proximity to Jax, how in the world was I going to make it through this class?

"Have you ever noticed that food just tastes better when it comes on a stick?"

Jax cocked a brow as he threaded red onions, pineapple and zucchini onto the skewer. "And what brings you to this theory?"

After adding the salmon, he set another finished skewer on the tray and I brushed the soy sauce marinade over it. We were making the main course, Asian salmon kabobs.

"State fair food. For instance, there are corndogs, deep fried candy bars—my favorite is the Milky Way. Then there's cotton candy, candied apples and chocolate covered cheesecake on a stick." My mouth watered thinking about the cheesecake.

"I don't think cotton candy counts."

"No?"

"Cotton candy comes on a paper cone, not a stick," he informed, placing the last kabob on the tray.

I rolled my eyes. "Okay, smarty pants. You just had to be technical."

"These look pretty good," he stated, adding a sprinkling of cilantro over each one.

"Once you've finished preparing the kabobs, set them aside and go back to your dumplings," the instructor announced from the front of the classroom. "Take the cabbage strips out of the water and wring out the moisture."

Jax worked on the cabbage while I prepared the rest of our filling. We'd already browned the meat. We made the executive decision to use turkey instead of ground beef. I took my time mixing in the ingredients: scallions, more cilantro, ginger along with the sesame oil and soy sauce.

Mixing was an easy job thankfully, because I couldn't take my eyes off Jax and neither could a number of women in the class. There were at least ten pairs of eyes on him at the moment. Smiling, I picked up a pineapple chunk and playfully coaxed him to take a bite. His mouth closed over the fruit licking the juice from my thumb. Jax smiled, slowly making my knees go weak and my head feel light. The gentle touch of his tongue against my skin prompted the ache between my thighs to return. I pulled myself together and resumed the task at hand—dumplings.

Clearing off some counter space, I set out the dumpling wrappers and then filled up a small bowl with water. The water was for sealing the dumplings. Jax finished with the cabbage and then combined it into our mixture stirring with a large spoon.

"To make basic dumplings, simply fold the dumpling into a half-moon and press closed." The instructor's voice cracked out in a high-pitch as she demonstrated the various ways to fold the wrappers.

Suddenly I'd lost interest in the task, as I watched Jax dip his fingers into the water and then working multiple pleats using his thumb and first finger. It was like watching an artist at work—he was simply too good. Skilled and precise, his dumplings looked like beautiful pieces of edible origami. By the time I was able to finish one of mine, he'd already made five.

"Here let me show you." His voice was low and seductive. After scooping some filling onto the wrapper, he took my fingers in his hands and then dipped them into the bowl of water. A shiver climbed up my legs. As he moved to stand behind me, he guided my fingers to the wrapper, interlacing his fingers with my own. I never knew a simple touch could be so erotic. Our wet fingers slid across the smooth wrapper, folding and then pinching it closed. His fingers caressed mine as we smoothed the edges together in a fluid movement.

Tingles shot everywhere, from my fingertips to my toes,

making a few stops to settle in other places. Jax's cock pressed against the small of my back.

"And as you can see once you pinch it closed then you slide it . . . in this way, zipper the dumpling closed." The sound of the instructor's voice boomed out.

Jax wiped my hands on the towel and then his own. After he turned off the burner, he clasped my hand in his and led me out the door.

Once outside in the hallway, he pushed me up against the wall and kissed me hard. The tile was cool, but it did nothing to quiet the alarms going off in my body. My hands snaked around his neck, and his tongue slid into my mouth.

He shoved his hands into my hair, holding me tight as he sucked on my tongue. My fingers dug into his shoulder blades as he deepened our kiss. His hands drifted up and down my back, eventually falling to my ass. A growl rattled his throat as he urged my hips forward. The sound was deep and pleasurable, causing the pressure between my legs to tighten.

My eyes flew open at the sound of footsteps echoing off the walls.

"Someone's coming," I whispered, our mouths a hair's breadth apart. "Should we go back inside and finish what we started?"

Saying nothing his eyes darted around the space. He pulled me down the hallway with him, as he turned the handle on several doors, finally finding one that opened. Jax dragged me inside, and then locked the door. Lights from outside splashed across the room. As he took a step toward me, his hands landed on my hips.

"I'm giving the tutorial now," he said coolly, but there was no mistaking that wicked gleam in his eyes.

CHAPTER
Thirteen

Jackson

A S THE OLD SAYING GOES, IF YOU CAN'T TAKE THE HEAT GET your ass out of the kitchen. It was too damn hot in that room, and I wasn't hungry for food any longer. I wanted something sweeter than the pineapple juice that I'd licked off her fingers. I wanted to taste Stevie.

Her tongue darted over her bottom lip as she studied me for a moment. I didn't give it another thought, and I hauled her ass up onto a prep station table. There was a mirror attached. *Fucking perfect.*

I lifted my hands to her face and kissed her, sucking her bottom lip into my mouth. It wasn't enough just to kiss her, I needed to *taste* her. I wanted her—to consume her. My fingers worked the tie at the side of her dress, and with a quick pull the fabric fell away exposing her silken skin and pink lace. I could only assume she needed the same contact when her hands slipped under my shirt. Her fingers skated across my abs as my hands tangled in her hair pulling her closer. Breaking our connection, I gazed into Stevie's heated eyes. She was breathless and flushed.

I eased her back onto the table. I kissed every inch of her, trailing my tongue across her abs and coming to rest just above her thong.

I inhaled her scent savoring her exquisite flavor. My fingers dug under the strings, taking note that the fabric wasn't stitched together very well. I wanted to rip them off, but I stopped myself. French lace and silk should cover the most intimate parts of Stevie's beautiful body. Not this cheaply made scratchy sorry excuse for lingerie.

I pushed the fabric away revealing her glistening pussy. My eyes lifted to the mirror above and Stevie's eyes snapped shut.

"No, sweetheart, open your eyes," I ordered, before dragging my tongue through her slit. "You're going to watch me eat you."

A soft wail slipped from her lips, and her nails dug into my scalp when my tongue circled her clit. Arching against my mouth, she moaned and shifted her hips.

Fuck, she is wild.

My eyes flicked up to the mirror meeting Stevie's blue ones staring back at me with a blistering heat. With my eyes locked on hers, I drew her folds between my teeth nipping gently before returning to her clit. Her hands fisted my hair, tugging and pulling at the roots.

"Oh *yes*, Jax," she moaned.

That was the most beautiful sound I think I'd ever heard.

"That's right, sweetheart," I said, twisting my wrist slipping a finger inside her. She was tight, hot, and slick. Seeing Stevie unravel was going to be the highlight of my day. Making her come—seeing her flushed and panting would be more satisfying than making a million before breakfast.

"Oh . . . *shit*," she moaned as I sucked her clit.

Her hips undulated while breathy pleas and curses fell from her lips. My tongue lashed over her sensitive skin, and she cried out my name. Adding another finger, I began fucking her intently. Soon it would be my cock inside her, stretching and filling her—this was just a small preview. *No pun intended.*

For a moment, I thought about dropping my pants and sliding into her neatly trimmed pussy, but this was all about her. I wanted her to remember this tomorrow—the image of my face between her thighs and my fingers deep inside her.

"I love the way you taste," I growled against her skin.

Stevie's nails bit into my scalp, and I lifted her leg over my shoulder. I sank my tongue inside her wet heat. She writhed and moaned as I plunged deeper before dragging upward to swirl around her clit.

"Please. *Oh please,* Jax. Please."

I replaced my tongue with two fingers and my tongue teased over her clit. Nipping at her folds, I felt her pulsing against me. Latching onto her clit, I sucked greedily and increased the rhythm of my fingers.

"Don't stop, *yes* . . . right there."

With her gorgeous eyes trained on me, I devoured her—licking and tasting her sweetness. My tongue swirled over her clit once more, and my reward was a shuddering moan as she came all over my fingers.

"Oh, it's all too much," she gasped, as I licked her slowly, drawing swirling circles on her clit.

Stevie laid there panting, finally closing her eyes. It gave me a moment to adjust my cock, freeing it from being choked out by my belt. My eyes roamed over her, watching the rise and fall of her chest.

Fuck she's beautiful.

"Holy shit," she rasped, crossing her arms over her body.

I chuckled, admiring my handy work on her thighs—red rashes from my stubble marked her creamy skin.

She sat up, taking a deep breath.

"Are you okay?" I asked, pressing my palms to the table on either side of her hips.

Pushing her hair back, her eyes met mine and a wide lazy grin spread across her face. "You might have destroyed some brain cells. All I can hear is the blood rushing in my ears."

I lowered my mouth to her ear. "And just think I haven't even fucked you, *yet*."

CHAPTER
fourteen

Stevie

A<small>N HOUR OF YOGA WAS SUPPOSED TO CALM MY MIND AND</small> body. All I could think about was Jax's lips on mine, and other places. I thought I knew what an orgasm was before I met Jax. Orgasms before I was introduced to his experienced tongue and magic fingers were like riding a bike with training wheels. This was full-blown, look ma no hands and then soaring off into the sunset.

After a long shower, I slipped into a pair of denim shorts and my favorite slouchy sweater. I opened the door to the fridge, and then pulled out all the ingredients to make a salad. Chopping up celery and dicing tomatoes couldn't hold my attention long enough to stop thinking about Jax.

I didn't see him at work earlier, and when Carol said he'd gone out of town on business, I felt a twinge of sadness. Why didn't he let me know that he was going out of town? Just because the man had gone down on me and in a public place no less, that didn't earn me the right to daily comings and goings. Then I was back to remembering his tongue sucking my clit while his fingers drove inside me.

Focus, Stevie.

I was all set to settle in for the evening and binge watch a few episodes of *Good Bones*. Gran's kitchen was in serious need of a makeover. The current palette of mustard yellow, forest green and rich browns was too dark and it made the space feel small. I'd found these cute white and teal retro barstools at an antique store and the colors inspired me to brighten up the space. Bought them right on the spot, and after that I started recording anything that was home renovating inspired.

When the door slung open, my thoughts scattered like the crumbles of blue cheese over the lettuce.

"Hey, lady," Megyn said, dropping her handbag to the counter.

"Hey, are you hungry? There's plenty for two." I shook the bottle of dressing and then drizzled a fair amount over the bed of greens. If there is one thing I cannot stand it's too much dressing on salad. I can't eat things that are soggy. Like when people drown pancakes, waffles or french toast in syrup. I don't get it. It feels as if they are taking away from the purity of the food.

She lifted a brow. "We're meeting Krystle at Pints and Paints tonight. We have to be there in like twenty minutes."

Oh shit.

"I totally spaced that was tonight."

Popping a cherry tomato into her mouth, she breezed past me towards the hallway. I shoveled a few bites of salad into my mouth and then washed it down with half a bottle of water.

"Get your buns in gear," she called from her bedroom.

So much for my night in, oh well, going out with friends will keep my mind off Jax, his lips, his hands and his whereabouts.

"Does this look like two flowers?" Megyn asked pointing to her canvas.

Krystle laughed. "It looks more like two mirroring vaginas."

A laugh bubbled up from my throat causing me to cough. I choked and sputtered on my beer. They both turned to face me staring at me wide-eyed and then Krystle rubbed my back.

"Are you okay?" Megyn asked, pushing to her feet.

I took a paper towel from the bin and then wiped my mouth and chin. Luckily the apron I was wearing caught most of the beer remnants. It was borderline criminal to waste this perfectly lovely pale ale.

I tossed the dirty paper towels into the garbage. "Yeah, I'm fine."

"Okay good, now back to the mirroring vaginas," Krystle said, and pointed her brush at Megyn's art piece.

I pressed my fist to my mouth to keep from smiling. Heat spread over every inch of my skin, and I shifted in my seat.

"What is with you and the giggles?" Krystle asked, before taking a sip of her beer.

"I am *not* giggling."

Megyn pointed at me with her brush. "Something is definitely up. Her face is as red as that paint."

Krystle glanced at me sideways. "What was it that got you all choked up?"

A few thoughts circled around my brain. First, and for obvious reasons, was Jax. My thighs burned but in the most delicious way. Like a psycho, I stood in the bathroom staring at the marks on my skin for a good ten minutes. Second, I could ask them their thoughts on Milo Moiré, the Swiss artist, and her "Mirror Box" performance piece. Krystle would call bullshit on that.

"Oh my God, you had sex and with *him*," Krystle stage-whispered.

The ladies at the table next to us tossed glaring glances in our direction. My heart hammered its way up my throat, and my palms misted over with sweat.

"Him who?" Megyn asked, waggling her brows.

"Would you two keep your voices down?" I asked, rolling my shoulders back. I wanted to shove Krystle's face into the palette of paint and wipe the smug look off her face.

"For your information, I did *not* have sex. However, an orgasm was involved. Actually, there were two and they were both mine."

Krystle stood in a rush, taking her apron off in the process. "That's it. Come on we're leaving, let's go to Quench. I need all the details and like now."

Our drinks practically poured themselves and our conversation took a hard left from demanding details about my evening of oral delight to Krystle confessing her displeasure of committed relationships.

"This one here turned down friends with benefits because it was too much commitment," Megyn said, pointing her fry at Krystle.

Krystle lifted her shoulder. "At that point when you're scheduling sex, you might as well be married."

I laughed. "So you never want to get married?"

"I'm much too young to think about marriage," she huffed. "I have a travel bucket list a mile long."

"And let's not forget her bingo card," Megyn reminded, arching a brow. "Krystle still has to sleep with a Spaniard, an Aussie, and if memory serves she still needs two of the Canadian provinces to complete the card."

Krystle tossed a fry at Megyn. "Three provinces, for your information."

"Okay, okay, but let's get back to the matter of Stevie . . ." Megyn eyed me over her mug of beer. "Getting hot and heavy with Jackson James Hart."

"Yes, it is a fascinating story," Krystle said, tapping the side of her beer glass. "Stevie catching the eye of the guy who was at the top of *Florida Business* magazine's forty under forty list, last year."

I shrugged. It was the first time I really thought about Jax being *older* than me. I guess age shouldn't matter though, unless it comes to cheese and wine. "Since when do you read business journals?"

She lifted a shoulder. "What? A girl can't stay informed with the happenings of the business world. I have career aspirations too, that is precisely why I signed up for community college for the spring semester."

I shot her a wide-eyed look. "That's awesome, Krystle. What are you studying?"

"I think I've narrowed it to either business management or accounting. But, nice try, back to Jackson James Hart, is he a good kisser?" she asked, tearing her chicken strip in two pieces.

Waggling my brows, I tilted my head in her direction. "What do *you* think?"

Megyn pulled out her phone and started furiously tapping away. "He's so handsome. I read an article where he attended a fundraiser for the Children's Hospital earlier this summer. He had a hot brunette on his arm. Guess she's history now that he's gone down on Stevie."

I closed my eyes at the memory of his lips on mine and his fingers inside me. Were Jax and I exclusive? We'd only had a few dates, but I really liked him. From the events that transpired I gathered that he liked me a lot too. I sounded like a teenager with a crush.

"Jackson Hart is the kind of man you allow the pleasure of taking your ass virginity," Krystle declared.

And once more this evening, I nearly choked on my beer. Little did Krystle know that I've finger fucked myself practically every night since meeting him. The sounds Jax made while he licked and sucked my skin were burned into my memory. Still today, I could feel his hot mouth on me.

I shot her a pointed look. "Ass virginity, wow, have you ever let a guy take your ass?"

Krystle shook her head. "No, I've not met anyone that deserving, *yet*."

Megyn cleared her throat. "If you're quite finished talking about the ass play, let's get this conversation back on track. The guy attends practically every swanky party on the planet. Here's a picture of him at a scotch tasting at the Ritz."

Krystle grabbed the phone from her hand. "Oh my God, some of those bottles cost as much as I make in a year."

I barely registered the rest of the evening's conversation. My thoughts bounced back and forth between the differences in our age and social backgrounds. Jax was the CEO of a resort, a company that he'd built from the ground up and at such a young age. There was also the fact that he was my boss, while not directly, the lines had been blurred.

On my drive home, I thought that perhaps I needed to re-inforce them—the blurred lines. The fear of not being able to fit into Jax's world crept in, and I never thought I could ever feel unsure about any relationship or in my case potential relationship.

When did I become this insecure girl?

CHAPTER
fifteen

Jackson

I SAT IN THE BACK OF THE ROOM WATCHING JASON AS HE SHUFFLED his shackled feet across the dull brown carpet. The guards escorted him down the center aisle to his seat where he was greeted by his lawyer, Mick Stano. My brother looked as if he'd aged ten years since the last time I saw him three years ago. There wasn't too much of my brother that I recognized, at least not the brother I'd known. His skin was ashen, and he was at least twenty pounds thinner.

As Jason scanned the room, his haunted dark eyes met mine. The wrinkles in his forehead were more pronounced, as were the creases around his eyes, affirming the years of doing hard time had taken their toll. He nodded giving me a tight-lipped smile.

My leg bounced up and down as I stared at the clock on the wall. The parole board could begin this little soiree at any time. The sooner the better, and then I could be on my way back home and away from this hell hole.

The board members recite various statements all involving the same words—murder . . . drugs . . . robbery . . . killed . . . mother.

I've heard the story for what feels like a hundred times and it never changes. My brother was armed with a gun, and robbed two drug dealers, Joshua King and Anthony Flores, at a home in the Coral Way district. Jason managed to escape, but the dumbass stopped off at a convenience store where his Escalade was spotted. A call was made—a call for his murder.

"You murdered the two men who killed your mother, do you feel any remorse?"

Waiting for him to say the words, I squeezed my eyes shut tight.

"No, I do not feel any remorse for killing the two men who *murdered* my mother."

"You do realize that you are admitting to this board that you have no guilt about taking two mens' lives."

His lawyer leaned into him and Jason shook his head. "They took my mom's life, eye for an eye." The words were delivered cold and flat.

Stano pushed to his feet, and cleared his throat. "My client's brother is here today to speak on his behalf."

Jason grabbed his wrist and shook his head. They exchanged a few words, I couldn't hear exactly what was said, but it was clear that I had wasted the trip.

"The state of Florida hereby has no choice but to deny you parole at this time."

I stood and then strode towards the door. "Mister Dennison, please wait," Stano called out. I turned to face him, and he stopped short of me to straighten his jacket.

"Don't you want to say anything on Jason's behalf?"

"It's Mister *Hart* to you, I cut out the Dennison part a long time ago. If Jason wishes to remain in jail, then who am I to change that?"

It was just after eight in the evening when I landed back in Amelia City. A heavy rainstorm kept us from flying out of Lawtey on time. My first thought was to call Stevie, but I wasn't sure unloading family baggage was the right thing to do this early in our relationship.

Stevie probably had a wonderful family. I could only assume since she had been so close with her grandmother that the rest of her family was tight knit. Once I hit the interstate, I flipped on the Bluetooth and called my sister. She'd want to know how things went down in court today with Jason.

"Hey, Jax, I didn't think I'd hear from you until tomorrow."

I smiled at the sound of her sweet southern accent. After graduating high school a semester early, she moved to Austin for college, then onto law school and never left. "Hey, Sis, how are things in Legal Aid these days?"

"Still fighting the good fight, I am one step closer to getting my client out of her abusive relationship."

Janessa decided that it was her destiny to help people. Instead of becoming an entertainment lawyer she shifted to Legal Aid.

"That's good news," I replied, while merging lanes.

"Is Jason out of prison?"

No beating around the bush for Janessa, she was always direct. Just like a lawyer to get right to the matter. "No, he showed no remorse for his crimes. I think he wants to die in there."

She sighed heavily. "The last time I visited him, his eyes were soulless. His light just burned out. Not that he really had any before."

"I know what you mean." I ran a hand through my hair. "I didn't even speak on his behalf. Jason must have told Stano he didn't want me to."

"I'm sorry, so what do we do now?"

I blew out a harsh breath. "As hard as this is for me to say, I think we have to let him go. He obviously doesn't want us in his life or our help, for that matter."

Janessa would never admit it, but the sniffling told me that she was in tears. If I knew my sister she'd pour a glass of bourbon and flip on her favorite country station after we hung up. I hated the thought of her being sad and alone, but she'd handled everything up to now with incredible strength. There was no reason to think she'd crumble upon hearing what we'd already suspected from Jason.

"Okay, Jax, what if he calls?"

"Then you decide whether or not you want to take the call. I'm not going to tell you *not* to have a relationship with our brother," I answered truthfully.

There was a long pause, and finally she said, "Well, that settles it, it's just you and me from now on."

"Seems it's been that way for quite some time."

She huffed out a quiet laugh. "Yeah, I suppose it has."

"Hey, let's chat sometime next week about you coming out here for Thanksgiving," I interjected, shifting the topic to lighten the mood. "That is, if you don't have plans already."

"I'm not sure. I'll have to let you know a little closer to the holiday."

I ran my hand along the steering wheel. "Fair enough."

Janessa didn't particularly enjoy coming to Florida. Usually, I stopped over in Austin whenever I could. At best we would see each other a few times a year.

"That's my other line, Jax, I need to go. Love you."

"Talk to you soon. Love you." Twenty One Pilots' "Heathens" filled the car when my Bluetooth disconnected. Despite the fact that this had been one long ass day, I had a ton of energy. I wanted to work out the energy with Stevie, but instead I opted for a workout in my home gym. Forty minutes later, beads of sweat poured down my face as I pushed myself on the last mile of five on the treadmill.

My lungs burned and my quads ached. It was as if I was training for the New York City Marathon. I ran it once during college, and I vowed never to do it again—merely a bucket list moment. It was no wonder I was working so hard, I hadn't been able to stop thinking about Stevie. Ever since I tasted her, I wanted more. Needing to cool down I slowed my pace to a jog. Pulling out my earbuds I directed my attention to the television. The Business Insider came on and they highlighted a story about the Maddox Hotel in London filing for chapter eleven bankruptcy.

Shit. I *wanted* that hotel. It was a perfect piece of real estate to launch Hart Hotels internationally.

I hit my lawyer's number on my cellphone. "Pick the fuck up, Gael," I muttered.

"Good evening, Hart. It's nice to hear from you at this late hour," he drawled in his elegant Spanish accent.

"Hello, Gael. That is why I pay you the big bucks to take my calls whatever the hour. I need everything you can get me on the Maddox Hotel in London. It's ripe for the taking and I want it, but at a very *inexpensive* price."

"Of course, that is no problem at all. I'll get right on it."

I killed the call and stripped out of my sweat soaked clothes and headed for the shower. I thought about jerking off. Instead I took a cool shower and tried very hard not to think about Stevie's sweet lips wrapped around my cock. I hadn't been this amped up over a woman since my ex, Alison. I'd been heartbroken when she'd been offered her dream job in Paris, but she said that we could make the long distance thing work. For about eight months we had been able to, but our phone calls became few and far between and trying to plan weekends together proved to be even more difficult.

There had been a fair amount of women since Alison, but I was only interested in an hour or two between the sheets and they were only interested in my bank account. I know, poor me.

After my shower I slipped into bed foregoing my usual scotch and cigar nightcap, even though after today's events I could have used that drink. It had been a day of hard truths. I hated reliving the details of Mom's death, and seeing Jason broken into a shell of a man didn't help matters. I let out a deep sigh and pushed the darkness out of my mind. Then I did something I hadn't done in a long time, I sent a goodnight text to a woman, that woman being Stevie. Tomorrow couldn't get here soon enough.

CHAPTER
sixteen

Stevie

GOODNIGHT, BEAUTIFUL, I'M LOOKING FORWARD TO OUR DATE. Jax's words, so simple and I couldn't stop staring at them on the screen. They lingered in the back of my thoughts leaving me feeling edgy and excited. I spent most of the morning distracted, but a phone call from my mother snapped me back to reality.

"Hey, Mom, how are you feeling?"

"I'm good," she answered through a cough.

"You okay? Is Dad helping you out?"

"Yes, nothing to worry about, just allergies. Your father is at work. Tell me what is going on with you?"

Mom sounded tired, and it was a safe bet that Dad wasn't helping her as much as she would have me believe. I should make plans to visit her soon.

"Do you want me to come home on my next day off?"

"Do not be silly, I am fine. How is your job, sugar? Have

you heard anything from the museum lately?"

"The job is good. I can't complain. I haven't heard anything from the museum yet, I am hopeful."

I'd been so pre-occupied I hadn't checked to see what was happening at the museum. I walked into my room and stared at my closet. Should I wear shorts over my bikini or the striped dress? I thought about telling my mom about Jax, but I just wasn't ready. Instead, I filled her in on my remodeling plans for Gran's place.

"That sounds like a nice project for you to take on. I found new curtains for the living room, and your father promised me he would hang them this weekend."

"Yeah, sure he will," I scoffed. My hand flew to my mouth. I hadn't meant to say that out loud. My mother was very much aware of how much I disliked my father.

I used to blame her for not leaving him.

I used to beg her to leave him.

I used to tell her how much I disrespected her for staying in an abusive relationship.

Frustrated, I called Gran. She said that I needed to realize that my mother was never going to leave my father. I tried to argue, pleading my case to Gran that I knew he was cheating. Gran told me to stop disrespecting my mother and grow up.

Then my grandmother said something that I'd never forget. "Young lady, you are wasting precious time carrying on like this. In your mother's eyes everything is fine. She married into a Southern family and by God her life *is* perfect. I told her not to marry that man, but she didn't listen to me and she sure as hell isn't going to listen to you."

"Uhmm," I said, smacking my forehead. "Sorry, Mom, I didn't mean that the way it sounded."

"Oh, Stevie, this isn't news to me, I understand the way you feel about your father."

My mouth fell open. Never had my mother ever said that she understood why I felt the way I did. "You understand?" Cradling the phone, I pulled out my dress inspecting it for wrinkles.

"Yes, I understand. That is all I will say on the matter and it warrants no further discussion," she said with finality.

I didn't ask any further questions, I closed out our conversation telling her about my attempt at painting and how I'd went to an Asian fusion cooking class.

I thought it was best that I leave out the sordid details with Jax.

Shortly before four my phone buzzed with a text. I smiled knowing that it was probably from Jax.

Jax: Are you ready for our date?

Me: I am. I missed you today.

Jax: I missed you too. There's a black town car waiting for you outside your apartment. You'll be greeted by a man named Mitch. He's going to drive you to meet me.

Me: Okay, you're very mysterious about this date.

Jax: See you soon.

A man named Mitch . . . I remembered Jax had called him the day at the gallery. I peered outside my kitchen window, and sure enough there sat a black town car. In front of the back passenger door stood a tall man with dark hair and broad shoulders. I drew in a deep breath as I studied my reflection in the mirror. I'd showered, shaved my legs, and trimmed up the downtown area for good measure. Today was a good hair and makeup day. I tried on at least six different outfits, eventually settling on the black and white striped dress I originally picked out.

Tonight could be the night I have sex with Jax, and every cell in my body is lit up like the night sky on the Fourth of July.

I scooped up my bag, and made my way down the staircase to the car. Mitch had a wide smile on his face as he opened the door for me. "Miss Brockman, good afternoon."

"Hello and thank you," I replied before climbing inside. My fingers danced over the white leather stitching and the supple black leather. Nervous knots formed low in my belly. Insecurity and doubt washed over me. Was this something Jax did often? I wondered how many other women had sat in this very seat.

Perhaps I've made a huge mistake?

Okay, stop it.

The inner voice was not my own, but rather Gran's. In this moment I could feel her disappointment in me, second guessing myself as if I was Andie's character from *Pretty in Pink*. The girl who everyone said wasn't good enough for the handsome wealthy Blaine.

Not even twenty minutes later we arrived at the marina. Ah, yes, the yacht Jax had mentioned. Once Mitch parked the car, he opened my door.

"Miss Brockman, you'll be looking for Hart's Desire."

Of course I would be—a fitting name.

Hauling my bag higher onto my shoulder I smiled. "Thank you."

He tilted his head. "My pleasure, miss, enjoy your evening."

Wringing my hands together, I strode down the wooden pier resisting the urge to skip. My eyes lifted to see Jax standing at the bow of his boat, wearing a navy tee, and a pair of stone colored slacks rolled up to his ankles. For a moment, I stopped my stride just to admire him. With his arms crossed over his broad chest, he stood tall looking out across the bay. The wind whipped up tousling his brown hair, the sunlight reflecting the hues of gold. My fingers curled inside my palms, remembering the feel of his hair scraping against my thighs.

As my last step connected with the wooden boards, Jax turned to face me. My eyes met his in a blistering heat turning my blood into liquid fire. He smiled that slow, heart-stopping, sexy smile, stoking the flames. Propelling himself forward, Jax effortlessly floated to the stern of the boat as his hands grasped ropes and gripped the railing for support.

"I'm so glad you're here," he said, reaching out to help me climb aboard. I grasped his hand, and my legs shook as I took a step forward.

"I'm happy to be here."

He pressed a kiss to my lips. "Come on, I want to show you around before we set sail," he said, sliding his hands down my arms. Once more I slipped my hand into his, my body buzzing with too many emotions, colliding like billiards across a pool table.

As we walked along the side of the boat, the fire in my body was quickly doused when I saw two men approaching us. The taller of the two men was dressed in white uniform, the captain I presumed. The other wearing a red polo and black colored trousers, closely resembling the attire the staff at the Cabana Bar wore.

"Stevie, this is Jim, the first mate."

"So does that make you the captain?" I asked looking up at Jax. He nodded, and gave me a wink. "And this is Nixon, the steward. He runs everything aboard the yacht."

"Miss Stevie," Nixon greeted me in his elegant French accent. "I run as much as Mister Hart will allow."

Jax gave Nixon a rueful smile and it made me giggle. Apparently it was no secret that Jax was a bit of a control freak.

"She's all ready for you, Mister Hart," Jim interjected. "The coordinates are set and the weather report is clear. It will be a good night for sailing."

"And both the evening and breakfast menus are planned," Nixon added. "You will have no trouble preparing the items. Miss Martinez is finishing up the desserts, now."

Both dinner and breakfast? I guess I was spending the night. Dread tugged at the knots and nerves in my body. I should have told Jax that I had to work in the morning.

I leaned over and whispered, "Can I talk to you for a moment?"

"Thank you, gentleman, excuse us."

They nodded in agreement and walked away going off to do whatever it was that First Mates and Stewards did before the boat was scheduled to leave the marina.

Jax bent his head to me my gaze. "Hey, everything okay?"

I swallowed past the lump in my throat. "I can't spend the night with you."

He frowned, the look of disappointment hit me smack in the forehead. What a stupid thing to say.

"Of course I'd love to spend the night with you. What I mean is that I have to work in the morning."

He placed his hands on my shoulders. "No need to worry I took care of that, you don't have to work this weekend."

"What do you mean?"

"I had Carol take you off the schedule for weekend rotations. I told you that you would need your weekend free."

My heart slammed into my ribs, and embarrassment washed over me. "What? How could you do that? Carol is my boss. I don't need her knowing the details of my personal life."

He shoved a hand through his hair. "Carol is my most trusted employee. She won't tell a soul. You have nothing to worry about. Besides I thought you'd enjoy having your weekends free."

"Have you learned nothing?" I asked, finding it hard not to laugh.

His eyes narrowed as he blew out a harsh breath. "I've learned lots of things in my thirty plus years on this earth. I managed to turn a failing hotel into one of the most exclusive resort and spa destinations in the world."

"Noted. Jackson James Hart—Hotelier Magnate Extraordinaire. I'll be sure to have that printed up on a banner and hang it over your desk."

His mouth curled up, and he shook his head in amusement. "What can I say? I'm proud of my accomplishments."

"That *is* something you should be very proud of, however, I'm gathering that because of that *very* thing you've developed a 'you know what's best for everyone around you' type attitude."

"Or maybe I'm just set in my ways." Jax rubbed his hand over the curve of his jaw and down his neck. Despite that statement, it seemed as if he was actually listening to what I was saying.

"Hey, I am all for change, but I need to work weekends," I replied, my tone sharp. "I *need* the tips."

His arms folded against his chest reminding me once more that he was a powerful man. Powerful and gorgeous and kind and now I was thinking about him naked.

"If I could arrange it so that you are scheduled to caddy at least one Platinum or VIP guest during the week, would that make you happy?"

"Do you know what the other caddies would think if they found out you were pulling strings and doing me special favors because . . ." I stopped short of tacking on any assumptions to that sentence. Abby already knew that Jax sent me flowers, and now Carol was aware of my scheduling changes. I twisted the silver ring on my right hand. This made for a difficult situation because I liked him more than I probably should.

"Ughh," I sighed. "I don't even know what to do with you."

Jax's blue eyes scanned my face, a wicked grin tugging at the corner of his mouth. "I have a couple of ideas for you."

I tilted my head and narrowed my eyes. "I'm sure that you do."

"I'm sorry." His hands fell to my waist. "Please don't be mad at me, even though my reasoning for changing your schedule *was* entirely selfish."

I dropped my forehead to his chest, and my hands smoothed over the fabric of his t-shirt. "I should find another place to work, things could get complicated quickly. Or maybe we shouldn't do this at all."

"No, the thought of it, please don't." The words came out, anguish rolling off his tongue. "This . . . it's barely begun."

His arms wrapped around me pulling me closer. I'm not sure how long we stayed like that, but I started counting the beats of his heart at one point.

"I think I have a proposal that you might like. Can we discuss it over dinner?"

"Having an actual discussion rather than you making a decision without running it by me first?" I smiled into his chest. "I think you can teach an old dog new tricks."

His hands stroked up and down my back. "Did you just call me old?"

I peered up at him, and pressed a kiss to his lips. "I would never."

Twenty five minutes later, Jax and I were cruising down the Salissa River. I decided to busy myself in the galley getting the food ready for our dinner. After I read over the menu card, I poured myself a glass of wine and then set the oven to pre-heat. The ingredients for a margherita pizza were measured and all I had to do was cut up the tomatoes and add the rest of the toppings. Easy as pie—pizza pie. I popped the pizza in the oven, and then grabbed the bottle of wine along with an extra glass.

The warm breeze drifted over my skin and for a moment I couldn't believe this was my life right now. I made my way back to the captain's station where Jax was steering the boat.

Captain's station?

That sounded ridiculous. I should really brush up on my boat lingo. I felt Jax's eyes on me watching my every move-ment. I placed the bottle of wine in the built in chilling bucket and nestled the glasses in cozy cup holders.

"How's it going, Captain?"

Jax grasped my waist pinning me between the steering wheel and his hard body. "See that spec of land out there?" he asked, slipping one of his strong hands over my shoulder.

I nodded, feeling the heat climb up my neck from the warmth of his breath fanning across my ear. The heat of his touch, his body against mine and the cadence of his voice stirred something inside of me—a fusion of electricity that zapped everything inside me to life.

"That's where we're going to dock for the evening."

"It looks perfect," I whispered. "Hey, I was wondering something."

"Oh, and what is that?"

"What's this area of the boat called?"

"This is the cockpit," he replied, smoothing his hand over the wheel.

Well that word didn't help in matters where thinking about Jax naked was concerned. I walked towards the seating area and table where I'd placed the wine. "And what is this area called?"

"You are standing in the upper salon."

"Then should I assume that there's a lower salon?"

He nodded. "You're good. We'll make a sailor out of you yet."

My eyes lifted to see the tiny piece of land coming into view. I felt the boat begin to slow its speed. Inhaling a deep breath, I took a moment to study the view. Had there been more to the land? Were there any treasures under the water holding valuable maritime artifacts? My phone pinged knocking me from my thoughts and alerting me to check on the pizza. According to Miss Martinez's directions it should be about ready.

"I'm going to check on the pizza. Will we be dining up here, in the *salon?*"

A few steps were all it took for Jax to wrap his hand around the back of my neck, and for his hands to slip into my hair. "Is that what you'd like?"

All I could do was nod. His lips pressed against mine with fervor, communicating the same intensity that spoken words somehow couldn't.

"Anything the lady wants, she gets."

"Does that include you?"

"Anything you want. I will give you *anything* you want, Stevie."

"Oh, think of the possibilities."

CHAPTER
seventeen

Stevie

ETWEEN THE PERFECTLY CHEESY, BUBBLY GOOD PIZZA, TWO glasses of red wine and the easy conversation, I'd nearly forgotten about my work problem. The problem being that I was dating my boss's boss, the CEO and owner of the company, and he seemed to want to control my work schedule. It was time to get down to business.

"So, Mister Hart, you mentioned something to me earlier about a possible solution to my work issue."

"Yes, I did. I've wanted to renovate our Park City resort for some time. In addition, I've acquired properties in Chicago, Whitefish and London. London is in the negotiation stage, but the other two are both finalized."

"Wow, when did all of this happen?"

"It's something I have been working on for a few months. The London property came up on my radar a few days ago."

"Okay, well, what does this have to do with me?"

"I'm going to need someone with an eye for detail. Someone with extensive knowledge of art comes to mind."

Tilting my head, I shrugged. "I'm not sure that I understand."

He leaned forward resting his arms on the tabletop. "Stevie, I want to bring you on to the executive team as a design consultant. I'd like you to handle the holiday and event installations for the hotel. Additionally, you'd assist me with acquiring art pieces for each of the locations."

My mouth gaped. "That *is* an incredible offer, but surely I'm underqualified. I'm only a few months out of school. My scope of work is limited to Maritime history and . . ."

"*And* this is a good opportunity," he interrupted, taking my hand in his. "I've seen your resume, and you are more than capable."

"But, I just don't . . . the museum . . ."

"Remember the day that I met you?"

"Yes."

"You impressed me with your marketing insight about the coldest beer in town. I told you had a knack for it. With your degree in Art History, I believe you'll find you're more qualified for this position than you think."

I wrinkled my nose. "That was just a few off-handed comments about beer, Jax."

"Give it a trial run," he interrupted coolly. "If it turns out that this is something that you enjoy doing, we can make the job permanent. If the museum calls and is able to offer you the curator position again and you want it, take it."

Why did he have to make so much sense? The truth of the matter was that it *was* a very good opportunity. To work for Hart Hotels in an executive capacity doing something that I loved seemed like a dream. I didn't bust my ass for the last five years to end up working the same job that helped me earn my degrees. Maybe I was meant to come here for *this* opportunity. On the other hand, would I have earned the job if I had gone through the formal process of interviewing as opposed to this *not* so formal one?

"I can practically hear you thinking." His voice was low and seductive.

"I'm going to need more time to think about this."

"No, you don't. Take the job, Stevie." He lifted his wine glass to his lips.

"What do you know about design and art history?"

He let out a hushed laugh. "Not much, why?"

"Well, you said that I'd be assisting you. That implies that you would be teaching me, which means that you have some level of expertise. If you have nothing to teach me, then I must decline the job offer."

His eyes met mine when the words "teach me" rolled off my tongue.

"Oh, I can teach you plenty, sweetheart."

In the next breath, he had pulled me to my feet and his lips fused to mine. My head was spinning and I felt like I was floating. In reality Jax had a firm grasp on my hips, propelling me backwards where we ended up near the front of the boat.

When his hands tugged at the hem of my dress, I murmured against his lips, "What are you doing?"

He dragged his fingertips up the back of my thighs, sending shockwaves of pleasure zapping through every cell in my body. "I'm getting you naked."

"Out here?" My eyes darted around the blackness of the sea and up to the sky where the twinkling of stars glittered over the waves soft beams of light shown across the boat.

He nodded, and yanked my dress up and over my head tossing it to the side. "For the last few weeks, I've wanted you in my bed, on my desk, on the table in my kitchen and the list goes on. However, the bow of the boat seems like a good place to start."

Standing in front of him in my bikini, I blinked swallowing down my nerves. Jax was direct that was for sure. I suppose that was how he was with all his endeavors—business and personal. *Fuck.* I wanted him too. I'd never had public sex fantasies, case in point the aforementioned peach margarita incident.

Yet, somehow Jax elicited new desires inside me. Maybe Krystle was onto something, I should consider making a bingo card and filling it up with sexual fantasies. His hands framed my face, the pads of his thumbs stroking my cheeks. I was a jumbled mess, and he was calm.

Determined.

Intense.

Focused—on me.

As he touched me, his hands sliding into my hair and then pulling me flush against him, I felt him everywhere. Somehow I managed to find my voice. "You must have taken a lot of cold showers."

My words made him laugh. It was a beautiful sound—rich and warm it rolled over me like the waves of the sea. "Maybe a few." His hands moved over every inch of my exposed skin, mapping over my shoulders and trailing down my back.

My need grew with each touch and graze over my skin and somehow I needed more. To be closer.

"So the bow, then what?"

His lips ghosted over mine, and then brushed against my

cheek. "Then, anything you want, which I believe will be the same thing I want—*more*."

"You're quite confident." I asserted.

"I am—*very*." Deft fingers worked the strings of my top, pulling until the fabric fell away. Instinctively I covered my breasts. I had no idea why. Heat spread across my cheeks and down my neck.

"I want to see you," he said. "I want to see everything."

With a nod, I did a quick scan of our surroundings once again. It was dead silent aside from the sounds of the ocean and the occasional rustle of breeze. My arms separated revealing my breasts, and I felt Jax's molten gaze on me.

"What if the sex is bad?" I barely got the words out, before his hands cupped my breasts. Slowly he moved his fingers massaging slow circles against my sensitive flesh. Everything inside me sizzled like a live wire, and when his thumbs lightly brushed over my nipples my hips rocked forward. My belly connected with his erection. *Shit*. He was thick and hard.

Jax shook his head. "Not possible, do I need to remind you of my oral skills again?"

I wasn't worried about *his* abilities. Up until Jax, I had only been with three men in my life. My high-school boyfriend, Kris, he was very sweet. Then there was Dylan, who I met in college and fell madly in love with, but I was a freshman when we started dating and he was a senior. When he graduated and moved to Charleston it was hard to keep our relationship going. I went home to work at the club, and that is when I met Cord. He mended my broken heart over Dylan, who I still loved or thought I did back then anyway.

"I plan to play out every fantasy that I've dreamed about you," he whispered into my hair, and a full body shiver rolled through me.

"*Jax.*"

He'd fantasized about me? That was an incredibly empowering feeling.

"Is there something you need, sweetheart?"

For starters your lips on mine. Your fingers inside me. *You* inside me.

"Just you."

"Good answer." His fingers tugged at the strings of my bikini bottoms and they fell to the floor. He bent down to pick up my swimsuit and then tossed it off the side of the boat.

"Uhmm, I kind of need those."

"No, I want you naked," Jax murmured against my skin. "You won't need anything the rest of the weekend."

I was fully naked and on display for the sky, the stars, the ocean and the heavens. Probably a few manatees and fish as well.

"Why am I the only one naked?" I teased.

Crossing his arms over his chest, he reached for the hem of his t-shirt, tugging and pulling it over his head. Next he unbuttoned his pants and shoved them along with his boxers to the ground. He was naked, and beautiful and standing before me looking like a sex god with the moonlight passing over his gorgeous chiseled features. My hands reached for his chest, my fingers grazing down over his broad chest and stroking lower to his abs—the kind of abs women dream about.

His hand brushed the hair away from my face and then spun me around propelling me forward. When his hand connected with my ass, my fingers curled around the railing in front of me.

"Your ass is perfect," he rasped in my ear.

Not only was he a dirty talker, but he just revealed his kinky side. Slowly he moved his palm over my skin rubbing the pain away. Perhaps I had a kinky side, because I really liked the sting of that, and I shouldn't because this man signed my paychecks.

He dragged his fingers through my wetness, and before I knew it he was there at my most sensitive spot. No one had ever touched me there. His cock, so hot, so thick pressed against my ass.

Fuck.

Before I could finish overthinking the entire thing, his hand connected low with my backside once more. Everything tingled and burned all at once. Instead of delivering another smack to my overly heated skin, this time he pulled up my hips and dipped two fingers inside me.

"Ahhh," I cried out, shifting my hips craving the friction.

"You're a greedy little thing, aren't you?"

With his lips trailing kisses across my shoulder blades, his fingers stroked me slowly. Anticipation wound through me.

Unable to find my voice, my entire body shook with need. He asked the question again. No thoughts. My mind was blank, like an untouched canvas. There was nothing except my want for him.

"I guess I am when it comes to you."

"Good answer."

I shivered when Jax folded his body over mine, bringing his hand around teasing my clit with his thumb. When he slipped his fingers back inside me, moans of pleasure spilled from my lips breaking the silence.

The pressure began to build, his fingers increased their sensual rhythm as his lips teased and nipped over my shoulders and up my neck. Lust consumed me, spilling over every nerve ending in my body.

"That feels good," I whispered.

"This is just the beginning." he rasped, his hands gliding up the sides of ribcage and then cupping my breasts.

I turned around, needing to see his face. We hadn't even had sex, yet he was whispering dirty promises. Rolling up on my tiptoes, I pressed a kiss to his mouth. My fingers trailed down his chest and over his abs once more, still lower moving my hands over the deep lines of his hips. My eyes never left his as I took his cock in my hands stroking him slowly.

"Christ, *Stevie*," he hissed.

I'd never gotten off on giving a guy pleasure. Blowjobs weren't my thing either. However seeing Jax's eyes brimming with lust and hearing the sound of his breathing growing ragged had me yearning to take him deep into my mouth.

"Do you have any idea how much I want you right now?" he asked, his voice was raspy and filled with a tormented edge.

I palmed his cock, pumping him with long strokes drawing out the torment—relishing in the seduction. Another groan fell from his lips, and then his hands were all over me.

"Change of plans, the bow can wait. I'll fuck you here soon. Tonight, I want you in my bed. In my bed *all* night where I can tease you, taste you again. I'll fuck you all night, and then you'll wake up with my cock still inside you wanting more."

"Well, what are we still doing standing here, stop talking and fuck me already."

He didn't think twice, he picked me up carrying me over his shoulder. My bare ass exposed to the world. We reached the master suite and he dropped me to my feet—more staring, more caressing and kissing.

Oh the kissing.

His lips ghosted over mine as his hands tangled in my hair. It was a blur of movements, but the soft fabric touching my back registered that I was in Jax's bed. He sucked my nipple into his mouth and gave the other the same care, this time biting softly. My back arched as I rubbed up against his erection, a silent demand for him to fuck me. Licking every inch of my neck and shoulders, his mouth worked an erotic magic. That light stubble of his chin scraped along my skin and I fucking loved it.

He pulled away from me, the sound of a drawer opening and then a foil pack being ripped open sent a shiver racing up my back.

"Do you know how long I have wanted this?"

Needing to hear him say the words, I shook my head. I was beginning to crave his filthy words. Suddenly, I wanted to hear him tell me in explicit detail all the dirty things he wanted to do to me. I blamed it on the anal sex conversation.

"The first time I saw you, I couldn't take my eyes off you, and now I can't look at you without wanting to kiss you."

Desire wound through me like a drug. His lips pressed against mine, causing my whole body to tremble with need. He kissed me, his mouth plundering mine. It was intense—a glimpse of what was to come when he was inside me. My pounding heart shifted into overdrive. Every inch of his body seemed to cover mine, promising me the best sex I'd ever had. This wouldn't be a fumbling sloppy fuck, this would be toe-curling orgasmic pleasure.

"Need you inside me, now," I whispered.

He rolled up to kneel between my legs, and then his cock was inside me, filling me, stretching me wide—tearing me apart thrust by thrust.

Every time he pushed into me, I felt my eyes roll back. My nails dug into the muscles of his back. "Oh, yes, Jax."

He was thorough, his movements unhurried, and every nerve ending in my body felt it. I relished the enduring strokes as we found our perfect rhythm. My legs wrapped around his waist drawing him closer.

He continued pumping into me and whispered, "Fuck, *Stevie*. You feel so good."

The muscles in his neck pulled tight. My hands smoothed over his chest, and his lips crushed to mine. Tingles of my budding orgasm radiated, taking hold of my thoughts. I wanted this to last, to savor this moment, but I didn't see that happening—it had been too long.

"I need you to come with me."

"Does that even happen? Is that even possible?" My voice was barely a whisper.

"Again, questioning my abilities?" His hips churned, working a little faster hitting my sweet spot with exact precision. This was my undoing, my surrender and everything went blank.

A long moan was my only response because waves of pleasure ripped through me, every inch of my skin blazed. It was hot, beautiful bliss. He fucked through my orgasm, driving harder. My nails dug deeper into his hips, wanting . . . *needing* more friction to savor those tingles.

"Fuck, *Stevie*." Thrusting deeper, his release was heralded by a sound that I could only describe as a primal growl. It was incredibly sexy. His lips rained kisses across my collarbone and down my chest. He slid out of me, and then out of the bed. The absence of his warmth, his touch, left me aching.

"Do *not* move. I'm not even close to being done with you." He pointed at me as he walked towards the bathroom.

My head fell deeper into the pillow, as I pressed a fist to my mouth to suppress a smile. His promise of more left me trembling with want. As much as my thighs hurt, I would happily do *that* again.

CHAPTER
eighteen

Stevie

THE NEXT MORNING, I WOKE IN JAX'S BED ALONE. I SANK deeper into the mattress, pulling the comforter up my body and covering my mouth. I inhaled deeply, the smell of freesia and fresh pear washed over my senses. The down was incredibly plush and the white sheets were buttery soft. Last night I barely had time to take note of the space, it was a grand master suite, bigger than my living room and kitchen combined.

The walls were a warm shade of beige which perfectly off-set the rich dark wood fixtures. Still life artwork hung on the walls, and fresh orchids sat in glass vases all around the room. It was the perfect blend of masculine touches with hints of femininity. I wouldn't mind calling this my bedroom, but no this was Jax's bedroom—his bedroom on *his* yacht.

Holy shit.

I rolled to my side and buried my face into the pillow.

Naked, that was the way I'd woken up in Jackson James Hart's bed and the night before had been . . . amazing. No, scratch that, it was mind blowing. Which of the two was higher on the scale? I didn't even know.

Looking at the clock on the nightstand, it was a quarter before nine.

Damn. I'd slept in and that was the first in a long time.

I wondered what Jax was doing. My stomach rumbled as I eased out of the bed setting my feet onto the thick carpet. My overnight bag sat on the floor next to the dresser, but all my clothes, the few I'd packed, were all neatly folded into the top drawer except for my dress from last night which hung in the closet alongside Jax's clothes. The man had an entire wardrobe complete with dress pants and shirts.

"Ready for business at a moment's notice," I mumbled, as my hands drifted over each item of clothing.

"That I am."

The sound of Jax's voice brought a smile to my face. I stepped from behind the closet door. He stood in front of me, dressed in a pair of blue and white striped shorts and a Yale University T-shirt. I let my eyes trail over his thick, corded forearms. His hair was perfect, if not a bit windblown. Those blue eyes dazzled like the ocean, and that neatly trimmed five o'clock shadow made it nearly impossible for me to think about anything other than his mouth on me—everywhere.

"Good morning."

His lips curved into sexy smile. "It's a good morning indeed when here you are standing in front of me naked."

"Not for much longer," I said, reaching for one of his dress shirts.

His smiled deepened. "Here allow me." Stepping towards

me, his fingers brushed against mine as he pulled a blue and white striped shirt from its hanger. "This one will look sexy on you. Any of them would really, but this one's my favorite."

As Jax's hands slipped over my shoulders, I struggled to focus on anything other than how good his touch felt and how much I wanted him again. My body was sore, and my mind was a swirly haze of all things Jax. I was afraid I might say something stupid. Caffeine was in order.

"Are you ready?"

I gazed over toward my bag. "Not quite, I need something to cover my . . ."

"No," he said, grasping my elbow and pulling me to him. "I said that you wouldn't need to wear anything else this weekend."

Damn, he was serious. I thought that was something he muttered in the heat of the moment. Braless sure, I do that most weekends and nights, but panty free, that was something else entirely.

"Come on, the coffee is ready and so is our breakfast."

"What are we having?" I asked, as we walked past the guest cabins and through the salon.

"We have fresh fruit, croissants, and yogurt. I can make you an omelet if you prefer. There's also my personal favorite: Cinnamon Toast Crunch cereal."

My eyes took in the elegant spread on the dining table. "That is quite the breakfast menu."

He tucked a strand of hair behind my ear. "Anything the lady wants, she gets."

"So, I've heard."

"Here, sit, please," he said, while pulling out a chair. "So what can I get you?"

"This is all wonderful," I replied, gesturing around the table at the pastry and fresh fruit. "I don't eat breakfast most days."

"Yes, I know this, but today you will."

I wasn't shy as I loaded up my plate, and then I poured a cup of coffee and settled back into the chair blowing the steam away from the cup.

Grabbing a croissant, Jax eased into the chair beside me. "So, you haven't officially accepted my job offer."

Inwardly I rolled my eyes as I took a sip of coffee. Could I really take this job that Jax offered? Was I capable? Nerves settled in the pit of my stomach.

"I don't think I can take the job."

"And why not?"

"It's a very good offer, and I thank you so much," I began, as I tore off a piece of croissant. "However, do you really think after what happened last night between the two of us, working together would be a good idea?"

His brow scrunched together, and he shook his head. "What happened last night?"

I tore off another bite of the flakey pastry and tossed it at him.

"I'm only kidding. Last night happened multiple times, I am very aware." He leaned in capturing my lips with his.

My body was all too aware of how many times we had sex and *that* was a problem. It was written all over my face and marked on my skin. How would I be able to work with Jax, be great at the job and keep it hidden that I was screwing the boss? No one would respect me. Maybe I shouldn't care.

"I can't take the job, because you wouldn't be able to keep your hands off me," I said, giving him a smirk. "Everyone would know our little secret. The interoffice emails practically write themselves—Stevie Brockman screwed her way into the job. You could print that on my business card, too, if you like."

His burst of laughter kept me from proceeding with my speech. "I'll search the email servers daily if I need to, and fire anyone who insinuates such a rumor. And for that matter, anyone who insults your capability will be fired."

"The lengths you'd go to defend my honor are quite impressive."

"So does that mean that you'd be accepting my offer?"

For a moment I thought about my student loans and the monthly bills that never failed to disappear. It would be nice to have an increase in income. "I still think that you are better off with an art dealer, someone more experienced or at the very least a decorator who has contacts at *Town & Country Magazine*."

He lifted a shoulder. "For what possible reason?"

"For an Ivy Leaguer, you're kinda clueless." I shook my head. "Did you really go to Yale?"

"I *really* did."

"The reason being is that you should have your properties photographed as you have them completed. It will be good visibility. In fact, someone in your PR department should line up an interview for a feature in a few publications."

Smiling, he leaned back in his chair. "Well, look at you, and here you thought that you're underqualified for this position. I'm going to remind you once more that you are completely qualified. More impressive are your *brilliant* marketing strategies, and that is something that I didn't see on your resume."

"I wouldn't say brilliant. It's basic marketing one-oh-one."

"Perhaps, but I think it just proves that you should take the job that I am offering," he said, taking my hands in his. "Don't overthink it and don't stress the things you can't control."

There was no use in fighting him any longer. With those dangerous blue eyes of his staring at me, it was hard to say no. "Okay."

"Okay? Really, are you really saying yes?"

"I still think this is a terrible idea, but I'm willing to give it a try."

"Maybe you should just trust me, my instincts are never wrong."

"Never wrong, huh?"

"Never."

"If I screw up, you'll have no one to blame but yourself."

"Oh, you'll definitely be screwing—me." He pulled me onto his lap, his warm breath fanned over my ear, and his fingertips inched up my thighs. "Your body is your own, but when you're in my bed it belongs to me." His gravelly voice was filled with promise. My thighs pressed together at the sudden rush of heat.

"You're staking your claim?" I teased, recalling our alpha male conversation from our first date at Hokaido Grill.

His nose grazed my cheek. "Spread your legs and I'll show you."

My hands pushed beneath his t-shirt. "If you promise me, no one gets to have your body, but me."

"All of this is yours, and only yours. That I can promise, Stevie."

His words soothed me. I was old enough to realize the difference between sex and fucking. Fucking was just an itch that needed scratching. Sex was something reminiscent of a craving—a want, multiple times over. At this point I was ready to explore all facets with Jax, and I had no desire, no want for anyone, but him.

Propping myself up onto my forearms, I gazed out at the ocean—not a soul in sight. Part of me wondered if perhaps Jax brokered some deal with the coast guard to keep every sailboat, ski boat, and yacht off the water today. The tips of his fingers brushed over the small of my back and I shivered.

"I don't know if I can stay naked for much longer, it's a little breezy for my liking." I pointed to the goosebumps decorating my arm.

He levered onto his side and continued trailing his fingers along my skin. "But, I really like you naked."

"I like you naked, too," I admitted, although he wasn't naked at the present moment. My eyes trained on the deep lines of his torso, I studied them as closely as a Ritchie Allen Benson watercolor.

I shifted closer to him. "Tell me about Yale."

"What do you want to know exactly?" he asked, the pad of his thumb stroking over my nipple.

"I want to know your story, the in depth details that I can't read about online or in the company manual."

"I studied International Business at Florida International University, and then there was Yale Business School. And that is about it."

"Unless you want me asking twenty questions, you better start filling in the gaps."

"Undergrad was typical college theatrics—parties, studying, long hours at the library and study labs, more parties. Yale was an experience, and I loved every minute of my time there."

"Did you have a job or anything while in school?"

"Not exactly."

"I had to work at the country club and then I was able to land a job at a local art gallery during my senior year. I really loved working there."

"Where was the art gallery?" he asked, brushing his knuckles up my arm.

"No redirecting the conversation. Answer now."

Smiling, his fingers tugged at the loose ends of my hair. "Me and a buddy, we organized poker nights. Tuesday nights started as friendly games. At first, the bets were low. Usually, it was a small group of us gambling away a few hundred dollars here and there. We changed the location each week to keep it secret."

"Sounds like a lot of work."

"At times it was, but after we got in the groove of things, it became easier. The future CEO's and Wall Street brokers became regulars and then we knew we had to start charging more."

"What was the buy in?"

"It started at a thousand dollars on Tuesday nights and on the weekends it was ten-thousand. Over the years the buy ins went up."

The chill of the wind kicked up, and I snuggled into his side for warmth. Leaning up, Jax grabbed one of the throws from the chaise. I shifted upright shielding my naked body from the world.

"Come here, let's get you warmed up."

I leaned against his back, and he engulfed the two of us in the blanket. "With all that money, is that how you were able to buy and build your hotels?"

"Uh huh," he whispered into my hair, as his hands rubbed my arms.

I attempted to open my mouth to ask another question, but when Jax's fingers drifted along my ribcage I closed my eyes. His heart beat against my back filling me with the most amazing sensation. Right now, it was the two of us and the whole world failed to exist. Monday would be a different story. This man, Jackson Hart, would officially be my boss.

In his arms—I wanted to stay like this forever, as if that was even an option. But, I knew I could enjoy this moment a little while longer.

"In case I didn't mention it at any point, I've had a really wonderful time with you, Jax."

He whispered into my ear, "Me too, it's been . . . perfect."

Yeah, I would say the same thing, but I didn't.

CHAPTER
nineteen

Stevie

D O NOT PICTURE HIM SHIRTLESS. D O NOT PICTURE HIM NAKED. I sat in the large conference room listening to Eric, the head of finance for Hart Hotels, discuss the specifics of the acquisition for the Maddox Hotel in London.

Distracted, completely distracted. It wasn't Eric that I needed to keep from picturing naked, obviously. My mind was on the weekend replaying a slideshow of images—Jax's naked body above me, thrusting into me and his mouth on mine.

I was hyperaware of Jax's presence. How could I not be?

I'd spent the majority of the morning in meetings with him staring at the curve of his mouth, his hair and his eyes, and every time that he picked up a pen I couldn't help remembering his hands all over me.

Being this close to him, I was afraid everyone in the room could read me as easily as the portfolio in front of us. Could they sense that I had been screwing Jax's brains out?

After we docked on Saturday afternoon he asked me to spend the rest of the weekend with him and I declined. I actually said no. That should have earned me a medal of achievement. Resisting Jax was seemingly impossible.

Instead of spending the night in his bed, I was in a warm bath and then in my own bed with a heating pad on my ass and thighs. The combination of ibuprofen and two shots of tequila temporarily erased the after effects of having sex with Jax.

Now I sat here pressing my thighs together, as if that would somehow quell the desire I had for all these people to leave and for Jax to lock the door, lower the blinds and bend me over this table. Within a matter of days, he'd managed to turn me into this woman—achy, needy . . . *horny*. Any way you sliced it at the end of the day, I wanted him twice . . . *thrice* as much as I had previously and he was my boss.

Screwing the boss. Yep, that would be the title of my memoir.

My hands shook as I lifted the bottle of water to my mouth. I needed some air and now.

"That wraps up the meeting. Does anyone have any questions?"

At that point I had completely tuned out and gathered up my belongings, shoving my notepad and the file folder into my bag. Once I saw Sharon, the VP of Human Resources, exit the room I followed suit.

My legs carried me down the hallway, past several conference rooms. Where was the elevator bank? As I turned on my heel, I saw Jax standing there with his hands in the pockets of his dress pants looking delicious as ever.

"The elevators are this way," he said, giving a nod. For a long moment, his eyes locked on mine. My cheeks and neck flushed as those illicit thoughts surfaced—lean muscles, chiseled abs, his narrow waist. My body betrayed me with every step I took, inching ever closer to him.

Giving a tight smile, I walked past him.

"How are you enjoying your first day, Stevie?"

"It's going well, Mister Hart," I replied, keeping my pace.

I turned the corner, expelling a deep breath as I pressed the down arrow. My eyes landed on the floor, and I studied the patterns on the carpet in an effort to direct my thoughts of going back and pushing Jax up against the wall and ravaging his mouth with mine.

"Fuck me," I muttered.

"Are you offering?" he asked, coming up to stand behind me. The rich sound of his husky voice slid through my veins charging every nerve and cell in my body. He was so close to me smelling perfectly divine. My lips parted and my nipples hardened against the soft fabric of my bra.

"Because if you are," he rasped, in my ear. "I'd graciously take you up on that offer."

I barely registered the sound of the elevator's arrival. The shiny chrome doors parted and I heaved myself inside. Jax stepped on, and then pressed the button for the twenty-first floor. Heat prickled across my skin and all my thoughts ran away from me.

"Relax, Stevie, I'm not going to fuck you in the elevator."

"But you intend to fuck me at some point today?"

His mouth pressed into a hardline as he pulled his phone from the inside of his jacket pocket. I studied him watching as his fingers flew across the screen. Impressive, this man was certainly a multitasker. Taking care of business, all the while making me incredibly wet. The car stopped and the doors opened. I stepped out in a rush and Jax followed keeping his pace in step with my own.

I'd like to say I was surprised when I felt his hand wrap around my arm and led me into his office. I was even less surprised when he closed the door and locked it. My heart galloped in my chest when he pinned his dreamy blue eyes on me.

"The answer to your question is yes, I intend to fuck you today."

○

Jax

My resolve to stay away from Stevie lasted longer than I expected—a full five hours.

Impressive.

Today for her first day of work she wore the same dress she'd worn the night we took the cooking class. When Carol brought her into my office, my dick rose to attention. The dress taunted me all through the morning, teasing me with the memory of her body—every beautiful inch of her curves that I had previously explored with my mouth and my hands. I'd been half hard just sitting across the table from her.

It took only a few steps to sweep her into my arms pressing my lips to hers.

"This . . . *this* is a very bad idea." Her voice was breathy, expressing need despite the words she'd spoken.

I took her bag and dropped it into a chair near my desk. My hands tangled in her hair as I kissed her lips again.

"I need you. I'm going out of my mind seeing you in this

dress again."

I reached between us, taking her hand and pressing it against my cock. She moaned licking her lips. Any fucking sanity I had took a flying leap out the window. There was only one thing I wanted and I was certain she wanted it too.

"Tell me what you want," I prompted. My fingers dug into her hips, and she rocked forward rubbing herself against me.

"Did you wear this dress for me?"

Instead of waiting for an answer I crushed my lips to hers. Sliding my tongue into her mouth, I deepened our kiss.

"Jax, we shouldn't—*ah*," she purred, when my fingers teased along the edge of her panties.

"Tell me that you touched yourself yesterday wishing it was my tongue on your clit, my mouth wrapped around your nipple as my cock pounded into you making you come."

I stroked her back and forth and then slipped my fingers inside her, relishing the soft little gasps that fell from her lips. *Christ.* She was hot and wet. "All morning I wondered if you were wet like this, for me. All for me."

I worked a third finger inside her, my thumb ghosted over her clit. Her eyes met mine they were hazy, brimming with lust.

"Yes, I can't think . . . you drive me crazy."

"And?"

"Yes, all for you. I'm wet for *you*."

"Good."

Blood rushed through my head and my dick like a steam engine barreling full speed. My fingers left her body, and her head fell forward. With a quick movement I spun her around, and her palms slapped against my desk. Inching her skirt up over her hips, the view of red cotton nylon reminded me to gift her with fine silk and lace.

Dropping to my knees, the desire within me grew. My hands stroked up and down her slim legs as I envisioned them encased in varying designs of thigh-highs. With her panties now balled up on the floor, I rose to my feet to stand behind her.

Condom.

"Don't move from that spot."

I walked into my private bathroom and rummaged through my drawers. Fuck. Not one single condom. Although, to be fair I hadn't fucked anyone in my office ever, that could be part of the issue.

"Jax, what are you doing?"

"I was looking for a condom, but apparently I'm out."

She pushed off my desk, stood tall smoothing her dress down over her beautiful skin. "Is this part of a regular work day for you—fucking in your office?"

My eyes narrowed. "No, it's definitely a first for me."

Turning away from me, she reached for her purse. *Shit.* No wonder she asked. If she thought that I kept condoms on hand here in my office, she would absolutely wonder if I did this all the time. I scrubbed a hand over my jaw. "Stevie, this is not a regular thing, I swear to God." I stumbled over my words sounding like a damn teenager.

She turned back to face me holding a silver foil packet between her fingers. "Lucky for you, my gran, and yes, I know this will sound weird, but she taught me to always be prepared."

I smirked. "I've always liked that Grandmother of yours."

With a devious smile playing on her lips, Stevie sauntered towards me. "You know I've always liked it when you stopped talking and fucked me."

Shit. This boldness was incredibly sexy on her. She set the condom on my desk as if the gauntlet had been thrown. Her eyes locked with mine as she unzipped my pants.

"I want you inside me, *now*."

When her arms snaked around my neck, I picked her up and then dropped her ass onto my desk. I kissed her hard, fucking her mouth driving deep. Our movements were hurried and unapologetic. Hooking my arm underneath her knees, I pulled her to the edge shoving her dress up and over her hips.

She took my cock in her hands, giving me a few pumps before opening the silver foil and expertly sheathing me. I cupped her face and kissed her again, drawing her bottom lip into my mouth. Her eyes were wild, filled with lust. My hands traveled up her thighs and beneath her skirt. Stevie moaned, working her fingers through my hair pulling me close. I settled between her legs, and she worked her hips to fit me in.

"Stevie," I groaned, pushing deeper.

My hold on her hips was punishing as I rocked into her body the way I needed it. I moved harder, deeper with each movement. She fisted my hair meeting me thrust for thrust. My mouth sealed over hers as I rocked in and out of her squeezing her ass. Her inner muscles gripped my cock, and pleasure spread from every cell in my body and went straight to my balls.

When her eyes squeezed shut, I knew Stevie was about to lose it. She whispered my name and came so perfectly around my cock. I slid deeper, and at the feel of her squeezing the entire length of my dick I found my own release seconds later.

Anything beyond the four walls of my office ceased to exist—all of it was cast out into the ocean, falling deeper into the abyss. The hotel could be crumbling around us and I wouldn't care. Right here, now it was the two of us and I was perfectly fine with drowning in her for the rest of the day.

CHAPTER
twenty

Stevie

AFTER A RESTLESS NIGHT'S SLEEP I CAME INTO THE OFFICE early. My first week had breezed by without any major disasters. The work was challenging and interesting, yet at the same time really enjoyable. I had to admit I was glad to not be caddying.

The position itself entailed a lot more than just acquiring art pieces. Each hotel had a specific interior design and installation concept and Jax wanted my input on everything right down to the types of floral arrangements. He had more faith in my abilities than I did, but as it turned out I had an eye for details.

At present I was in the middle of décor plans for the Azore spa at the Chicago hotel. Samples of orchids, green trick dianthus, smooth rocks, and four kinds of vases spread before me, as I tried to create a design aesthetic that would be used throughout the hotel for fresh floral and foliage. My plan was for the décor in the treatment rooms to differ slightly from the reception area.

"Are you avoiding me?" Hearing the gravelly tone caused the hairs on the back of my neck to stand on end. I didn't have to look up to know that it was Jax standing in my doorway, but I did anyway. He stood before me wearing a dark striped suit with a grey tie offset against a crisp white shirt. I didn't want to think about floral arrangements on coffee tables or credenzas. I only wanted that voice, his voice whispering dirty promises into my ear. I wanted his mouth on mine, his lips peppering my neck with kisses and drifting up to my lips. It was all kinds of wrong.

"I'm not avoiding you," I replied, returning my eyes to the grid sheet in front of me.

I registered the sound of my door catching in the latch. From the corner of my eye I watched as he placed a muffin onto my desk.

"What's this?"

"A muffin."

"I know that, I mean what is it doing on my desk?"

"Consider this my peace offering."

"I was unaware of a war. Unless we're talking *Game of Thrones* and winter is coming. In that case I can talk GoT all day long."

His finger pressed to my lips. "You're babbling and that muffin is breakfast."

I lifted a shoulder. "Then what the hell was all the war and peace talk about?"

"Let's just say that I have a feeling that you're avoiding me, because of the sex, the incredible sex we had in my office and the sex we could be having right now."

I felt the blush in my cheeks rise. "Tempting offer, but to be clear, I'm not avoiding you."

"I'm glad to hear that," he said, sliding a piece of paper across the surface of my desk. "Here's another tempting offer, this is the alarm code and directions to my home."

My fingers smoothed over the paper, and Jax pulled a silver key from his pocket placing it next to the piece of paper. "House key, in case there is a problem with the code."

Before I could say anything, Jax brought his hand to my hair and crushed his lips to mine. Our mouths moving together in sync and my hands fisted into his hair.

I pulled back. "See this was what I was trying to avoid. No kissing in the office. No making googly eyes in the office and definitely no *sex* in the office. Those are my terms."

"Googly eyes?"

I waved my hand at him. "You know what I mean. I can't resist those eyes of yours and . . . and I can't think now because you've kissed me and I have a lot of work to do, so kissing in the office is a big no, no."

A slow sexy smile spread across his lips. "Fair enough. I accept your terms."

"Good, I'm glad we agree. Now tell me about this," I said, tapping my pen to the paper.

"You can use the key or the code any time that you like, even if I'm out of town and you just want to take a dip in my pool."

I didn't say anything. Words seemed to escape me and forget about having a rational thought. Then he smiled at me, and suddenly the words came. "Thank you and I'd really like that."

"I'd love to see you later if you're free."

"I have plans tonight, but maybe this weekend?"

"I'm late for a budget meeting." Jax leaned over the front

of my desk. "This would be the part where I'd kiss you goodbye and tell you to have a good rest of the day, but the treaty is iron clad."

Before I could think or blink, Jax slipped out of my office and I was alone. Sagging into my chair, I tossed my pen onto the desk. Heat, lust, passion, call it what you wanted. Every time that Jax kissed me, it reminded me of butterflies. That feeling never grew old and it clung to every cell in my body.

There was something wonderfully wicked knowing that I had Jax's alarm code and the key to his house in my purse. After a long week adjusting to a new job, the comforts of Jax's house sounded like heaven. Much better than this techno club with overpriced, watered down drinks that Megyn's friend, Angela, insisted we hit up for a night out. Megyn axed Beau and she was ready to dance the night away. That basically translated as: Megyn would like to get drunk and make out with some hot dude.

"What can I get you?" the bartender asked, as he continued pouring shots for another patron.

"I need a lemon drop martini, a cosmo, and a glass of chardonnay. House is fine."

"You don't want to try one of our Halloween cocktails tonight?"

"No thanks, maybe later."

Glancing around I wondered why Angela wanted to come to this place. It was a new club that had opened at one of the hotels on the beach. There wasn't anything special about the place—it looked like any other bar with loud blaring music and colorful lights zipping around.

After I paid for our drinks, I made my way through the crowd, trying desperately not to spill the drinks. It wasn't as crowded as I anticipated for a Friday night or an opening week, but then again it was early.

"Here you go, ladies," I announced, setting the drinks on the high top table.

Angela and Megyn were deep in conversation something about Beau sleeping with a hostess from the restaurant where they worked. I sipped my wine and tried to listen to their conversation, but truthfully I'd lost interest in the drama. Enthusiasm for girl's night out was lost on me tonight. My mind was anywhere but here, and admittedly club hopping wasn't my thing. If that made me sound old, I didn't care.

Half a pitcher of margaritas later, both Megyn and Angela were shaking it on the dancefloor. I switched to vodka needing something stronger to endure this night in which I was notably the third wheel. Earlier I tried to say goodnight, but Megyn begged me to stay and do shots with them. I didn't partake because I didn't want to be sick in the morning. Yoga was calling my name.

They kept trying to coax me onto the dancefloor and each time I declined. Sitting on the outside watching as guys rubbed up on the two of them made my stomach turn, or perhaps it was the booze.

From behind me I heard chants and singing, I turned around and a sugary sweet concoction sloshed and spilled down my arm splashing onto my skirt. Glancing up I saw a red head wearing a pink glittery tiara and the button on her white dress said: "Buy Me a Shot I'm Tying the Knot."

"Oh my God, girl, I am *so* sorry. First, you have to let me take care of this stain on your skirt. Second, I'm replacing your drink."

"Please, it's no trouble," I replied, pushing to my feet. "I can just take care of it in the ladies room."

"No arguments. Sit your butt back down on that stool." She was methodic in her tone ordering her bridesmaids to hand her club soda, a soft cloth and something else. It was like watching a surgeon at work. "What are you drinking, doll?" she asked, dabbing at the spot on my skirt.

"Something called a Smoked Pumpkin. It's one of the specialty cocktails."

She then proceeded to announce to someone named Kia, to grab another martini as well as my drink.

"Would you ladies like to sit with me?" I asked, motioning to the empty barstools.

"We would love to," she answered, setting her purse on the table. "I'm Kim and as you can tell I'm getting married."

Smiling and clapping in between a litany of appreciative thank yous, the rest of the Kim's friends ditched their jackets and party favors at the table and then made their way to the bar.

"Stevie, and congratulations, when is the big day?"

"Two weeks from tomorrow." She tucked her long dark hair behind her ear and that's when I noticed the ring.

"Oh my God," I yelped, grabbing her hand and gazing at the sparkling diamond.

"Here you go, Kim," Kia chirped, placing our drinks in front of us. "Anything else?"

"No," she blurted, rolling her eyes. "Go away. Go drink. Go dance."

My eyes popped wide, but I couldn't help but laugh when Kim turned back to face me smiling.

"Annoying—A F." She sipped her cocktail. "Everything is 'penis this' and 'penis that' and it's so tacky. I just wanted a nice bridal brunch—bottomless mimosas and plenty of food. Kia, she's my sister, insisted on a stripper, a limo, and all this garish shit."

I shrugged. "It sounds like she just wanted to make it special for you."

"She means well, I know that, but I think this would be her ideal last hurrah party if she was the one getting married." She plucked an item from her purse. "Penis straws? Seriously, who knew this was still a thing?"

I laughed as Kim waved the plastic phallic with misshaped balls in my face. "Penis cupcakes, condom corsages, and penis jello shots," she rattled on swirling the lemon slice in her glass. "Ughh, I am so sick of me already, I can't wait for this whole thing to be over, at least the wedding part. I'm looking forward to the marriage part, but first the honeymoon."

"And where is the honeymoon?"

"Aruba. Sun, fun, surf, and sand—just the two of us for ten days."

"Sounds heavenly."

I hadn't had a vacation in a long time, but when you live in Florida with beaches surrounding you, it was hard to think about planning a getaway. I couldn't afford Europe. At this point my next vacation might just be my honeymoon, and that is even if I end up getting married.

She bumped my arm. "So what brings you out tonight?"

"My roommate ditched her guy, I guess she caught him cheating and so here we are drinking and dancing the night away." I lifted my glass in Megyn and Angela's direction on the dancefloor.

"And after a long week you've had enough of it. What would you rather be doing?"

"Honestly, I'd rather be binge-watching *Grey's Anatomy* and eating my way through a pint of double fudge ice cream . . ." I hesitated for a moment not wanting to overshare. "Or spending the evening with the guy I've been seeing."

I had mixed feelings about ditching my girlfriends for a guy. I'd never been that girl, but somehow here I sat wanting to be with him instead hanging out with them.

"Oh, there's a guy?" Kim lifted her brows. "Tell me more."

"It's a *new-ish* relationship. He's smart, he makes me laugh and he's very sexy."

"And how is the sex?"

"Really amazing, incredibly super-hot," I admitted.

"Good for you." She tipped her glass to mine. "Jared and I agreed to a 'no sex until the wedding night' pact. I understand the sentiment, but now I'm re-thinking it all." She paused to take a drink. "You should get out of here and go have amazing, incredible super-hot sex."

"And just ditch my roommate? No, I couldn't possibly."

"Your roommate is grinding up on some guy, and she hasn't been over here since I sat down. Look at her, she's having a good time. Go tell her goodbye and let's get you to your guy. Besides one of us should be having sex."

Kim rallied her bride tribe while I shimmied through the small crowd on the dance floor to tell Megyn that I was leaving. Megyn was at that level where she was coming off her buzz and the two of them were responsibly hydrating with bottles of water. Apparently the guys they were dancing with were work friends, which made me feel less guilty about cutting out early.

"Ready?" Kim asked, looping her arm with mine.

"Yep."

We walked outside and a limo pulled up to the valet stand. I was about to ask for a cab, but Kim told me to get inside.

I gave the driver the address and listened as Kim and Kia discussed what bar they should hit next. The conversation teetered between choosing a tiki bar or an out of the way quiet dive bar.

"My friend, Krystle, is the bartender at Quench," I chimed in. "They have great coconut shrimp and you need the loaded fries in your life. The juke box is filled with Jimmy Buffett, the beer is ice cold and the rum drinks are a specialty. Just tell Krystle 'Stevie sent you' and she will hook you up."

"That sounds perfect," Kim said, and the others nodded in agreement.

A few moments later the limo came to a stop. "O-M-G, is this your house?" Kia asked pressing her hand to the glass.

Unable to speak, I stared up at the massive structure, my eyes darting from the wood to the concrete to the glass. I didn't know how to describe the sleek beauty of his home.

"This is where her man lives."

The door opened and I barely registered the sound of Kim's voice. Hugging her, I wished her tons of wedding day happiness. After saying goodbye to the rest of the ladies, I stepped out of the limo and practically skipped up the stairs to the front door.

As I fished the key out of my purse, I heard them chanting and cheering. Laughing, I turned back and whispered yelled for them to keep it down.

Kim waved and then disappeared behind the glass. I watched until the taillights faded into the night. For a moment I hesitated as I tried pushing the key into the lock. My body swayed a bit as I peered through the door's side window. I didn't have that much to drink, did I? Leaning against the doorframe I recounted how many drinks I had over the course of the evening—definitely not enough alcohol that I'd be drunk, or even tipsy. It had to be nerves.

"Are you going to stand there all night or come inside?"

Startled I jumped and then looked up for a camera or intercom. "I was thinking about *coming* . . . inside."

The door opened and there stood Jax with a pleased expression. "You better get in here."

"Hi," I said, leaning forward and wrapping my arms around his neck.

"So you changed your mind about coming over tonight?"

Nodding, my fingers scraped lightly up the back of his neck. My ears perked up at the sound of running water. My gaze travelled up a large wall made of glass and brick to a sleek waterfall feature. It was gorgeous, and the sound was soothing.

"Would you give me the grand tour?" I asked, motioning around the well-lit space.

He led me through the foyer and my jaw hit the floor. I didn't know what to focus on first, the huge colorful mural that hung above the rectangular fireplace. The ginormous plush grey sectional sofa adorned with deep plum, burnt orange and steel blue decorative pillows. The hues obviously mirrored the mural.

Then I caught sight of his bar and the entire wall of wine enclosed behind a glass wall. This led my eyes upward, taking in the soaring ceilings only to find more glass and wood that surrounded the railing. The entire house was work of art, it wasn't overly masculine. My fingertips brushed over the couch, as I admired every straight line and angle. This was the ideal bachelor pad—simple design with robust details that made it warm and inviting.

"Impressive." I placed my purse onto the table behind the couch. "My entire apartment could fit inside this living space."

"You're welcome to fit inside here anytime."

I rolled my eyes. "As much as I love your pervy innuendos, that wasn't very good."

His hands fell to my waist, as his lips ghosted over mine. "Guess I'll just have to take you to bed and work on my innuendos."

"I'm perfectly fine with good old-fashioned dirty talk." His hands worked the buttons on my white shirt.

"Noted."

Climbing the stairs, Jax took my hand in his. We had to walk around the upstairs to get to his bedroom on the other side of the house, since it was an open-air concept design. Once we reached the master suite, Jax busied himself with the task of stripping me out of my clothes.

I steadied myself as I slipped out of my heels, and I had an excellent view of Jax pulling his grey Henley tee over his sculpted shoulders. It wasn't my only spectacular view. The ocean was spread before me with twinkling lights bouncing off the waves.

"I'm glad that you're here," he said, discarding his dark jeans on the chair where his shirt lay.

"Me too," I admitted.

"I missed you." He approached, threading his fingers through my hair.

"Me too."

CHAPTER
twenty-one

Stevie

I AWOKE IN A HAZE FROM A DREAM DRENCHED IN SWEAT. JAX SLEPT peacefully next to me. Careful not to disturb him, I eased out of the bed and then walked to the doorway scooping up my underwear and bra along the way.

Shuffling down the hallway to the guest bathroom, bits and pieces of the dream came into view. It was one of those dreams straight out of a Lifetime movie, the one where the girl marries the guy only to find out he has some mysterious past filled with dark secrets. A total cliché.

I pulled my panties up over my hips and then clasped my bra. It dawned on me that I barely knew the man that I had been sleeping with these past few weeks. Turning on the faucet, my brain went into overdrive thinking about Jax as a possible serial killer or a polygamist hiding in plain sight. It was entirely possible that the reason he acquired several hotel properties all over the country was because that's where his other wives lived.

As I dried my hands, I stared at my reflection in the mirror. "You need to stop drinking vodka. You have crazy dreams when you drink vodka."

While statistically the chance that Jax was a serial killer, or married to multiple wives, was low, at six-thirty on a Saturday morning it gave me just enough cause to bolt and fast. I plodded down the stairs and found my dress, shoes and handbag. Fishing out my phone, I called a cab and then finger combed out my hair, applied some lip gloss making myself look less walk of shame-*ish*.

When the text from the cab company appeared, I slipped out the door. In my mind I decided that this wasn't running away, I was gaining some perspective. There was only one person who could give me perspective.

After a shower and a quick change I hopped in my car and headed towards Amelia City. I stopped off for a coffee and fresh flowers. The coffee was for me, the flowers were for Gran.

Jax: Where did you go?

I stared at the text message thinking of something to say that didn't sound insane. As I pulled onto the road that led to the cemetery, I came up with a few responses. The drive gave me a lot of time to think about how silly I'd been leaving. I knew that I could talk to Jax. After all *he* was an adult. My behavior on the other hand resembled nothing of adulthood.

Me: Home for clean clothes. I had an appointment this morning.

Jax: A work appointment?

Me: No. Personal matter.

Jax: Will you be coming back? I wasn't finished with you.

Me: Is that what you'd like?

Jax: Yes, I would like that very much.

Me: In that case you'll be seeing me in about an hour or so.

I slipped my phone into my purse and headed down the path to Gran's grave. Dusting off the headstone, I forced all the sexy time thoughts from my mind. I replaced the dying peach roses with an assortment of orange, yellow and red mums.

"Gran, it's Stevie. Things have been insane, so I apologize for not visiting last weekend. I have a new job, not at the museum but at the hotel." I plucked the copy of *Hollywood Wives* from my purse as I situated myself on the bench. "So, should we read first or do you want to hear about the dream I had and how I ran out on *my* . . . the guy I'm dating. Anyway, I don't know what I'm doing. I'm dating my new boss, and I thought instead of waking up next to him and having a conversation the better option would be to run away like a child." My gaze travelled around the grounds to headstones, the trees and the flowers.

"Jackson, that's what everyone calls him, but me, I call him Jax. He's charming, handsome and funny; at least *I* think he's funny." I stood, and ran my hand over the stone and the letters of her name. "He also holds a lot of similar qualities to the men in this book." I laughed and thumbed at the pages. "*None* of that matters. At times I can't tell if I'm in over my head. It's like am I dreaming or drowning?" Sighing, I slumped down onto the bench. "I like him a lot, Gran, and I think you'd like him too. So that about sums it up, I'm dating my boss and it's crazy scary but also amazing. And now on with the book, let's see what Gina Germaine is up to today."

CHAPTER
twenty-two

Jackson

MY FINGERS TAPPED AGAINST THE BOARDROOM TABLE waiting for the rest of the executive team to filter in for the meeting. As Carol sifted through her file folders, her assistant, Beth, passed out the agenda. Stevie breezed through the door wearing a black and white dress. She looked beautiful. Her blonde hair fell in loose waves over her bare shoulders and her lips, her perfect kissable lips, were bright pink. She took a seat next to Eric, and he stared at her a little too long for my liking.

When I cleared my throat her blue eyes met mine. I smiled and her cheeks tinged as pink as her lips.

I called the meeting to order by welcoming everyone and then gave the floor to Eric. Halfway through the analysis of the monthly financial statement, Stevie's eyes met mine again. Her teeth sank into her bottom lip, registering my dick to life. I tried to stop the images of me bending Stevie over this table and fucking her while she cried out my name begging me for more.

"And that is all from me," Eric said.

"Thank you, Eric. Okay, Carol, what do you have for us today?"

"As you can see we need to finalize the events for the holiday season," Carol began. "More specifically, the details regarding our Merry and Bright Christmas brunch."

"The Winter Wonderland tea event begins the first week of November," Beth interjected. "As you can see, we are almost sold out of our afternoon tea event packages through December."

"That's good news, but aren't we normally sold out of this event within the first hours of the press release?" I asked, leveling my gaze towards Carol.

"Yes, however this year," Carol replied tapping her pen against the table. "We've had an unusual number of inquiries for children's activities during the holiday season. It seems the Surfcomber is offering a variety of holiday movies, baking classes and ornament making packages for kids while their parents attend afternoon tea."

"So the Surfcomber has decided to up their game and take our annual afternoon tea event and put their own spin on it?" Kenzie, the director of marketing asked.

"Hart Hotel is an upscale resort and spa, not a babysitting service," Eric scoffed. "If they want that kind of treatment why don't they head north and stay at Disney?"

"Absolutely, I agree," Carol said. "As much as I adore children, our patrons come here for the experience. We've never had a children's club or anything of that nature."

"It's *never* been a part of the Hart Hotels Inc. branding," Kenzie reminded. "Changing our image now could jeopardize our expansion."

Stevie raised her hand. "You have something to offer, Miss Brockman?"

"Yes, sir," she answered.

"*Fuck me.*"

Carol pinned me with a sharp look. No one else in the room seemed to have heard. While we were in this room, I needed to stop seeing Stevie as the woman I was currently sleeping with and refocus. She was an employee. At the same time we were executive associates in the same meeting.

"I have an idea that might be able to satisfy the issue at hand and still remain true to the Hart Hotels Inc. brand."

"Please, by all means the floor is yours," I said, leaning back into my chair.

"What about offering story time with Missus Claus?"

"Additional cost, we'd need to hire an actress to play Missus Claus," I pointed out.

"Right, okay, what about just having a member of the staff? The Revel Club Lounge would provide the perfect space. Pair it with a giftwrapping event. Instead of the parents having to schlep out to separate events so that Tommy can get daddy a gift and Suzy can get mommy a gift. Have the kids purchase items from our gift shop."

"So you're suggesting that little Suzy and little Tommy take their parents credit card and buy some Waterford Crystal for holiday gifts?" Carol challenged.

Carol brought up an excellent question. Outwardly, I displayed zero emotion. Inwardly I was cheering for Stevie to solve it.

"Actually, I was thinking one gift, the same gift—a silver picture frame," Stevie said, holding up her phone. "An elegant frame that will display their holiday memories."

"Oh, yes, I love those silver frames in the gift shop," Beth mused. "I have at least five in my house."

"Think of it like a gift with purchase. It saves the parent's the time and the hassle of driving the kids to the mall to find the perfect gift at the same time filters money back into the hotel."

"It's not a bad idea, not at all," Kenzie said. "I like it."

"Do you have any more suggestions?" I asked.

Stevie tucked a loose strand of hair behind her ear. "What about having a hot chocolate bar for the kids?"

I watched as she answered the follow up questions with ease. She barely blinked or faltered with any of her answers. The more she spoke the more it confirmed that I was right to trust my gut in offering her a position on the executive team.

CHAPTER
Twenty-three

Stevie

I T TOOK EVERYTHING INSIDE ME NOT TO SLAM MY NOTEPAD ONTO my desk. Cursing Jax under my breath, I slumped into my chair. Was he trying to teach me something by putting me on the spot and challenging me? He was different in the meeting. Of course he was different—it's his company. You asked for this, Stevie. No preferential treatment.

"Miss Brockman, may I have a word with you?" Carol's voice brought me out of my thoughts.

"Sure, what can I do for you?"

She stepped further into my office and Beth appeared by her side. "Miss Brockman, you are in violation of the employee dress code."

My eyes popped wide and I froze. "What?"

"I'll speak slower this time," she answered, taking a ruler from Beth's hands. "You are in violation of the employee dress code."

Beth stared at the floor as Carol approached me. I was officially confused as hell.

She dropped to her knees in front of me, steadying the ruler from the hem of my dress to my knee. "Exactly as I suspected a quarter of an inch."

"I don't understand."

"The hemline of your dress is two and a quarter inches above your knee. Company policy states 'hemlines may not be shorter than two inches.' Not only that, but your shoulders are bare." Her gaze never left me as she traded Beth the ruler for a booklet. "Miss Brockman, can you tell me what floor we are on?"

"The twenty-first floor."

"Very good, one of two executive floors," she replied, handing me the booklet. "The next time I see you here, perhaps you'll be dressed more like a professional and less like you're going to a casual backyard barbeque. Pages ten and eleven will provide you with the appropriate information. I suggest you drop by one of our four boutiques and use your executive employee discount. Do you have any questions?"

"No, I do not." I kept my tone even.

She looked at her watch. "Well, now I can finally go to lunch." They walked away without another word. Fighting back tears, I smoothed my palms down my dress. I shuffled back to my desk and dropped onto my chair wishing I had a pillow that I could scream into.

After lunch, I walked through the windowed hallway towards the boutique on the mezzanine level. Stopping for a moment,

I admired the artwork and paintings that decorated the wall, taking note of the special sunlight reflective frames. *Nice touch.*

My phone pinged alerting me to the auction that was ending in two hours. I had my eye on a collection of tintype photos for the Park City property renovation. A vintage collector had some beautiful casual photos of celebrities at the Sundance film festival. At present, I was the highest bidder. As I shoved my phone into my handbag I felt someone grab my arm from behind, spinning me around.

"Hey, how's your day going?" Jax's blue eyes stared into mine.

Jerking from the hold he had on me I stumbled backwards and my ass connected with a wooden door.

"Are you okay?"

"I'm touched by your concern, *Mister* Hart."

He narrowed his gaze at me. "Is something on your mind, *Miss* Brockman?"

"Yes, it seems that I have violated the company dress code and I need to purchase something with a longer hemline."

"This dress?"

I nodded.

"Says who?" he asked, slipping his hand under my skirt.

"The company manual, specifically pages ten and eleven. Since this is your company, I'm only to assume that you made the rules."

His fingers traced the lace edge of my panties. "I do make the rules, but I can also change the rules."

"Don't do me any favors."

"Is there a reason for your hostile attitude towards me this afternoon?"

"You put me on the spot in that meeting earlier. Were you

trying to embarrass me?" Anger vibrated in my voice.

Footsteps echoed in the hallway accompanied by voices. His hand slipped from beneath my dress and landed on the handle of the door. "Let's chat." Jax grasped my elbow with his other hand, propelling me backwards into a dark a room.

The lights flicked followed by the door catching in the latch. "You think that I put you on the spot in the meeting?"

Nodding, I crossed my arms.

Jax fixed his gaze on me. "Honestly, Stevie, all I was trying to do was challenge your line of thinking. I was really proud of you in the meeting."

"Really?"

He stepped forward rubbing his hands up and down my arms. "*Really*," he repeated. "You came up with some excellent ideas and it was very sexy to watch you hold your own in that room."

Embarrassment flowed through me, evidenced by the heat rising in my cheeks. In this moment, I was acting like a brat and showing my age. If I was being honest, I was ticked about how Carol had treated me and I was taking it out on Jax. A small part of me wanted to tell him everything, but that would be tattling. I'll be damned if I was going to be that woman running to her boyfriend and getting him involved with petty inter-office squabbles. I violated the dress code, I needed to own up to that mistake.

His mouth curled into a smile, and he stole a kiss, tugging my bottom lip. "I should write you up for mouthing off to the CEO."

Uncurling my arms, I smiled against his lips. "I'm sorry for my attitude, Mister Hart."

Smirking, he waved me off and then his lips landed on

mine. His palm connected with my backside. "If I didn't have a meeting in ten minutes, I'd teach that mouth of yours a lesson." He slid his hand between my legs rubbing my clit through my panties. My heart hammered in my chest, my eyes dropped to his lips. "Say my name again."

I sucked in a sharp breath. "Mister Hart, you're in danger of violating our no sex at the office rule."

"Yeah," he murmured, pressing his forehead to mine. "Are you coming home with me tonight?"

I laid my hands on his chest, feeling his heart beating a slow steady rhythm. "I suppose I could sleepover."

He waggled his brows. "Who said anything about sleeping?"

CHAPTER
Twenty-four

Stevie

Four weeks later

"Hey, Mom," I said, cradling the phone between my chin and shoulder.

"Stevie, when will you be coming home for Thanksgiving?"

Scrambling around my bathroom, I pushed the speaker button and then proceeded to grab my toothbrush from the holder.

Thanksgiving? Is that coming up already? My current project was keeping me busy. The Thanksgiving installation at the hotel was coming down early Friday morning and I would need to be there to oversee the Christmas installation. I had a twenty-five foot Christmas tree that would be set up in the lobby. Twenty-two birch trees, more than sixty thousand twinkling lights and three hundred feet of pine needle garland all waiting to transform Hart Hotel into a winter wonderland.

"Stevie, did you hear me?"

My fingers squeezed the tube of whitening paste. "Uh, yeah, I guess I hadn't given it much thought. I figured that you'd being going over to Aunt Darlene and Uncle Roger's place."

Darlene was my mom's younger sister and Uncle Roger wasn't my uncle, not really. He was Darlene's second husband, now divorced, but after I graduated they decided to start dating again—too complicated for me.

Relationships should be easy. Most people will tell you that relationships are hard work. I think that a relationship with the wrong person is hard work.

"Well, your father, he decided that we should host this year. Darlene and Roger will be there, the older kids won't be around. Your father, he wants to deep fry a turkey."

I rolled my eyes, and shoved the toothbrush into my mouth to keep me from saying something offensive. My father was notorious for leaving every family gathering and holiday. Sometimes it was to go hunting, so he claimed. One Easter, I followed him. All he did was go around town to the car washes, which was nothing out of the ordinary.

"I'm ordering some pies, from Handel's bakery, but I will be making your favorite sweet potato casserole."

At twenty-four, could I finally tell my mom that I hated sweet potato anything? I really did. I'd lied my entire life about loving sweet potatoes and when someone added brown sugar or marshmallows, just no. No, I would take it to my grave. There was no reason to give her anymore grief, I'd done that plenty where my father was concerned.

"Anyway, we'd love to see you, sugar."

And by *we*—she means her, which is totally fine by me. "I'd love to see you too, Mom," I said, smoothing my dress over my hips. "I don't know about Thanksgiving because I am oversee-ing the Christmas installation at the hotel."

"I understand," she said. "With a new job comes major responsibility. You definitely need to keep up your exemplary work ethic."

"Maybe you could visit before Christmas," I suggested be-fore muting the phone to gargle some mouthwash.

"I'll take a look at the calendar. I have a meeting with the principal at your elementary school. There's an administrative position open after the winter break. And I'm overseeing the Christmas bazaar and holiday bake sale at the church."

"Busy lady. That's really awesome about the school job, Mom. I wish you good luck."

"Thanks, sugar. That's the other line, I better take the call."

"Okay, talk soon."

I ended the call and stuffed my phone into my purse. Looking at the clock on the wall, I had fifteen minutes to make it to work. After grabbing my keys, I pulled open the screen door to find my father standing on the porch.

What the hell? Shock is all I felt, but I don't want him to know that or hear any kind of tone in my voice, so I faked a smile as wide as the delta and put a sing song pitch into my voice.

"Hey, Dad, what brings you down to Florida?" I asked, locking the door.

His fingers rubbed the greying black stubble of his jawline. His hands were ashen, and held more spots than I remembered. Hard to believe they were the same hands that used to hit me when I made too much noise playing with my toys.

As he stepped towards me, the scent of menthols and too

much Brut cologne invaded my senses. "I need a couple thousand dollars." He jutted his chin. "Can you help your old man out?"

I kept my tone even. "What makes you think I have that kind of money?"

His brows drew together, as he nodded. "Little girl, I know that old bitty that you call Gran, left you this place and I think she left you a hefty sum of cash."

"No, she really didn't and if she had I would have paid off my student loans by now and my car," I replied, gesturing towards the Focus.

His expression went dark as his green bloodshot eyes met mine. "Right, and by the looks of your fancy dress, you're telling me you don't have any money?"

"Does Mom know that you're here?" I bit out.

"What I do is none of your mother's concern."

I sidestepped him, and headed towards the stairs. "I need to be going. I have a meeting at work. Thanks for stopping by, Dad."

He took a step backwards wrapping his hand around the railing keeping me from moving down the stairs. "If you're hiding money, I'll find out, and you'll wish you hadn't lied to me." His words were menacing. Disgust lurched in my stomach and the tone sent shivers racing up my spine.

Lighting up a cigarette, my dad descended the wooden stairs and walked to his orange Chevy pickup. Thank goodness Megyn was staying at a friend's house. I didn't need her hearing my dad's threats. As I climbed into my car, I watched as the truck drove down the alley.

When I got to work, I logged into my bank account from my personal laptop. I had a few thousand dollars in my account.

It wasn't much, but there's enough to pay bills and some extra to put towards renovating Gran's place.

I stared at the framed picture of mom and me and sadness swirled inside me. Earlier on the phone, she was so happy asking me to come home for the holiday weekend. After the visit from my father, it reminded me of all the reasons I wanted to avoid Kennesaw.

Slouching back in my chair, my fingers pinched the bridge of my nose. I let my dad's earlier words roll around in my head. Why would he think that Gran had given me a large sum of money? Better yet, what would lead him to believe there was a stash of cash somewhere? Perhaps I should revisit the file folders in Gran's desk.

"Why is this my life?" I whispered.

"Miss Brockman," Jax's assistant, Ingrid's voice drifted over the intercom of my desk phone.

"Good morning, Ingrid."

"Oh good, you're here. Good morning, Mister Hart would like to remind you that you will be meeting with him and the President of the Salissa Island historical committee this week. I've forwarded the details to your email."

I felt my brows pinch together. "I thought Carol was attending that meeting with Mister Hart?"

"Conflict of scheduling," she answered.

"Okay, thank you, Ingrid. I will add it to my calendar."

I couldn't say that I was upset about attending this meeting. I'd always had a fascination with the history of the island. When I'd come here to visit, I would beg Gran to take me to the Landmark District. I loved taking carriage rides through the brick streets and looking at all the early English architecture. It was a special treat when Gran and I would have lunch at the Orange Tree English Pub and then walk around downtown. Somehow we always end up at Baker's Art Gallery.

Knock. Knock.

My eyes flicked up to see Jax standing in my doorway, filling the space in a pinstriped suit his hand smoothing over his silver tie.

"You were late this morning," he said.

I blew out a harsh breath. "Family stuff." It's all I could bear to say because the thought of telling Jax about my father was an embarrassment of riches.

Riches.

"You want to tell me about it?"

"It's some pretty ugly stuff. My family life isn't all that great. You'll probably want to run the other way."

"I'm not in the habit of running away from unsavory family issues. I've got some of my own."

My brows lifted at his admission as I leaned forward in my chair. "My father paid me a visit this morning and I don't particularly care for the man. He wasn't exactly the kind of father who taught me how to ride a bike or help me up when I'd fall. He was more the kind of dad who kicked me when I was down."

Unbuttoning his jacket, Jax took a seat in front of my desk. "Are you saying that your father hit you?"

My fingers splayed across my forehead. "Yes, and my mom. He's a drunk and I am pretty sure that he cheats on my mom." My voice shook as the last few words tumbled out. I didn't open up to people about my home life. Until Krystle, Tiffany was the only person who knew all my dirty little family secrets. Megyn doesn't even know.

His thumb grazed along the stubble of his jaw. "Did he lay his hands on you this morning?"

Shaking my head, my eyes dropped to my lap. "He yammered on about Gran having money stashed away and something about him needing money."

"Hey, look at me." Jax's blue eyes searched my face. "Do you think he'll come back to your place?"

"Only if he finds out I've got a big pile of cash lying around."

"Yeah, when they find out you have money that's all they see." He stood, and buttoned his jacket. "Do you feel safe enough to stay at your place?"

I swallowed harshly. "I'd be lying if I said that this morning didn't have me on edge."

"If you'd like I can stay with you, or you can stay at my place."

"I don't want to leave my roommate, Megyn, alone, but at the same time I don't want to alarm her or disrupt her life."

"I understand." He glanced at his watch. "I've got a meeting, but I'll check in with you later."

As he walked out of my office, I smiled and tried to think about the last time someone cared this much about my well-being. Jax didn't treat me like a damsel in distress; he asked how he could help me. *A refreshing approach.*

As soon as I pushed open the door to my apartment, the sound of loud moans echoed through the small space.

"Oh god, yes!" Megyn called out. "Yes! Right there!"

My eyes squeezed shut, and I quietly slipped off my heels. I tip toed over to the mail bin, and shuffled through the contents. Moans turned into screams. Seconds later I heard the sound of iron tapping against the wall.

Did she make up with Beau?

"You fuck good, baby."

That was not Beau's voice, but it was all I needed to exit stage left to my bedroom. Closing the door behind me, I dropped my purse onto my desk. Then I shuffled towards my closet and placed my heels back into their rightful shoebox.

My phone pinged with a message from Jax.

Tell me the details of your father's vehicle. Car? Truck? SUV? Anything you have, along with his description.

Me: Here is a picture of my father. It was taken just before my graduation.

Jax: What is his name?

Me: Martin Brockman.

Me: He drives an orange colored Chevy pickup.

Jax: Thanks. I have a guy who is going to keep an eye on your place and your roommate, Megyn.

Before I could respond, my phone chimed and Jax's name flashed on the screen. I hit the call button.

"I've been thinking and I want you to stay with me. My reasons are selfish—I don't like the fact that your father has a history of abuse where you are concerned. If he hurt you. If he hit you, Stevie. I wouldn't be able to . . ." his voice trailed off. "I'm concerned."

The pain in his voice was obvious.

"I'm concerned too, but you promise me that Megyn will be okay?"

"I've got my best security guy looking out for her."

I stared at my suitcase and my eyes darted to my pile of laundry. "Do you mind if I do some laundry at your place?"

He laughed. "Not at all. I need to finish up a few things here and then I will pick you up. Say in about an hour."

"No, let me drive to your house. I'm not carpooling to work with you."

"As you wish," he replied. "See you later."

I ended the call and tossed my phone onto my bed. The sound of Megyn's door opening and heavy footfalls crossing the hardwood told me the romp was over.

"You were fantastic," a gruff voice said. "I really enjoyed that, babe."

"Me too," she said, opening the door.

I rushed to my window to see if could catch a glimpse of her new guy. Long jet-black hair shielded his face. The only thing I could see were the brightly colored tattoos that decorated his right arm. Lights to a white Escalade flicked on and he opened the door.

Okay, enough spying.

My fingers grasped the zipper on the back of my dress.

"How much of that did you hear, Stevie?" Megyn called out and tapped my door.

A loud laugh burst from my throat as I slipped my dress over my head. "Enough to know that you had a good time."

"I'm sorry," she breathed. "This guy has been coming into the restaurant for weeks. Every time he sits in my section. I never had the nerve to carry on more than casual conversation—until today."

I tossed my dress into my laundry bag. "Why today?"

"Well," Megyn began, expelling a deep breath. "Beau was

being a real dickhole today."

Pulling on a pair of leggings and my favorite logo tee, I already knew where this was going. "Ah, I see."

"I can practically hear you judging me." She laughed.

Smiling, I opened the door. "No judgement. I am all too familiar with dickhole ex-boyfriends. So if you want to get your rocks off with someone else—I say, you do you girl."

She crossed the threshold and then flopped onto my bed. "The sex, it was really good—leg shaking good."

I walked into my bathroom and then busied myself with the task of packing up my toiletries. "Do you think it will be more than sex?"

She groaned. "He said he wanted to see me again, but who knows if he meant it or not."

"Well, you're young, hot and single," I said, crossing back through my bedroom. "Go out there and have as much sex as you want." I grabbed my suitcase and propped it open.

Megyn levered up onto her elbows. "What are you doing?"

"Jax invited me to stay with him for a few days."

"Wow." She raised her eyebrow. "Are things getting serious between the two of you?"

I shook my head and continued packing. "No, it's only been a couple of months. How serious can that be?"

"Yeah, I suppose you're right. Although I think I could fall in love with Jackson Hart pretty easily."

"But, you my friend are an Aries so you are most likely to fall in love easily."

"While that is true, I believe that right in the middle of everyday life, sometimes love can surprise us with a fairy tale."

Pulling open my dresser drawer, I raised a brow. "See, that right there—you really are a dreamer."

"Well, I will hold down the fort while you're away." She readjusted her position on my bed, tucking her legs against her chest. "I don't know when you'll be back, but I am leaving Wednesday to go home for Thanksgiving and I won't be back until Sunday night."

On a long sigh, I tossed some intimate pieces into my lingerie bag. "Speaking of family, my dad showed up here this morning."

"Oh really? Do I get to meet him?"

Leaning against my dresser, I shook my head. "No trust me. Martin Brockman is the last man I'd ever introduce you to."

"Eeekk, not a good dad, huh?"

"Not in the least." After I zipped up my suitcase, I set it up right onto the wheels.

She bopped her head. "Yeah, I can relate. My mother is a real pill sometimes, but my sister excels at being an uber bitch. You're lucky that you're an only child."

Sometimes I wished that I had a sibling. Other days I was grateful I didn't because that would have been one more person that my dad could punish.

Megyn swung her legs off the side of my bed. "Well, I need to shower. Have a great time with Jax." She stood and then wrapped her arms around my shoulders.

I hugged her tight. "Have a safe trip home and a wonderful Thanksgiving."

CHAPTER
twenty-five

Jackson

"MISTER HART, WE HAVE OBTAINED THE LICENSE plate for Martin Brockman's pickup. Currently the vehicle is parked at a small diner just outside Bonita Springs."

"Where is Mister Brockman?"

"He's inside the diner—alone."

"Thank you, Archie. Keep me updated."

"Will do, sir."

Curiosity had the better of me and I wondered why Stevie's father was headed south instead of back to Georgia. I clicked my inbox, seeing an email from Florida International at the top.

Subject: Annual Winter Fundraiser and Gala.

Mr. Hart,

Firstly, we thank you for your generosity and sizable donations to our University through the years. Your continued support of our academic programs has helped in countless ways.

Attached you will find the formal invitation to our Winter Fundraising Gala. This year, we'd be honored to have you as our keynote speaker. To say that we are impressed by your accomplishments in the Hospitality and Business industries is an understatement. We cordially invite you to Florida International University as our Keynote Speaker for our Annual Winter Fundraiser and Gala.

As you know, the Chaplin School of Hospitality and Tourism Management consistently ranks as one of the top programs in the nation. Our attending students, alumni and faculty would be honored to gain insight of your experiences that have propelled Hart Hotels into the upper echelon of the hospitality industry.

On behalf of Florida International University, we look forward to the prospect of you speaking at our annual event.

Bradley Andre M.S.

Director of Conference Services

Chaplin School of Hospitality and Tourism Management

Shock and surprise wound through me as I stared at the invitation. I'd given dozens of lectures and speeches over the years but to be invited to my alma mater was quite the honor. Did I really want to go back to Miami? I'd been run out of town and forced to sell my hotel all because my brother murdered the mayor's criminal son.

I dialed Archie. "I need up to date information on Anthony Flores Senior, the former mayor of Miami and anything you can get me on the Rojas drug cartel. I want it all."

"Will do, boss."

I put the matter of the RSVP out of my mind, returning focus to the next item on my to-do list—an evening with Stevie. And as if she heard my thoughts a message appeared on my phone.

Stevie: I'm all alone in your house. Are you done perfecting your golf game? If you are, perhaps you can come home and play with me?

My phone pinged again. An image of Stevie lying in my bed wearing one of my white button-down shirts and nothing else came into focus. Only a tiny corner of the comforter covered her pussy.

"Holy shit," I mumbled.

Her fingers dug into my skin as I gripped her thighs moving her up and down my cock. Stevie's lips covered mine and my tongue slid across hers. Each time we had sex was far more intense, for more explosive than the time before.

On a long moan she writhed above me, tossing her head back. "Oh *yes*," Her nails bit into my skin as she came around my cock. The sight of her coming undone above me was beautiful. Stevie collapsed in my arms, struggling to catch her breath. I kissed her softly as my hands glided up and down her back.

Sex with Stevie was something of an addiction and I never wanted to be cured. Oddly enough, the word addiction shifted my thoughts to Miami.

"Jax?" She looked down at me, her blue eyes hooded. She squeezed her inner muscles making me aware that I was still buried deep inside her. I lifted Stevie up, pulling out and then rolled out from underneath her and off the bed to discard the condom.

Climbing back under the covers, Stevie shifted and then snuggled into my side. "Are you good?" I asked.

"Yes," she replied, smoothing her fingertips along my abs. "Can I ask you something?"

"Sure."

"Thanksgiving is next week," she began. "Do you invite your family here or do you go *home*?"

I let out a deep breath. "My family consists of me and my sister, Janessa."

She looked up at me, her brows pinched together in confusion.

"You're not the only one with a less than awesome father," I replied. "My father left when I was in college. I came home for Thanksgiving break to find out he'd served my mother with divorce papers. I haven't seen or heard from him in years." Truth be told I didn't know if he was dead or alive. I could have looked. I could have checked up on him. After all I had the resources. The money. What I didn't have was the gene that allowed me to care about him.

Stevie sucked in a breath. "I'm so sorry."

"Although I appreciate the sentiment, you don't need to apologize."

She tilted her mouth to mine, kissing me.

"And my brother," I said, skimming my fingers along her ribcage.

"You have a brother?"

"Jason, yeah, he's in prison."

Stevie propped herself up onto her elbow, looking at me with those beautiful blue eyes that captivated my soul. "That was the last thing I expected to hear. What happened?"

"He was involved in a drug deal gone badly—a robbery, actually." My hands shook as I remembered the sight of my mother lying on a slab of metal all life drained from her face. "It ended up costing my mother her life. The guys killed my mother instead of my brother and then Jason killed them."

Stevie twined her arms around my torso. "The loss and the

pain, I can't imagine what you've been through."

"Like anything, I just try to deal with it when it hits me and let it go when I can."

"Do you ever see your brother?"

"He was up for parole some weeks ago, I saw him for what I believe to be the last time."

"He didn't get out, I assume?"

"Nope." I pulled Stevie up my body so that her back was pressed against my chest.

"How often do you see your sister?"

"A few times a year," I said, kissing the back of her neck. "She's a lawyer in Austin."

"Will the two of you be getting together for the holiday?"

"No, she has other plans," I whispered in her ear. "Why all the questions about Thanksgiving?"

She shrugged. "No reason."

I shifted, pinning Stevie beneath me. "Now, why don't I believe you?"

Stevie smiled, snaking her arms around my neck and rubbing herself against me. "Fine, you called my bluff. I'm not going to Kennesaw for Thanksgiving. I was wondering if you'd like to spend the day with me?"

Shaking my head, I slid my cock against her wetness. "No, I want to spend the entire weekend with you."

She leaned up brushing her lips against mine. "I'd like that."

"Good." I fished another condom off the nightstand and rolled it down my length. "Hold on because I think you'll like this more."

"*Ahhh,*" she cried out as I pushed into her. I gripped her hips and made her take every inch of my cock for the rest of the night.

CHAPTER
Twenty-six

Stevie

THIN LINES OF YELLOW SPLASHED ACROSS THE ROOM. SORE and dehydrated, I eased out of bed carefully, hoping not to disturb Jax sleeping. When I focused on the left side of the bed, it was empty aside from a handwritten note.

Had to take an early conference call.

See you at the office. Help yourself to coffee and breakfast.

Note the "and breakfast" part – Jax

My tired legs carried me into the shower and I let the hot water do its job. Twenty minutes and an ibuprofen later, I made my way into Jax's walk-in closet. A cream colored box with a giant black ribbon sat atop the dresser with a small envelope attached.

These are for you.

I plan to fill this dresser with more—for you.

Personally, I'm a fan of the pink lace. – Jax

Lifting the lid, I then pushed back the black tissue paper.

My eyes widened at the sight of beautiful silky colors of pink, lavender, white, and black lace.

"Holy crap."

I winced as the hot coffee splashed onto my shaking hand. My muscles had yet to recover from gripping the bookcase in Jax's office while he tongue fucked me into an epic orgasm. The CEO of Hart Hotels Inc. was on his knees begging to see my pussy covered in fine silk. *I literally brought the man to his knees.*

In between meetings and conference calls with national and international art galleries, I spent the majority of my day perusing online auctions. Staying busy was good for my peace of mind and kept me from marching back down the hallway and familiarizing myself with every flat surface in Jax's office. So much for not breaking the no sex at the office rule.

"Good afternoon, Miss Brockman." Carol stood in my doorway holding a file folder in the air.

"Hello, Carol," I replied, dabbing a napkin onto my skin.

"It's Miss Edgerton, not Carol."

"Very well." I tossed the napkin into the trash as I rounded the corner of my desk.

"I see that you've scheduled the visual display team to tear down the autumn installation beginning at five A.M. Friday morning."

"Yes, that is correct."

"The Friday morning after Thanksgiving Day."

I stood my ground. "Is there a point?"

With a flick of her wrist she tossed the folder onto my desk. "In the past we have scheduled this as an overnight project. This is due to the fact that many of our visual display team members are also maintenance team members." She crossed her arms. "Not only that, but it is usually a six hour project, starting at five in the morning takes the installation well into midday hours. The lobby will be filled with guests maneuvering around ladders and pallets of décor. It's a lawsuit waiting to happen."

I felt the blush rising in my cheeks. "I didn't realize."

"With your multiple college degrees, certainly you should have realized." she replied, narrowing her eyes at me.

"Miss Edgerton, I am happy to—"

She held up her hand. "I expected more from you. Has he screwed you senseless?"

Carol didn't wait for my answer. Instead, she walked away, leaving me in total shock.

I spent rest of the afternoon trying to coordinate the visual display team schedule with Maria, the head of the engineering department.

"Lucy, Terri, Sarah, Britannia, and Thom are all available to work from midnight until the project is complete. Hector and Brad will come in two hours early to help finish up the installation."

She nodded. "Yes, all the shifts are covered."

I clasped my hands together feeling relieved that we'd been able to make the schedule changes on short notice with ease.

"It was a pleasure working with you, Stevie." Maria pushed to her feet. "Enjoy the holiday."

"You too, Maria."

After Maria left, I checked my calendar. No meetings for

the rest of the day. I fired up my computer and then scanned my email. Nothing pressing.

At the sound of laughter in the hallway, I glanced up seeing Eric and Beth gliding by my office. "A few of us are grabbing drinks at The Rusty Anchor, you want to come along?"

I wondered for a split second if Carol was going to be there. She didn't strike me as the type to socialize over drinks with co-workers. "Sure, I'll meet you there."

"Great, first round is on me."

Eric strode away and I powered down my computer. I grabbed my handbag and my cardigan out of the coat closet glancing at my reflection in the mirror. "What a day," I mumbled.

It was nearly five o'clock by the time I got to the bar. With the holiday traffic it was a madhouse on the highway.

Wild beats of music pumped through the speakers as I pulled open the heavy wooden door. The space was illuminated by the soft glow of electric blue and yellow lights. The scent of fried food and stale beer hung in the air as I maneuvered past a few empty bar tables to the back where I spotted Eric and Beth playing darts. My smile grew wider when I saw Abby sitting at a table talking to Maria and Thom.

A hand brushed around my hip. "I was starting to think you were going to stand us up." The familiar voice sent anger funneling through my veins.

I took a step forward putting distance between Cord and me before turning to face him. "What did I tell you about touching me?"

Not giving him a second more of my time I strode towards Abby. She jumped up and hugged me. Eric asked me for my drink order and then I greeted everyone else.

"Let's grab this booth," Abby suggested.

"So how have you been?" I asked, sliding against the red pleather.

"Good, really good and you?"

"Same. How's your sister? Did she have her baby?"

"Not yet, only a few more weeks." She smiled over the rim of her glass. "Oh, I received a promotion at Tonic Volley."

"That's awesome. What's the job?"

"Assistant Graphic Designer," she answered. "It's full-time and came with a big pay increase."

"Congratulations."

"Yeah, and I didn't even have to sleep with anyone to get the gig." She gave me a crooked smile and then tossed back her drink. Eric sat my cocktail in front of me, giving me a moment to formulate my response to Abby.

"I can't tell if you're being serious or not."

"Of course I'm only joking, Stevie."

Smiling, I relaxed into the booth taking a sip of my martini. "So why don't you tell me more about this new job and if you're dating anyone, I need all the details."

I managed to keep Abby talking through another round of drinks. She informed me that she was dating a new guy and that she had officially given notice to Carol that she was leaving.

"How did Carol take the news that you were moving on?" I asked.

She hiccupped through a laugh. "Carol was her typical self, saying that she'd miss me, blah, blah. I don't care. I loved working at Hart Hotels, but if I'm honest, Carol's an asshole."

I leaned forward clicking her glass to mine. "Can't argue with that—she's reprimanded me twice, and was a total bitch about it."

"Did you tell your boyfriend?"

I waved her off. "Not worth it, besides Carol is Jackson's 'most trusted employee'."

Abby side-eyed me.

"His words, I swear."

"Carol the *cuntasaurus*," Abby staged whispered. "She needs to get laid."

"Isn't that the truth," Beth agreed, sliding beside Abby. "I'm sorry she's been so awful to you both."

My brows lifted. "It's not your fault, Beth."

"I know," she commented in a low whisper. "I don't know why she has such a stick up her ass. When I first started working for her, she was pleasant. I can't say why she changed."

We shifted the conversation to a non-Carol, non-work topic—holiday plans. Beth was going to Tennessee for Thanksgiving, while Abby was running in a five mile race for charity before going to her mom's place in Jacksonville.

After my second martini I needed to use the ladies room. Excusing myself, I disappeared into the restroom, which was surprisingly clean and chic. The line was four deep. Ten minutes later I made it through the line and stood washing my hands. I toweled off my hands and pulled my phone from my purse. I had a text message from Jax that was sent an hour ago.

Jax: I've got a call with the Project Manager for the Park City renovation. We're executing a few change orders.

Me: Sorry I am just now seeing this message. Partaking in happy hour with Eric, Abby and a few more work people.

Reaching for the door, I kept my eyes focused on the screen. I stepped into the hallway and found Cord leaning against the wall. "Are you texting your *new* boyfriend?" Light from the red lamps that lit up the hallway passed over his face as he approached me.

"That is none of your business."

"Rumor has it that you're screwing the boss." The smell of beer and smoke was heavy on his breath.

"You know what they say about rumors," I shot back.

"Please enlighten me."

"Rumors are spread by fools and accepted by idiots."

"Well then, let's put the rumors to rest—are you or are you not fucking Jackson Hart?"

"Charming." I tried pushing past him, but he didn't move an inch. "Get out of my way, Cord."

"You didn't say the magic word." His hot breath fanned across my ear.

"Get the *fuck* out of my way," I snapped.

He held up his hands in mock surrender and slithered back until his hip bumped the wall. As I moved past him, the beer from his mug splashed onto my skin.

When I returned to our table, Abby was engrossed in a conversation about tattoos with a guy that I didn't recognize.

"Hey, I think I'm going to take off."

She gave me a frown. "Oh no, do you have to?"

I fished my keys from my purse. "Yeah, lots to prep for tomorrow. I'm making a turkey and it's my first time."

She slipped out of the booth to give me a hug. "It was great to see you, Stevie. Let's not wait so long to catch up."

"I agree. I'll text you soon."

On my way out the door I waved to everyone and told them to have a nice holiday. As I walked to my car, the conversation with Cord replayed over in my mind. He had some nerve. Too many variables were working against me and Jax. Abby, Carol, and Cord all knew about the two of us. Who else knew?

CHAPTER
twenty-seven

Jackson

"**W**ELL, IT'S OFFICIAL. I'VE WRECKED Thanksgiving." Stevie tossed the charred meat into the trash, and I pulled open the sliding glass door in the kitchen.

"You didn't wreck anything."

She pressed her fingers to her temples. "What was I thinking trying to cook an entire feast? I am a takeout girl, not Betty Crocker."

Along with the pearl earrings, the apron she wore over her black skinny jeans and white sleeveless, lace blouse might have suggested otherwise. Laughing, I leaned my hip against the counter. "Hey, most days I don't cook either. I'm not sure that I could have done much better."

"All we have is pie, rolls and potatoes." She leaned forward and scooped up her wine glass from the counter. "It doesn't make for a great meal."

"As much as I love carbs, you're right." I took a drink of whiskey watching as Stevie swirled the contents of her glass. I had a feeling that she was contemplating how to save the meal.

I walked over to the sliding glass door and pulled it shut. "I have an idea. I know a place we can go."

"Where?"

"It's a surprise."

She eyed me over her wine glass. "What do you have in store for me, Jackson Hart?"

Stevie rarely called me Jackson. Admittedly, I liked it—really liked it.

The streets of Salissa Island were nearly desolate. I let Stevie drive my Mercedes over to Amelia City. She took me by surprise when she veered left onto Emerald Avenue.

"These are not the directions I punched in," I pointed out.

She smiled. "I know. We're taking a quick detour. I want you to meet someone."

Stevie maneuvered along the streets of Amelia City with ease and then pulled up to the cemetery. "Okay, this is a little frightening."

"Don't be scared, it's not like its Halloween," she mocked, turning off the engine and then handing me the keys.

We trekked along the brick walkway lined with trees hand in hand arriving in front of a grey marbled headstone. In the distance, another family stood together hugging and taking photos. Brightly colored balloons dotted the sky above them.

Ruby Marie Harrison
Beloved Wife, Mother, and Grandmother

"Hi, Gran," Stevie said, brushing the debris from the top the gravestone. "It's me, Stevie, and this is Jackson, the guy I told you about."

I leaned closer, whispering, "You told your grandmother about me, should I be worried?"

She nudged her shoulder into my bicep. "I did, and I *believe* she approves."

"I'm glad to hear that."

"I'm positive that she would have liked you. I come here every Saturday morning, when I'm not working."

"This is your personal appointment? The one you said you had when you snuck out of my house that morning."

She nodded. "Yeah, sorry about that."

We stood in silence for a few moments. I hadn't been to a cemetery since my mother's funeral.

Too many flowers.

Too many people.

Too much rain.

Too much noise.

Everything from that day came barreling back at hyper speed. I tipped my head to the sky watching the clouds float by. Stevie curled her hand around my forearm. "Is this too weird for you?"

I shook my head. "I wouldn't say that at all. Honestly, I was thinking about my mother."

She smacked her palm against her forehead. "Oh, shit. I wasn't thinking in bringing you here."

I bent to meet her eyes. "Don't overthink it, Stevie. I wouldn't be here if I didn't want to be. I don't think much of my family on holidays. If you hadn't brought me here, this day might have passed without giving her a thought."

"Do you want to visit her today?"

I laced my fingers with hers as we walked back towards the car. "Well, that would be quite a trip because she's buried in Montana."

"I assumed she was here in Florida, I'm sorry."

We arrived at the car and I pulled Stevie into my arms. "You need to stop apologizing. Intimacy and sharing personal stuff, even though at times it's difficult, I believe that's what is called being in a relationship."

She smiled as the warm breeze toyed with her blonde hair. "Speaking of our relationship, I wasn't going to bring this up, at least not today anyway."

I tucked an errant strand behind her ear. "What, is it?"

"Yesterday, at happy hour with Abby and Eric, Cord was there, asking me if the rumors about the two of us were true. I managed to blow him off, but I am not sure that he believed me, and seeing as Abby and Carol know about the two of us—how long will it be before my mask slips and the whole company finds out."

Aggravation teased at my nerves. No way in hell was I about to let her asshat of an ex fuck with us. We'd tell people about us when the time was right. I hoped that my employees were smarter than to give into petty gossip.

"I'll have a chat with him on Monday."

"Oh no you won't." Stevie burst out with a laugh, her blue eyes sparkling with amusement. "If you talk to Cord he will know with absolute certainty that I told you. And why would I, Stevie Brockman the Design Consultant for Hart Hotels, be bothered to talk to my boss. . ." She jabbed at my chest. "About a silly rumor."

In my ideal world, my relationship with Stevie was the

best kept secret on the island. However, I was smart enough to realize at some point it would get out. "Good point. I'll keep my mouth shut for now, but if he steps out of line he's gone." Paying no attention to the public that surrounded us I threaded my fingers through her hair and claimed her mouth.

Stevie's stomach rumbled effectively breaking our moment. I smiled against her lips. "I'm going to feed you now. I don't need you passing out on me."

"Can I drive?"

I shook my head, unlocking my car. "In your condition, lack of nutrients and all, I'm not so sure that you should be operating heavy machinery."

"Wise guy."

"Yes, I am very wise."

CHAPTER
twenty-eight

Stevie

"I CALLED MY MOM THIS MORNING, AND HER EXACT WORDS about my dad were—he went to Florida to view a few properties. Apparently he's expanding the business." I wrung my hands together as Jax pulled onto Emerald Avenue.

"You don't believe her?"

"It's not that I don't believe her, I believe that's what he told her."

"Maybe that is why he came to you for the money," Jax asserted, flicking his turn signal to change lanes.

I shrugged. "Well, he could have been nicer." Uncertainty coiled in my veins and I couldn't help but wonder if my distracted thoughts were the cause for screwing up our turkey dinner.

We didn't say anything more for the remainder of the drive. Our destination was a magnificent high-rise building just over the bridge.

"What is this place?" I asked, as he handed the valet his keys.

"Come with me and find out," Jax whispered, resting his firm hand against my back leading me towards a bank of elevators.

The elevator deposited us on the top floor where the doors opened to a hostess desk for Masson's, an elegant Italian restaurant. I'd heard rumors about this place. A sleek rectangular fireplace was anchored in the middle of the space surrounded by tables covered in pristine ivory linens.

"Good afternoon, Mister Hart, we have your usual table ready for you."

As we moved through the nearly empty restaurant, Jax kept his hand on my lower back. To my surprise, his usual table was a private room. I walked towards the windows taking in the view of Amelia City, Salissa Island and the ocean spread before me.

"It's breathtaking."

"Not half as striking as you," he remarked, wrapping his arms around my waist from behind.

"I feel really underdressed. Why didn't you tell me to change?"

He moved to stand in front of me. "You look beautiful. Now, shall we sit and order some appetizers?"

Eight handstitched ivory, leather chairs were positioned around an oval table and a glass chandelier hung from a tray ceiling. The adjacent wall was finished with a glass paneled black wine cellar door.

After we ordered two buffalo caprese salads and eggplant bruschetta, we perused the wine selection. We settled on a bottle of red wine that cost as much as my car insurance. Jax swirled the contents before taking a drink. A nod was the signal of approval and then he poured the cranberry colored liquid into my glass.

"Johnnie Walker black, rocks," he said to the server.

"You aren't having any wine?"

"I'll have a glass with dinner."

"So," I drawled out. "Do you come here often?" I laughed at my own question.

"Not as much as I would like," he replied. "I was here in June for Carol's birthday."

Jealousy spread through my chest at the thought of Carol sitting here with Jax in such an intimate setting laughing and talking. Had they been an item?

"Is that something you do often, join your employees for birthday dinners at expensive restaurants?"

"Not particularly," he replied. "But, when the woman I'm seeing asks me to accompany her to her sister's birthday dinner. I'm obligated to go."

I stilled, my heart galloping in my chest. "Carol has a sister and you dated her?"

My mind raced thinking back to the article for the Children's Hospital fundraiser and the brunette on his arm. Was she Carol's sister? Why did they break-up? This could explain Carol's shitty attitude towards me.

"Yes, her name is Trina and we weren't in a committed relationship," he commented. "I had several charitable obligations and I was advised to be seen with someone on my arm."

"Why?" I pressed, my voice taking on shakiness.

He leaned forward. "I had been considering a run for the state senate."

I shook my head in confusion, and even though I heard him perfectly I still asked the question. "Are you serious?"

Before he could reply, our server breezed in depositing our appetizers, Jax's scotch, and then refilling our water glasses. My fingers tapped against my lips. A senator—he wanted to be a senator?

"I can tell this is all overwhelming, let me explain," he said, draping his linen napkin across his lap. "I was considering a run for senate, but then I decided that further expanding Hart Hotels was more important to me. I couldn't do both so I put my political aspirations on hold."

"On hold, as in you'd like to resume them at some point?" I stabbed at a tomato with my fork.

"I intend to, yes."

"And you need to be seen in public with someone on your arm, because it shows commitment, a dedication of sorts."

He nodded. "Being viewed as coupled as opposed to a single bachelor does appeal more favorably to voters."

"Jesus Christ, Jackson, when were you planning to tell me all of this?" My fork clanged against the salad plate and my words spilled out harsher than I intended. I took a hurried sip of wine.

"Are you mad?"

"Are you avoiding my question?" I shot back.

I was somewhat getting used to the idea of being in his world. Now, suddenly it didn't feel like Jax's world, the guy I'd met who helped me with my car and talked about state fair food. It definitely felt like Jackson James Hart's world, and I was plain old Stevie Brockman who lived in a two bedroom rental above a Chinese restaurant. Forget the staff at Hart Hotels finding out about the two of us. The press would have a field day with that information. I wasn't exactly the epitome of a senator's girlfriend.

"Look, Stevie, I am not sure what the future holds. What I do know is that I like spending time with you. I also like a nice glass of scotch, politics and playing nine holes of golf." He leaned closer to me. "And normally holidays are just another day for me. Sometimes I spend them eating alone at the hotel, but today I am with you and I'm happier than I have been in a long time—*happy* and not just going through the motions of the day."

My heart splintered at his admission. I couldn't help feeling like shit, because I could relate on some level. Holidays back home were spent mostly avoiding my redneck cousins and listening to my dad and his hillbilly brother talk about the good old days—it was the same ten stories repeated every time. Depending on the holiday I could pick up a shift at the country club. I'd spend the day waiting on other people and their families. After the restaurant had closed, the serving staff would haul ass down the buffet line filling our plates with French toast, extra crispy bacon and mushy eggs.

"Sorry, I just felt a little blindsided," I said, picking up my fork and returning to my salad.

"I'm sorry. I didn't mean to make you feel that way."

"You're forgiven and, for the record, I'm happy too, I'm really glad to be here with you."

"Good."

The sun dipped behind the clouds casting a shadow over the room. I studied Jax, watching him eat, and I wasn't thinking about apologies, or home, or work or the future. For a moment I enjoyed the way his lips closed over the tines of his fork and the way his blue eyes sparkled even in the dim light.

Jax leaned closer, threading his hands through my hair. "Kiss me."

My lips moved over his, he tasted like olive oil and red wine. He took his time, tugging at my lower lip, licking his tongue against mine. Time stood still, and I barely remembered ordering dinner, yet here I sat in a private dining room sharing a meal with the man who dominated conference rooms. A man, who could order an entire meal in Italian as fluidly as he could chat about golf statistics. A man, who I was very much starting to fall for.

"So, what are you doing the weekend of December sixteenth?"

"Let me consult my secretary," I answered, twirling the linguine around the tines of my fork. "Why, what's going on?"

"I've been invited to speak at my alma mater and I'd like you to go with me."

"That's exciting. Yale or Florida International?"

"FIU, but I'd love to take you up to New Haven. I haven't been there in a while."

Jax wanted to take me to Connecticut. I suppose for him that was like me meeting his family.

"You realize that you're inviting me to a public event. We risk being exposed. Anyone could take our picture."

Jax nodded, his jaw pulsing. "I want you with me, by my side, at this event. Pictures and press, I'll handle it."

I expected pressure to build in my chest or a panic freak out to arise, but there was nothing. Only calm. Only him and I.

"What should I wear?"

"It's a fundraising gala, formal attire is required."

"Well, then, I guess you've got a date for your big night."

CHAPTER
twenty-nine

Stevie

D ECEMBER WAS OFF TO A CHAOTIC START. MY GAZE travelled around my apartment eyeing the scene splayed before me. It was a toss-up—either a hurricane had blasted through or I'd been robbed—thankfully neither was the case.

Boxes were stacked everywhere on the new hardwood floor. Part of the kitchen wall was tiled, the other half bare. White subway tiles, paint cans, paint brushes and paint rollers lined the new island. My new cabinets sat covered in plastic wrap.

"Okay, I got most of my clothes packed away and I ordered the pizza. It will be here in twenty." Megyn emerged from her room piling her hair on top of her head in a bun.

"I still can't believe that you're leaving. I will miss our pizza and Netflix nights."

She grabbed a beer from the fridge and popped the cap. "I

know. It's the end of an era."

I laughed at her *Friends* reference. Megyn had given me thirty days' notice that she was moving out. After Thanksgiving, she'd been recruited by some guy who was in need of an executive assistant. He'd been dining at the restaurant where she worked for a few days. Apparently, Megyn had impressed him with her attention to detail and impeccable people skills. I couldn't blame her for taking the job. The pay was nearly six figures and she had the use of a town car at her disposal. So come the new year, I'd be living alone.

The good news was that my holiday bonus was enough to cover the renovations and makeover this place needed in the kitchen and living room. Jax had put me in contact with someone to do the flooring, and his appliance guy was more than gracious in giving me a fair price to replace the fridge, microwave, dishwasher and stove. The bathroom and the bedrooms were next on my list. I had a lot of work to keep me busy.

"So, Miami, huh?"

Megyn nodded and planted herself on a barstool at the island. "Yep, but I am going to miss this place. I can't thank you enough for the last months. You're a great roommate, Stevie."

I pulled a bottle of wine from the fridge. "You too, and you will do great things in Miami. I just know it."

She smiled, and pulled at the label on the bottle. "What will you do when this place is fully made over?"

I took a seat next to her, and poured the wine. "Honestly, I think I might try and sell. Rumor has it that Mister Lin is shopping buyers for the restaurant. If that is true, I kind of want to ask Jax if he would consider loaning me the money to buy it."

Her eyes popped. "You want to buy a Chinese restaurant?"

I gulped my wine and laughed. "I want to turn it into

another apartment or an art gallery."

She tossed her head back her body shaking in laughter. "That's actually brilliant. Do you think that he would give you the money?"

"I think *give* is a strong word in this scenario. I think Jax would consider it, if he thought it was the right business move."

She shot me a knowing glance. "I think he'd give you your own island if you asked for it. From my where I'm sitting, you've done what most women could only dream of."

I swallowed another swig of wine. "Oh yeah, and what would that be?"

She pointed her bottle at me. "You've kept Jackson Hart, one of the most eligible bachelors in Florida, off the market for months."

Has it been that long? Months? I swallowed the rest of my drink allowing that thought to sink in.

"Don't you think that means something?"

I dangled my empty glass in my hand. "Well, he did ask me to go away with him next weekend. He's the keynote speaker for a fundraising gala at FIU."

"A big important speech and he wants you there," she remarked. "Do you *love* him?"

I pushed up from my seated position. "I need more wine."

"Are you avoiding the question?"

"You're asking me if I love Jax. Couldn't you have asked me an easier question, like—what's new with you?"

"Well, I would have but that dreamy look on your face at the mention of his name—the issue needs addressing."

Holding my breath, I turned back to face Megyn, who was grinning like an idiot with her chin propped in her hand.

"Enlighten me, please," I said, uncorking the wine bottle.

Megyn smiled and nodded. "He makes you happy, and as soon as you start talking about him your whole body lights up. You're falling for him, either that or you've already fallen and you haven't admitted it to yourself."

My whole body lit up? *Like I'm a damn Christmas tree?*

What I felt between us, was not a spark, but a bonfire roaring through every fiber of my body.

Filling me.

Consuming me.

It burned so hot, I feared that I wouldn't escape it, but at the same time I needed it, craved it.

Part of me wondered what it would be like to have those flames burning my soul forever. If those flames were extinguished, my heart would live in darkness and I'd have no one to blame but myself.

Megyn licked her lips, while a broad smile spread across her face. "Well, I won't look for a couples Christmas card from the two of you, *yet.*"

I gulped my wine. "Yeah, well, what you can do is help me look for a dress for the gala. Actually, I probably need a few."

"You should wear something in winter white. Give him a preview of what you'd look like as a blushing bride."

Megyn wasn't wrong about the blushing part, she was however, wrong about the bride part. "I'm not even twenty-four yet, no way in hell I am ready for marriage."

"So what do you want out of this relationship?"

"Honestly, I'm trying to wrap my head around all of it. On Thanksgiving, he told me that he considered a run for the senate. He has political aspirations. I feel like I have only scratched the surface with this man."

I skimmed through the highlights of my conversations

with Jax, keeping the sex as PG-rated as I could. The Jax I knew was funny and generous and above all a gentleman. He was the kind of man you dreamt about as an actual Prince Charming, except I was certain Disney princes didn't say depraved and dirty words in bed. Perhaps, William and Harry did. *Okay, Harry did.*

There was a loud knock at the door, most likely the pizza, but for safe measure I peered through the peephole to confirm.

After I paid for the food, Megyn and I settled in for a night of *Fuller House* and online dress shopping. My phone buzzed and I studied the screen.

Jax: Wish you were here, but I know that you need your girls night.

Me: Don't you have guys nights, like ever? Do you even have friends?

Jax: I do. You wouldn't believe me if I told you.

Me: Try me.

Jax: Matthew Barber is one of my closest friends.

I screeched out loud nearly spilling my wine and avoiding major disaster by saving my laptop from crashing to the floor.

"What the hell?" Megyn called out.

I shoved my phone in her face and her expression confirmed we both had some questions for Jax.

Me: Are you telling me that you are friends with one of the most popular movie stars on the planet? If you are lying to me.

Jax: I'm not lying.

Me: How did you meet him?

Jax: I met him in grad school. Matthew was visiting a friend at Yale and he played in one of our casino weekends. This was before he was famous.

Me: How was he able to afford the buy in?

Jax: I am not allowed to reveal those details.

Me: I respect that, but holy shit, Jax, you're friends with a celebrity?

Jax: I am. Right now, I am having dinner with a non-celebrity, but I wanted to say goodnight and I will talk to you soon.

Me: Goodnight xx

CHAPTER
Thirty

Jackson

THE WEEK FLEW BY IN A BLUR. A GOOD PORTION OF MY TIME outside work was spent writing my speech for the FIU winter gala. Between meetings and holiday lunches, I had zero time to shop for a new suit. My assistant, Ingrid, managed to have a few racks of suits delivered from Neiman's for me to try and I added ten more to my wardrobe.

We landed in Miami, the familiar scent of swampy humidity welcoming us with open arms. I had a town car waiting for us upon arrival. We checked into the hotel and, out of habit, I inspected every aspect of the Presidential suite. The space was impressive with its bi-level floor plan and dramatic ocean views. The art deco style was fitting, and I quite liked the terrazzo floors and massive aquarium wall.

"Damn, this place is nice," Stevie remarked on a whistle. "I love the domed ceiling."

"It's okay."

"Okay," she repeated cocking a brow. "Okay is the Hilton Garden Inn at the Tampa Airport. This place is something out of a dream."

"I'll take your word for it." I poured a glass of red wine for Stevie and then made myself a drink.

"I like reading travel blogs, and this one writer did an entire post on the okayest hotel in Florida. It was a great read." Her laugh boomed through the space.

I loved her laugh and I needed it right now. Irritation consumed me, and it had nothing to do with Stevie and everything to do with being back here in Miami. I hated that this city was a stain on my memory. Being back here after all these years left me feeling an odd mixture of anger and sadness.

She grabbed the bottle of wine from the bar. "I'm going to start getting ready for the evening. That massive rain shower is calling my name."

I nodded, lifting the glass. "Enjoy." I watched as Stevie climbed the stairs to the master suite. Once she disappeared, I walked onto the balcony. Even in the afternoon, the city was alive with energy. I watched as people hurried inside cafes and bars for tapas and happy hour drinks. Everything and nothing had changed. The last time I had been here was the day I sold this place. Stevie had no idea this was my former hotel. Thankfully, no one had recognized me when we checked in. Although, it had been years and my new last name wouldn't raise any chatter.

For another thirty minutes, I watched more people slip inside places guarding their designer clothes from the afternoon rain shower. The lightning flashing in the distance was my cue to head upstairs to shower and change.

"Why didn't we stay closer to the university?" Stevie asked, as we stepped out of the car. "I mean, why didn't we stay at this hotel?"

"How can you come to Miami and not stay near the beach?"

"Good point."

Inside the banquet room, ornate chandeliers hung from the ceiling drenching the room in a soft glimmering light. Ivory clothed tables surrounded the room decorated with floating candles and lush greenery runners with baby's breath.

A giant screen flashed black and white photos of me and my work including my philanthropic endeavors. All of it I had pre-approved.

"Very impressive, Mister Hart." Stevie nudged my arm with her shoulder. "I'm going to find the ladies room."

"Okay, I'll get us some drinks and meet you over at table one."

I made my way to the bar, pushing through the crowd. When I ordered our drinks, I felt someone tapping my shoulder from behind.

Turning around, I found myself face to face with my ex-mentor, John Wright. He had been like a father to me, now he was only a man who I hated slightly less than my own father.

"Hello, Jax," he said, stepping closer to me.

"John." I glanced at his lapel. "So you're a professor now? I hope that you're not teaching business ethics."

He chuckled. "I wasn't sure that you would recognize me."

"Well, John, you never really forget the face of man who walks into your office and tells you to get the hell out of dodge."

"That was a long time ago, kid, and it was just business. You're not still sore about that are you?" he asked, gesturing around the room. "Look at all you've accomplished in three years. Perhaps you'll be thanking me in your speech tonight."

"Unlikely, you might have been a mentor to Jax Dennison," I replied smoothly, trying to maintain my cool. "But to Jackson Hart—you're no one special."

My fists clenched as I picked up the champagne glasses and walked away before I said something that drew attention to the two of us.

Across the room I spotted Stevie standing by the table. She looked gorgeous wearing a red sleeveless dress. It was inspired—classy and elegant, reminiscent of Jackie Kennedy or Audrey Hepburn. The lights danced off her diamond earring when she turned her gaze towards mine.

I handed her a glass of champagne. "You look stunning, if I haven't mentioned."

"Why thank you, and you look handsome—*dashing* in this navy blue suit.

We took our seats and were joined by the head of the department and the president of the university and their respective dates. Throughout the dinner we slipped into casual conversation. It was pretty painless.

Stevie was a natural. She worked the table like a total pro and they hung on her every word.

I signaled to the waiter and ordered a glass of whiskey. The lights came up slightly, and a spotlight shone on the stage at the lectern.

"Ladies and gentleman, welcome to our annual winter fundraising gala. It is an enormous pleasure to have you here. Tonight, it is our honor to welcome Mister Jackson Hart, the

CEO of Hart Hotels Incorporated and Florida International University graduate, as our keynote speaker."

I smoothed my tie and buttoned my jacket as the room filled with applause. The crowd pushed to its feet as I made my way to the podium. The applause grew louder as I positioned myself in the spotlight—some clicked cutlery against their glasses. My gaze swung to Stevie who didn't stand, but offered me the brightest smile and a thumbs up.

"Good evening, it is a tremendous honor to be here with all of you. When Bradley Andre asked me to speak at tonight's event I wasn't sure what I'd talk about. What bit of inspiration can I bring to this evening that isn't a meme on Instagram? What words of wisdom can I offer? Well here they are—choose confidence. Give up fear. Appreciate your failures as much as your successes. Learn from those failures, but never forget them. Never allow the taste of success to fool you in thinking that you have arrived—stay hungry. A few years ago, I was faced with a choice . . ."

I told the crowd about my temporary setback which gave birth to Hart Hotels Inc. My eyes focused on John for a moment and I ended my speech on a high note.

"Embrace the storms in your life. Nothing grows without rain. It's a simple as that. Thank you."

John raised his glass to me. While the crowd was on their feet with applause I looked towards Stevie who was on her feet this time. I took one last look at John and then shook Bradley's hand before leaving the podium.

"I had no idea about your first hotel," Stevie said, hugging me.

"Yeah, actually we should talk about that."

"Mister Hart," Bradley suddenly stepped between us. "We

need you for a few photographs."

"Go on, we'll chat in a bit," Stevie said, before brushing her lips to mine.

Bradley ushered me to the other side of the room and I smiled and posed for at least two dozen photos. I chatted with various members of the administration, answering questions and turning down a guest lecturer position.

When I was finally relieved of my photo ops, the hum of low music piped through the speakers. My throat felt like sandpaper and I made a beeline for the bar.

"Whiskey neat, please," I said, slapping down a ten.

"Excuse me, Mister Hart."

I turned to see a young woman, standing next to me.

"Yes."

"Hello, sir, I'm Riley Clark. I was wondering why you changed your last name from Dennison to Hart? In all the yearbook photos you're listed as Jackson Dennison."

"People reinvent themselves every day," I replied curtly. "Would you stay at a Dennison Resort or a Hart Resort?"

"I think I see what you're saying, sir," Riley fluttered her brown eyes at me. "Was this something that your public relations team told you to do?"

"Are you a journalist for the school, Riley?"

"No, I'm just curious as to why you changed your name after you sold your first hotel—the Magnolia," she pressed. "It was the hottest spot in Miami Beach, the profits that year you sold were the highest they'd ever been."

"Right," I said. "Buy low, sell high."

She stared at me for a moment. "That's it?"

"That's it. Nice chatting with you, kid."

She clenched her jaw, and I strode off. Calling her kid was

payment for calling me sir. I spotted Stevie across the room engaged in a conversation. She threw her head back in laughter. As I got closer, my feet stopped moving. My blood ran cold at the sight of the man in the grey pinstriped suit dancing with her. His gaze met mine, and I stared into the blue eyes that matched my own.

CHAPTER
thirty-one

Stevie

"I CAN'T BELIEVE THAT YOU'RE HERE, JAMES. I MEAN WHAT ARE the chances?"

Before James had a chance to respond I saw an intense Jax stalking towards us. His eyes narrowed and his jaw ticked making it quite clear that he was upset. James let go of the hold he had on me and I stepped back.

"What the hell are you doing here?" Jax asked pointedly.

Confusion flashed through me as my gaze pinged between the two men. "Do you two know one another?"

"Which question do you want answered first, Jackson?"

I'd never seen Jax so worked up before—well, I had in the bedroom, but not in a professional setting. At work if something was wrong he was always the calmest person in the room. I suppose that made him intimidating to most people.

My arms folded over my chest, I narrowed my eyes towards Jax.

Silence.

They kept their blue eyes trained on one another. The same shade of blue. A hint of smile crossed James' face and then Jax broke the silence.

"Stevie, this person is my father," he said, before tossing back his entire drink and then slamming the glass to the tabletop.

A gasp slipped from my mouth. The weight of the world crashed around me and my legs threatened to give out. Words failed me as I watched two men that I had known separately engage in a silent war. Jax shot icy glares at his father. *His father.*

My hand touched Jax's arm. "How can James be your father? His last name is Dennison."

"I had my last name legally changed a few years ago. I didn't much care for the name Dennison."

James' swung his gaze towards the dancefloor. It was the first time he'd broken eye contact with Jax. "I like Hart as a last name, excellent choice for you. Name change or not we're still family, Jackson. Like it or not I am your father."

"No, we're not family," Jax remarked, pointing a finger at his father. "The day you walked out on us was the day you made the choice to no longer be my father."

"No matter what you think, we're flesh and blood—we're the same."

The veins in Jax's neck throbbed, every part of him bristling with anger. "We might share DNA, but that is where the similarities end—strictly biology. Don't bother calling for a kidney, liver, or any other goddamn organ." Jax grasped my arm. "Get your purse, we're leaving."

James shoved his hands into his pockets, sadness creeping over his face. "It was nice to see you, Stevie."

"No fucking way." Jax sneered and shook his head. "You stay the fuck away from her, and you stay the fuck away from me. We're done here." Jax grasped my hand, pulling me through the room and into the hallway.

"Jackson stop, *please*, my legs aren't as long as yours."

When we reached the lobby he finally stopped, releasing me from his grip. He paced a small path, running his hands through his hair. "How the hell do you know my father?" His brows pinched together.

I held up my hand. "Firstly, I had no idea that James Dennison was your father. Secondly, he does business with *my* father."

Jax stilled, dropping his hands to his hips. "What do you mean business?"

"He's a sales rep for a car wash supplies manufacturer. Actually, now I that I think about it, he might be an executive, but James and my dad have done business together for years."

He let out deep breath. "Stay away from him."

"I wasn't planning on hanging out with him anytime soon."

"I need you to go back to our hotel."

"No, I want to stay with you."

"Dammit, Stevie, I need you to listen to me and go back to the hotel."

Shaking my head, I ignored the agonizing ache that bloomed in my chest. Emotion clogged my throat as I followed Jax outside. The smell of wet pavement and heat swirled around me when we pushed open the door.

Jax pulled his phone from the inside of his jacket pocket. "Yes, Fritz bring the car around please, I need to you to drive Miss Brockman back to the hotel. You escort her to the room. Then I want you stationed at that door until I get back. No one

goes in or out without my knowledge. Not even room service."
When the call ended, his fingers flew over the screen of his
phone and then he dropped it back into his pocket.

I swallowed past the lump in my throat, tightening the grip
on my clutch. "Jax, you're scaring me."

"I have some business to take care of and then I will see
you back at the hotel."

"Does this have something to do with your father?"

"I don't want you to worry about that."

My hand gripped his wrist and his gaze met mine. "You
gave a lovely speech tonight, it was the highlight of the evening."

Abruptly he cursed, and realized his phone was vibrating.
"I have to go." His knuckles grazed down my cheek. "I'll see
you later."

The car pulled up and then Fritz stepped out to open the
door. Jax's hand landed on the small of my back propelling me
towards the car. Saying nothing, I climbed inside and when the
door shut I felt a chill twirl up my spine. The car pulled away
from valet stand and my eyes focused on the rearview mirror,
he was gone.

CHAPTER
thirty-two

Jackson

STEPPING BACK INTO THE LOBBY, I KEPT MY EYES ON THE CAR AND lifted my phone to my ear. "What do you have for me, Archie?"

"Not much, yet," he answered. "Your father is a managing partner of an industrial chemical supply company in Boca Raton. No personal social media accounts. There is a short bio on the company's website. I have forwarded that to you. He is remarried."

"I want a recent photo of his new wife and a detailed rundown of where he's been the last week."

"Got it."

My fist curled at my side. "You call me immediately with anything on Martin Brockman. I want to know the connection to my father."

"Understood," he affirmed.

I ended the call and swiped to a photo of Stevie. I stared at her captivatingly beautiful face. It was a candid moment, one of her studying a piece of art at the farmer's market. Yeah, she had me going to farmer's markets on the weekends. I had her going to scotch tastings. My Netflix cue was filled with a plethora of rom-coms and teen dramas from the nineties. She spoke about the nostalgia of the era as if she hadn't spent a majority of it in diapers. I'd managed to convince her that the only acceptable dessert between Halloween and Thanksgiving was pie. She convinced me that sometimes you needed to sing a Taylor Swift song out loud.

Somewhere in between, memories and life before Stevie had slipped into the dark recesses of my mind. I never dreamed that my past and my present would collide.

"Jackson." My father approached me slowly, the light from the terrible fluorescent bulbs passed over the deep lines of his forehead.

"James." My voice seethed with disgust.

"Do you still prefer drinking coffee after dinner or have you moved on to something stronger?"

"You actually remembered something about me?" I held his gaze.

"Join me for a drink." He jutted his chin towards the bar area. "We have some catching up to do."

"There will be no catching up," I remarked, sidestepping him. "There *will* be questions asked by me and answers provided by you."

We grabbed a high top in the back of the bar. My father ordered a beer and I ordered a very expensive scotch—a double.

"I've followed your career—you've done very well for yourself. Opening two hotels in three years and three more scheduled over the next two years."

"If this is the part where you ask me for money, you can forget it."

He laughed, and sat back adjusting his cufflinks. The server placed our drinks on the table and then walked away.

"No, I don't need money," he replied, picking up his bottle. "I do okay for myself and . . ."

"Your new wife," I interjected. "You can spare me the sharing of family photos, because I don't give a fuck. How did you even find me?"

He took a long pull from the bottle. "It wasn't hard. Your brother was swayed with a carton of cigarettes and a conjugal visit from a friend of mine. One of the guards owed me a favor."

"I won't bother asking as to why a prison guard owed you a favor." I tossed back part of my drink. "Is that the kind of thing that you do, collect favors for information?"

He snickered. "Information is one of the most valuable commodities."

I eyed him over my tumbler. "Why did you leave?"

"I suppose I do owe you an explanation." He ran his thumb along his jawline. "Things with your mom and me, they weren't that great once we'd moved to Fort Lauderdale. She never wanted to move and I couldn't blame her for feeling the way she did. I picked you guys up and moved you across the country away from family and friends at an important time in your lives. As the years went by one thing led to another—finances were tight . . ." he hesitated. "With two kids in college, and then Jason's legal fees, and a second mortgage on the house, our paychecks just never seemed to be enough."

"So you left, great story. You left because things were tight financially." I tossed back the rest of my drink and then stood.

"Sit down, Jackson, I'm not finished."

"I am. This was a waste of my time."

He grabbed the sleeve of my jacket. "Please sit. That is *not* why I left." My father signaled to the server for another round as I returned to my seat. He waited until she was out of earshot before continuing. "In college, I sold drugs."

I laughed. "Wow, that is the last thing that I expected. You were a drug dealer?"

My father sipped his drink. "Yeah, it was the seventies—a different time. Anyway, a year after we moved here, I met up with some college buddies in Atlanta. I confessed things had not been so great and times were tough. He presented me with an offer I couldn't pass up. It was easy money—shipping drugs from Miami to Atlanta. Since I was already familiar with the business . . ."

"The business of drug dealing," I interrupted, shaking my head. "And how did you do this?"

My father cocked a brow. "The specifics aren't important here, and even if you are my son, I don't trust you. What is important is that your mother found out about what I was doing and then she kicked me out."

"That's very interesting. If you were in such financial despair, why didn't you just ask Uncle Robert or Uncle Larry for help?"

"Right, and have them hold that over my head for years, no thanks. Besides, it wouldn't have mattered, your mother was done with me and this was her way out. She agreed to keep the real reason from you, your brother and your sister if I'd just walk away."

"And you just went without a fight?"

"What was there to fight for, Jackson? She made her choice. We would have divorced eventually."

"Well, this has been enlightening. I think I'll be going now." I pulled my cell from my jacket pocket to check the time.

"A few months after Jason got out of jail in Montana for robbing the convenience store, he came to see me. He tracked me down and invited me to lunch, said he needed a job." He took a long drink. "So I got him a job at the chemical company I was working for in Miami at the time in the maintenance division."

"So while I was finishing up my time at Yale, you and Jason were in contact?" I pinched the bridge of my nose. "Never mind, I don't care. Cut to the chase."

"I'm trying here," he said, blowing out a sharp breath. "There are things you should know."

"And why is that, exactly?"

"I'm dying."

"Let me guess this is your deathbed confessional?"

"If that is what you'd like to call it."

"I think you sought me out at this event so that you could clear your conscience."

"I tried to keep Jason on the up and up, but he found out about the side operation and wanted in on the profits. So after some convincing on his part, Jason ran a crew for me, from Miami to Atlanta," he said, shifting to lean closer. "The mayor's kid, he was also part of that crew. Flores Junior was skimming off the top. Jason went to confront him and get the money back. What Jason stumbled upon was Flores Junior and King running a sex trafficking ring. That's why he stopped at the gas station that day—to call the police. It was a dumb move—thinking purely on emotion."

My mind was whirling. This was like a bad Lifetime movie or one of those cliché romance novels Stevie was always reading.

"Given what you're telling me—the incident that day with Jason, Flores Junior and King wasn't a drug deal gone badly?"

My father nodded. "The story was a fabrication by the press courtesy of the mayor's office. Better to have your son be the victim of a robbery than be forever remembered as a sex trafficker."

"Ah, yes, the hierarchy among criminals," I quipped.

"You must remember back then, and how Flores Senior operated, he ruled Miami, dictator style. There wasn't anything that happened in this city without his approval or disapproval. Flores Junior went to his father, told him everything. In an effort to avoid a major political scandal and keep his kid from going to jail, the mayor orchestrated a cover-up. All did not go according to plan."

"What wasn't part of the plan—Mom getting murdered or Jason murdering Flores Junior and King? Spare me the details. I've heard that story a thousand times."

"Your mother getting murdered was a fucking travesty. The mayor was hell bent on revenge, he wanted your hotel. He was going to set you up and then take the Magnolia."

"Set me up? Take the Magnolia? I had to sell the hotel anyway—on *his* orders. John Wright delivered the letter himself."

My father nodded. "That's right. You were able to sell it and leave Miami. I went to the mayor's office and attempted to get a meeting with him. I wanted to appeal to him one father to another, but he wouldn't see me. Not at first anyway. John ended up facilitating a meeting between the two of us."

"John Wright?"

"Yeah, he really liked you—knew you had great potential. John managed to convince Flores Senior to end his act of revenge. The mayor agreed on the terms—you leave Miami and never do business here again. You could have gone to prison just like your brother."

"Jesus." I eyed my father. "If you're looking for some kind of thank you . . ."

"I'm not, I swear. I get that I don't deserve it. But, Jackson, even though I left, I never stopped looking out for you, Jason and Janessa."

"Are you still running the side business?"

"No, I had to get out of Miami too—mayor's orders— which didn't make my partners in Atlanta happy."

Saying nothing, I sat back trying to absorb everything that my father had explained to me. I sipped my beverage while he sat quietly his gaze swung to the TV screen above the bar. Government officials like Flores Sr. made my stomach lurch with disgust. Why did everything regarding politics have to be so fucking ugly?

"Was Martin Brockman one of your partners?"

"Not a partner, but he allowed us to switch out the vehicles at his car washes for a small fee. Other times he let us to stash the cars and drugs in an empty wash bay. He'd shut it down for repairs."

I let out a deep breath. "I don't want Stevie knowing about any of this. I will tell her when the time is right."

"You have my word."

"I don't need your word. I need your silence."

My father looked at his watch and stood. "Well, it's getting pretty late. I should be going." He signaled for the server to bring the check.

"I got the check," I said, pulling my money clip from my jacket pocket.

"You don't need to do that, since I invited you."

"Thank you, both." She dropped the check off and then hurried back to the bar announcing last call.

My father picked up the check presenter. "For what it's worth, I'm proud of you."

"I'm going to stop you right there," I said, holding up my hand. "I appreciate you setting the record straight, but . . ."

"But, there won't be any shared holidays or invites to barbeques anytime soon. I understand." He tucked a crisp hundred dollar bill inside and then closed the case.

I nodded. "I'm not trying to be rude or cruel and I'm sorry to hear about your failing health."

That's all I could give the man at least at this point. If I decided to have a relationship with him in the future, it would be my decision. There was no need for an explanation other than and I wouldn't be forced into a situation based on guilt.

He extended his hand to mine and I shook it. "Goodbye, Jackson."

I watched as my father strode out of the hotel, and this time I witnessed him walking out of my life. Swiping my phone's screen to life, I dialed Archie. "Yeah, I know the connection between my father and Martin Brockman. Keep me updated on their daily whereabouts—for now."

CHAPTER
thirty-three

Stevie

"I**T'S ONLY ME."**

I awoke from a light sleep to those three words. Still in my dress, I dozed off waiting for him to return. Faint light surrounded us but I could see the conflict in Jax's blue eyes. Wrestling with something heavy—his emotions clear as day painted over his beautiful face. It was much like the day when I met him on his yacht.

"No, the thought of it, please don't." The words came out, anguish rolling off his tongue. *"This . . . it's barely begun."*

"I was worried about you," I said, through a yawn. "What time is it?"

"Almost two."

I rolled up to lean against the headboard. "Are you okay?"

He shrugged out of his jacket and then tossed it onto the wingback chair. "Yes."

Liar.

Saying nothing, he begged me to allow him this lie, and I did. When he was ready to talk to me about seeing his father after all this time he would.

The mattress dipped as Jax sat beside me. My fingers drifted over his chest, his muscles tensed under my touch. He inhaled, and pressed his forehead against mine. When he breathed, I wanted to be that air.

"I'm right here," I whispered, my hands framing his face.

"Good," he rasped, and his lips fused to mine, his hands pushing into my hair. "Ask me what I need."

"What do you need?"

"You, just you, you're the only one for me."

My entire body vibrated with heat hearing those words. He once said that my body was my own, but in his bed my body belonged to him. It was pointless to deny that this man didn't have my heart and my soul. I wasn't falling for Jax, I'd already fallen and all of me belonged to him.

Pulling me up from the bed, he worked the zipper of my dress. The fabric slid down my legs pooling at my feet. The moment his lips connected to mine, I was lost to him. My fingers brushed down the row of buttons on his shirt. He loosened his belt buckle and I pried open his shirt, stilling my hands on his bare chest.

With our clothes discarded, Jax wrapped his arms around me guiding me back onto the bed. My head hit the pillow and his mouth was on me immediately. Licking, sucking and nipping at all the right spots. He palmed my breasts, rolling my nipples between his thumb and index finger. I groaned, letting my eyes fall closed.

"I want you in my bed every night," he whispered, the hot tip of his cock nudging at my entrance. His fingers dug into my hips as he slammed inside me. I cried out feeling the delicious ache of him filling me and spreading through my body. The way I felt when I was with him, it consumed every part of me.

"Take all of me," I whispered.

His hips shifted and he drove into me, thrusting deeper. My arms found their way over his thick shoulders and I hooked my legs around him drawing him closer. We rocked together, moans of pleasure filled the space between us.

I flipped through memories of the past months—our conversations, the cooking class, our first kiss. He was sexy, and caring, and powerful and a bit mysterious. Jax had secrets, could I handle it if he never wanted to tell me those secrets?

He snapped his hips in a furious rhythm pulling me back into our moment. My gaze met his, his eyes seared into me.

"That's better," he groaned. "I like it better when I'm watching you watching me fuck you."

"Oh, Jax," I gasped, as he hit a new spot deep inside me. My fingers dug into his shoulders as I arched into him.

"You're so beautiful," he whispered, slamming his hips into mine.

Crests of my impending orgasm built low in my core. He caught my nipple in his mouth, quick and rough I moaned as he sucked harder making me burn with need.

"Ah." My voice shook. "Right there."

Dipping his tongue inside my mouth, I felt my insides clenching and tightening as he kissed me. My nails dug into the muscles of his shoulders.

"Fuck, Stevie, what you do to me." He breathed hard pounding into me.

I screamed his name as my insides exploded when his dick pumped into my sweet spot driving me home. Jax rocked into me hard, a litany of profanity spilled from his lips. My pussy tightened around his cock and he growled into my shoulder unleashing his own orgasm.

I tilted my head, finding his lips and getting lost in his soft kiss.

And in that moment it was clear, so obviously crystal clear—I never wanted to kiss anyone else ever again. Only him, only ever him.

This may take me down.

Jax's fingers glided up and down my arm. The sight of him lying next to me, his skin bathed in the early morning light, still seemed unreal. We'd spent the night together many times over these last months, but there were times I feared I'd wake up to a reality where this had all been a dream.

"About my father," he murmured. "When did you first meet him?"

My nails scratched up his chest. "I was wrapping up my shift at the country club one afternoon and he came in the restaurant with my dad. It was about three in the afternoon and I know this because the kitchen had just closed, so they could prepare for the dinner crowd. I think your dad was a little embarrassed that my dad brought him to a restaurant in the middle of a shift change, but when they paid, James left me a huge tip. Why do you ask?"

"I'm just trying to piece things together."

The cold, heavy ache of trying to understand what Jax must have been going through hit me in the chest. Minutes slipped by, and the strange echoes that lurked in this suite occupied the quiet. I didn't know if I should press on, remembering that Jax isn't one for answering questions at length. Given the colossal subject matter and limited time he's had to process seeing his father after all this time left me searching for the right words.

Jax expelled a deep breath. "He told me that he was dying."

I shifted, glancing up at him. "How do you feel about that?"

"As much as I hate what happened to our family, I don't wish the man ill. He is my father after all and if I'm being honest, there is a heavy weight there."

"Yeah, I get it." The words came out of my mouth, but did I really understand what Jax was feeling? All these years I wanted my father to go away and leave me and my mother alone.

"I never spent time or money looking for him and I could have. Apparently Jason found him and I guess from what my father said they worked together for a few years before Jason was arrested." He scrubbed his hands down his face. "I'm glad that Janessa and I weren't part of that Dennison family reunion." He leveled his gaze in my direction. "There are things that I need to tell you, about my past."

It was my turn to take a deep breath. "Okay, like what?"

"For starters we're staying in the hotel that I once owned."

My brows lifted. "This was The Magnolia?"

"Yeah, and I was forced to sell it by order of the mayor. I was told in no uncertain terms to leave Miami and never do business here again. An unfortunate side effect of my brother's crime, at least that was what I believed at the time. My father paints a deeper story, one that could have ended in me going to prison."

"What?" The question left my throat in a loud squeak.

"Apparently, Mayor Flores was hell bent on revenge. He wanted my hotel and he was going to set me up for a crime."

I rolled my eyes. "What kind of crime exactly?"

"Murder, drugs, extortion, prostitution," he replied with his arms outstretched. "Your guess is as good as mine."

"Well, for the record, I am very glad that you were not sent off to prison."

He laughed, it was a miserable laugh. "Yeah, you and me both, but as it turns out, it seems that my father was the one who convinced Mayor Flores to end his act of revenge."

"No way," I said, rolling up to my knees.

"They had a chat and the end resolution was that neither my father nor I do business in Miami ever again or until he was no longer running things here."

"So your dad was here in Miami the same time that you were?"

Jax nodded. "Not only was he working for a chemical supply company, he was running drugs from here to Atlanta and Jason ran a crew for him."

I blew out a breath. "Wow. This is so much to absorb."

"Tell me about it."

There was a long silence as I tried to wrap my head around everything Jax had just told me. I thought back to the few times I saw James in Kennesaw. How on Earth does the past collide with the present in such a weird way?

Jax's phone played a musical score from *The Phantom of the Opera*. I covered my mouth with the blankets to hide my smile.

"I didn't know that you loved musicals."

He tossed back the covers and stood. "I do," he answered. "Is that weird?"

"Not at all, I like a man who appreciates the arts."

Jax leaned down pressing his fists to the mattress. "And I appreciate you listening to me this morning."

"Thank you for being honest with me."

He stared at me for a long moment and then brushed his lips to mine. Our kiss deepened, his tongue licked mine, teasing me until my body was drowning in need.

He pulled back from our kiss. "How did I get so lucky to have you walk into my life?"

"As I recall, you walked into my life, Jackson Hart."

"I guess I did, it was good luck for me that you had car trouble that day."

Me too.

CHAPTER
thirty-four

Jackson

Two days before Christmas

"W ELL," I SAID TO STEVIE AS I LIFTED HER SUITCASE from the trunk of my car. "Have a safe trip back home."

"Thank you," she replied, pushing her sunglasses on top of her head.

"Are you sure that you don't want to take my jet?"

She chuckled grasping the handle of her luggage and propping it upright. "I can't show up in Kennesaw on a private jet. Paying for my first class upgrade was generous enough."

"I will miss you," I whispered, tucking her close to me.

"I'll miss you too, but I will be back the day after Christmas." She pulled back from our embrace to straighten my tie. "You have a safe trip to Montana."

She rolled up to her tiptoes and kissed me—hot and needy

and not at all appropriate for public. I heard rumblings from people and a few whistles of appreciation. Stevie smiled against my lips, and then pushed back from our embrace. I watched until she disappeared through the crowd of people. My heart was heavy with an ache that I couldn't describe.

I arrived back at my office just after four in the afternoon. Slumping into my chair, I began checking my emails. Somehow over the last months, Stevie had taken up permanent residence in my life and I didn't mind one bit. She was great at her job, the kind of fun that kept me feeling young, and very good in bed. Beautiful, educated and strong, the list was miles long.

Everyone slowly drifted out the office as I shifted focus to the reports in front of me. Ingrid walked in just as I opened the progress report for the Chicago property.

"Mister Hart, Miss Edgerton is here to see you."

I don't remember scheduling a meeting with Carol. I glanced at my calendar, my entire afternoon was free. "Send Carol in."

"Uh, sir."

"It's not Carol," Carol's sister, Trina interrupted as she strode in wearing a sleeveless green blouse and black pencil skirt. "Close the door, Ingrid."

Ingrid swung her gaze in my direction and I nodded. When she shut the door, Trina settled into one of the chairs opposite my desk.

"You're looking well, Trina," I said, rising from my chair. "May I offer you a drink?"

She smiled. "Sure, my usual."

"A vodka rocks, then?" I asked, confirming because I'd honestly forgotten.

"How sweet of you to remember," she cooed.

As I poured her drink, I wondered why she was really here. When I decided not to seek a political office, we parted ways. Trina was very nice, a straight shooter, but our relationship was never romantic. Our arrangement was of mutual benefit, her philanthropic work was given more attention and I had a pretty, Good Samaritan on my arm at events. We introduced one another to people and shared contacts. Trina respected our careers and there were zero complications to keeping our relationship casual.

I handed Trina the glass and sat on the corner of my desk. "What brings you by?"

She leveled her gaze at me. "My sister tells me that you're seeing someone."

This was a surprise. I'd never known Carol to spread office gossip. "And if I am, how is it any of your or Carol's concern?"

"Carol says she's very young." Trina licked her lips before taking a drink.

"You know what they say about age, it's only relevant to cheese and wine."

She shot me a knowing glance. "I'm intrigued, Jackson. It's only a matter of time before the public finds out that you're sleeping with a pretty young thing."

"We've been in public and no one cared," I shot back.

"Not that you know of." She waved a hand in the air. "I know you, Jackson Hart, and you have dreams of a political career. What do you think the voters will think of your—twinkie?"

I narrowed my eyes. "If it comes to that, I think that they would see that she's a lot more than her age."

Standing, Trina swallowed a drink and then placed the glass onto the coaster. "I hope so, Jackson, I really do." She tucked her Prada clutch under her arm and smiled. "Merry Christmas."

"Merry Christmas, Trina."

After she left, I let my eyes fall closed as I scrubbed a hand over my jaw. "Time for a drink." Her words replayed on a loop as I poured some scotch into a tumbler.

Carol had been my most trusted employee. Hardworking, dependable, and she knew her boundaries—or so I thought. Working with Carol had never been an issue, until now. Who I date and who I sleep with is my business.

My cell vibrated against the tabletop this time it was a call from Archie. "What do you have for me?"

"Miss Brockman's plane arrived safely in Kennesaw. I am forwarding you the latest updates regarding Martin Brockman and your father."

"Thanks, Archie," I said, pulling up my email. "Now, enjoy the holidays with your family."

"Yes, sir. Merry Christmas."

"Merry Christmas."

I scanned the report for anything out of the ordinary, nothing caught my eye. My father's daily activity was pretty uneventful aside from his trip to a clinic in Boca Raton. Martin had traveled from Kennesaw to his car wash locations in Marietta, Roswell, and Acworth. At this point, I wasn't sure what I was looking for anyway. My phone buzzed as I took a drink. Liquid heat ran through my veins when I saw Stevie's name on the screen.

Landed. On my way to baggage claim. She'd texted.

Me: Glad you made it safely.

Stevie: Let's hope I make it through these next days with my family.

Me: You will. If your dad gives you any trouble, just leave. I'll change your return ticket if you need me too.

Stevie: Thank you. Let's hope it doesn't come to that.

Me: Here's to drama free holidays with the family.

CHAPTER
thirty-five

Jackson

"WHAT CAN I GET YOU?" MY UNCLE LARRY CALLED from behind the bar. It was Christmas Eve and the house was filled with laughter as Bing Crosby's voice boomed from the sound system. I breathed deep getting my fill of cinnamon and pine. Being here was surreal. Janessa was settled into a corner reading a story to the younger kids while my aunt Kathy served hot chocolate. My uncle Robert and cousin, Austin, sat in front of the fire playing checkers, checking the Broncos score in between moves. This was my mom's side of the family and I was grateful to be here, although I wished Stevie was here too. I know that if she had come with me that she would have been interrogated by my sister. Janessa would want a complete history and timeline of our relationship and I wasn't about to subject Stevie to that kind of torture.

"As I recall you had a specialty cocktail last time that I was here. A whiskey concoction."

He drummed his fingers against the wood top. "Ah, you want the old Montana."

"Sounds familiar."

"How are things in Florida?" he asked, grabbing the bottle of whiskey.

"I have no complaints. I'm on track to have one of the best fourth quarters in years."

Cocking a brow, he continued pouring liquids into the stainless steel shaker. "Wonderful to hear. Beth and I are planning a trip to Park City real soon. We're planning on staying at your hotel out there."

"Let me know when you go," I replied, watching him pour the amber liquid into two glasses. "I can make sure you get the best room in the place."

"Perks of knowing the owner." He smiled and handed me the glass.

"Exactly." I tipped back my glass taking a large swallow. "That's the stuff."

I walked towards the window wondering how Stevie's yuletide festivities were going. This morning she texted me saying that so far she's managed to steer clear of her father.

Janessa shoved a plate of food in front of me. "Here, you gotta try this cheese."

"Vermont cheddar, thanks. What's new in legal aid?"

"I have jury selection for a case next week—ex-attorney who traded legal-aid services for sex with clients." She tucked her blonde hair behind her ears. "These women, their stories are gut-wrenching."

I took a sip of my drink. "Scumbag."

"Yeah, the bastard actually made video recordings of the

sexual encounters." Janessa moved, leaning her back against the window. "What's up with you? I can tell when something's weighing on you."

Something was bothering me. I had yet to tell her about my run in with our father. Did I want to? Was it worth it?

I expelled a deep breath. "I saw Dad."

"What?" she stage whispered, confusion painted all over her face.

"Yeah, he showed up at a speech I gave at FIU a week ago."

She nodded prying the glass from my hand. "Well," she paused, before taking a long drink. "That's the last thing I expected you to say."

I sighed. "I know, apparently he's been keeping tabs on all of us. He *says* that he's dying."

"Do you believe him?"

I glanced sideways at her. "Part of me wants to believe him, and the other part wants to take him to the best doctor in Florida for a series of confirmation tests."

She laughed, and shook her head. "I can't say that I wouldn't offer to drive."

For now, I decided to not share all the gory details with Janessa, leaving out all the parts of the drugs and his involvement with keeping me from an alleged revenge plot. With an important case coming up, I didn't want our family drama invading her focus.

"There's something else going on with you . . . I can't put my finger on it." Janessa snapped her fingers, her green eyes sparkling with amusement. "You're seeing someone."

I met her gaze. "There *is* someone."

Her dark brows rose. "You want to tell me about her?"

"Nope," I replied, and snatched my drink back. My uncle's

had moved the party to the deck and I decided to join them. The flames from the outdoor stone fireplace burned a blaze of orange and white.

"Jackson," Robert boomed out. "Join us for some holiday cheer and a cigar." He raised the bottle of whiskey in my direction.

"Don't mind if I do." I set my drink down to light the cigar and then planted myself in a chair.

Larry breathed in the night air. "There's snow on the way."

Robert tossed another log onto the fire. "The nose of the great north can tell you five days in advance when the snow's coming."

I laughed. "Or what I like to call the five day forecast."

"But the weather forecast can be wrong, I'm never wrong." He puffed on his cigar.

"Never, huh?"

"Nope. I got instincts and they rarely fail me."

Robert propped his feet onto the stone ledge. "You ever think about moving back here, Jackson?"

The question cut me off guard. To be honest no, I never thought about moving. I loved my life in Florida. The company needed me. Who would oversee day to day operations if I weren't there?

"Honestly, until this moment no, I never thought about it. Is there a reason you're asking?" I took a drink, feeling the chill of the winter air hit the back of my neck. I downed the rest to help stave off the cold.

"Yeah," he answered, inclining his head in my direction. "You know the governor's position is up for election. It would be the perfect time for you to entertain that career in politics."

My uncles were lifelong politicians. Robert was a

long-standing member of the Northern Plains Council for Resources. This organization was dedicated to the protection of Montana's water quality, family farms and ranches. The Brooks family was instrumental in establishing the first Montana chapter of the Federation of Fly Fisherman.

My grandfather opened a fly fishing outlet in 1953 and when he retired, Larry and Robert expanded and tripled the profits. My mother helped run the flagship store, but the riches came long after we'd moved to Florida.

"I don't have any political experience. Running for the Governor of Montana seems pretty lofty," I pointed out.

"In this race, it wouldn't matter," Larry said. "The left candidate is too far left. He has some good ideas on social issues, but he lacks a certain moral fiber. The conservative side is too conservative and stuck in the Dark Ages. Montana wants to move ahead not be stuck behind. Frank Barrister would be your only real competition."

"And he recently secured a million-dollar donation from the Collins Fellowship," Robert added.

I lifted the bottle of whiskey and poured a shot into my glass. It was a lot to absorb. "When would I have to announce my candidacy?"

Larry added another log to the fire. "You can announce anytime you like. In my opinion, it takes two years to run a successful campaign."

"What about residency? I haven't lived here since I was a teenager."

"I think we have a solution for that," Larry announced.

"Before your mother passed away," Robert began. "She came to me for a loan. Karen wanted to buy a piece of land. She died before we could complete the sale, so I bought the property." He reached inside his jacket pocket and then pulled out an envelope. "This here land belongs to you and Janessa." He slipped the envelope into my hand, and then took a long puff from his cigar.

"I don't know what to say."

His hand dropped to my shoulder giving it a squeeze. "We'll go to the courthouse day after Christmas and I can sign over the deed to you officially."

"You need to let me repay you."

"Nonsense, this is a gift. I knew your mother well, son, and she'd want you to have that land. You don't owe me a thing."

Larry chuckled, smoke rings billowing from his mouth. "Well, except to think about moving back here and running for governor."

A career in politics, was I ready for that now? I took a drink, the heat burning a trail down my chest. My eyes trained on the paper, looking for answers. The crackling of wood and howling from the occasional wolf filled the quiet. Snow began to fall coating the stone on the patio. This was my mother's way of telling me to accept the gift.

CHAPTER
thirty-six

Stevie

I'D SPENT MOST OF CHRISTMAS EVE IN MY OLD ROOM AS MY FAMILY went about their day without me. My mother had gone to the market for some last minute dinner supplies. I'd managed to avoid my father all morning, for which I was grateful.

Mom ended up getting that job at the school, and she was eager to get back to working again. After she picked me up from the airport yesterday, we picked up some fresh flowers from the market and then we stopped at the coffee shop. Things didn't change much around here.

After my shower, I reorganized my bookshelves. My fingers grazed over the spines of my vintage YA collection that sat on the top shelf of the wooden book case. Maybe I should take them with me when I leave. I dusted off one of my Sweet Valley High books and curled up in my window seat.

By one in the afternoon I was restless and bored. I thought

about calling Tiffany to see if she wanted to grab a coffee, but then I realized she was probably at her grandparents' house in Atlanta. When my stomach started growling I ventured downstairs to what I thought was an empty house.

Hushed chatter carried through the kitchen and into the front hallway. I heard my father's voice, hissing and snipping in sharp tones. Oh good, my childhood was rearing its ugly head. And I heard a woman's voice, low and angry and it did not belong to my mother.

"Keep your voice down," my dad whispered. "Danielle could be back any moment."

"I told you where the money was, Martin. I knew you would fuck this up. Couldn't you just be nice to that daughter of yours for five minutes?"

"If you want the money so bad, Darlene, why don't you just go to Salissa Island and get it from Stevie?"

Aunt Darlene? What the hell was she doing talking to my father? She barely tolerated the man. And about the alleged money at Gran's place.

"What I want is for you and me to leave this town and start our life together. I love you."

He sighed. "I know I love you too. I wish that things could be easier."

"They'd be easier if we had that money."

Bile bubbled in my throat. Gross. My dad and Darlene were having an affair. I took a deep breath and started to walk down the steps. There were two ways this was going to go, either I was going to expose them and blow up the family Christmas. Or I could slip my headphones in and pretend I heard nothing.

I was halfway down the staircase when I realized that my headphones weren't in the pockets of my sweater coat.

"It's never going to get easier, sweetheart."

I fumbled with my phone bringing up the video app. When my feet hit the rug in the foyer I found the two of them locked in each other's arms. Darlene's eyes went wide with fear when she saw me standing in the entryway.

"Oh hello, Stevie," she drawled out casually as if the two of them hugging was completely fucking natural. "We didn't think anyone was home. What a nice surprise."

"A nice surprise?" My gaze swung to my father's. He stood rooted to his spot like he hadn't had his hands all over a woman who was not his wife.

Darlene's gazed pinged between me and my father. "Your dad was just being nice and lending me and ear." Her hands wrung together.

"It looked like he was offering you more than his ear."

My father's jaw tightened. "It isn't what it looks like."

"Oh please, I heard everything." I shot back, feeling more confidence than I had in a long time. "What's funny is that I can't believe you would do this to your sister, Darlene. But, Dad, I totally knew you were capable of betraying Mom. I tried to tell her you were nothing more than a snake."

My dad laughed. "If I were you, little girl, I wouldn't breathe a word of this to your mother. Mark my words—you will live to regret it."

"I might keep my mouth shut, but first you're going to tell me about this money you think that Gran has stashed away." My words were flat and direct.

Darlene and my father exchanged glances. "Well, Stevie dear, we think that your grandmother has a large sum of money hidden away. We found a journal when we were boxing up her house in Acworth and there are certain entries that suggest she might have had more money than originally stated in her will."

Straightening my shoulders, my eyes narrowed. "And if there is a large stash of money, what do you intend to do with it?"

My father stepped towards me. "None of your goddamn business."

"Well, you can tell me or I'll just tell Mom about this little afternoon delight situation."

Darlene's face turned as red as Georgia clay. "You wouldn't dare do that."

"I can and I will. I have nothing to lose. If Mom finds out my father figure is a lying cheating bastard, I win. What do I care about what happens to her relationship with you?"

This was all very daytime soapy. The truth was I *did* care. I didn't want my mother to be hurt by her husband and her sister.

"I'm not going to be blackmailed by you," my father hissed.

I walked towards the refrigerator. "Well then, I guess you two should think about how you're going to tell Mom. I won't lie for either of you."

"So goddam righteous," Darlene muttered. "You think that you're better than all of us because you went to college."

I pulled open the door to the fridge. "Of course you think that," I paused, grabbing the jelly. "That's an ignorant thing to say."

My father turned to Darlene grasping her elbow. "Let's just give her time to cool off. Stevie will come to her senses."

Darlene ripped her arm away. "She won't. She loves every minute of this."

Brushing past my dad, I walked into the pantry to get the

peanut butter and bread. "I wouldn't say that I *love* any of this."

"I'm out of here," Darlene announced as the door to the back porch slammed.

When I emerged from the pantry my dad was sitting at the table with a cross look on his face. "You weren't meant to see us together."

I tossed the bread onto the counter beside the jelly. "No, I suppose that I wasn't."

"I'll tell your mother, just not tonight or tomorrow. I won't ruin Christmas for her."

"I'm surprised that you even care." I twisted the lid off the jars and then slapped a piece of whole wheat bread onto a plate. "Yet, at the same time just ruin her life completely," I huffed and busied myself with the task of making my sandwich. "You know, Mom loves you and I have no idea why. What I do know, is that you should divorce her because she will never leave you."

The chair screeched across the floor when he pushed back from the table. "I'm leaving, I have business. You would be wise not to mention this to your mother. We will get through the next thirty-six hours and then I want you out of here. Pack your shit and leave."

"With pleasure," I called after him.

The door to the garage slammed shut and I felt all the tension leave my body. I took a bite of my sandwich and then cleaned up the mess. The last place I wanted to be was here even if it was Christmas Eve. Swallowing another bite of my sandwich, I told myself that I could do this. It was thirty-six measly hours and then I would be back on a plane to Salissa Island. It wasn't my business how these so-called adults worked out their issues. I would support my mom whatever the outcome.

The garage door opened and closed shut. My mom

appeared hauling in a few bags of groceries. "Oh good, you're here. Would you mind grabbing the rest of the groceries from the car? I need to start making the pies for tonight."

"Sure thing, Mom." I tossed my napkin into the garbage, slapped on a smile and pushed down all the earlier ugliness with Dad and Darlene and vowed to power through the rest of my time here.

The ride to the airport was a quiet one. Christmas went off without a hitch and Darlene didn't even bother to show up. She called Mom and told her that she wasn't feeling so great. Dad was on his best behavior even helping Mom with the dishes afterward. All I had to do was make it through some light dinner conversation, opening presents, and watching "Scrooged." I happened to love that movie so it made sitting in a room with my father more tolerable.

"Well, Stevie, I'm really glad you came home for Christmas. Are you sure that you have to leave so soon."

I looked over at my mom from the passenger seat. "Yeah, Mom, I have to be back at work tomorrow morning." I clutched my phone in my hand and stared at the text from Jax. He said he had some exciting news that he couldn't wait to share with me. I wondered what it could be.

"Have you heard from the museum, yet?"

I shook my head. "No, and to be honest I really like the job I am doing now. If they called I can't say I'd take the job, plus I am making a lot more money at the hotel."

"Well, as long as you're happy."

"I am."

This was the happiest I had been in a long time. Work was good, despite the slight worry of people finding out about me and Jax before we were ready. I missed him. Emotion welled in my chest at the thought of seeing him soon. We agreed to exchange gifts after Christmas and tonight I couldn't wait to hold him in my arms.

My mom smiled and merged into the lane for the airport. "Stevie, I'm glad that we have a private moment. I wanted you to hear it from me."

My heart slammed into my ribs. Closing my eyes, I braced myself for the news. He did it, he actually told her about him and Darlene.

"Your father and I are getting a divorce."

My head snapped to look at her. "What? I have like a million questions."

"Caught him and Darlene together in his office around Halloween."

I swallowed past the shock. "Does he know that you know?"

"No, but he will soon. He's getting the papers today."

"You're serving him with the papers *today*?"

She nodded and I swore I saw a hint of a smile on her lips. I'm glad I kept my mouth shut. It could have ruined everything for my mom. I'm not sorry that I stood up to my father. I had a thousand more questions, but only one seemed to hold any value.

"Are you going to be okay, Mom?" I asked, as she pulled up to the curb.

She grasped my hand giving it a tight squeeze. "I'm going to be better than okay, I'm going to be great."

"I don't doubt that one bit."

Mr. Lin had called me and asked if I could come by the restaurant at some point. So once I unpacked, I trekked downstairs. The restaurant was relatively quiet, aside from music coming from the kitchen.

"Mister Lin, it's Stevie," I called out from the dining room.

"Oh hello, Stevie," he said, appearing from behind the bar. "Did you have a nice Christmas?"

"I did. What about you?"

"It was good, yes. The whole family gathered around the table, even my sister came all the way from New York." He smiled and gestured for me to take a seat in one of the booths.

"Full house, huh?"

He chuckled. "Oh yes. Good though. Children's laughter is good for the soul. Family is the most important thing in the world."

My family was never particularly close but I couldn't stop grinning, the joy in his expression gave me joy.

"Well, I will just get right to it," he said, sliding a manila envelope across the tabletop towards me.

"What's this?"

"Open, please." He gestured towards the package.

I cocked a brow and pulled back the metal clasps. What I pulled out was a very large check and some paperwork. My eyes scanned over the words. The bold face type explained that my grandmother and Mister Lin co-owned the restaurant.

"You and Ruby were business partners?" I shook my head in disbelief.

"Your grandmother was a silent partner." He tapped his finger against the table. "When I was about to lose this place your grandmother helped me out."

This must be the extra money that Dad and Darlene were talking about. How much did they know about Gran and the restaurant?

"Does anyone else know about my grandmother helping you out?"

He shook his head. "I don't believe that she told anyone, but her lawyer and now you know."

"And this very large check made out to me and signed by you? What is this from?"

"Per my agreement with your grandmother, this is her profit from the sale of the restaurant which as you can see belongs to you."

I blinked unable to process what Mr. Lin was telling me. My grandmother did a very generous thing by helping Mr. Lin. They weren't having an affair they were business partners. Megyn and I would have a good laugh about this situation.

"I have a confession to make, when I found out the restaurant was for sale, I thought about buying it from you."

Mister Lin cocked a brow. "Really? You wanted to run a Chinese restaurant?"

I waved him off with a laugh. "No, I wanted to turn this place into another apartment or an art gallery."

He smiled and stood. "New owners take over in thirty days. This place will be a cupcake shop."

"Great, the smell alone will cause me to gain ten pounds." I gathered the contents and shoved it all back into the envelope. One of his staff came out from the kitchen carrying a brown bag. "I put all your favorites in here, Stevie and *two* eggrolls."

"Thank you, but you didn't need to do that." I opened the bag and took a deep breath. I would miss these noodles.

After I said goodbye to Mister Lin I walked back up to my apartment. It was just after three in the afternoon. I devoured one of the eggrolls and shoved the rest into the refrigerator. I needed to get to the bank and deposit this check. Having that much money lying around my place wasn't the brightest idea. Flipping the check over, I smiled and signed the back.

"Thank you, Gran."

My phone buzzed across the counter.

Jax: My flight has been cancelled. Snow storm. I will call you tonight.

Me: Bummer. Do you have to sleep in the airport?

Jax: No. I'm at a nearby hotel.

Me: Stay warm. I miss you.

Jax: I miss you too.

CHAPTER
thirty-seven

Stevie

O
N FRIDAY, I ARRIVED AT WORK EARLY AND DROPPED JAX'S Christmas present along with a card onto his desk. He'd been snowed in for two days in Montana. It was slightly disturbing that four days without him left me feeling twitchy.

We talked briefly. I filled him in on the family drama saving the part about Gran's business and Mr. Lin for when he returned. Jax told me about his uncle gifting him a piece of land in Montana that his mother had originally wanted to purchase. Apparently, he spent a majority of the snowed in days working and looking at home designs via Pinterest with his sister. The thought of him making Pinterest boards made me smile.

When I got to my desk, there were several emails from Jax. The email he'd sent to the executive team outlined a portion of his duties be split between me and Carol in his absence. Carol took control of the weekly staff meeting, while I walked the property with Maria going over the maintenance checklist.

I powered through my morning, closing out an auction for a set of Japanese Cloisonné vases from the Meiji period. Things were all falling into place where the Chicago property was concerned. The hotel was slated to open this summer and I couldn't wait to tour the space.

"Miss Brockman, it's Calvin at the front desk. The weekly floral delivery is here, but my paperwork shows berries, greenery, and pink ranunculus. The flowers on the truck are white. I wanted to double check with you before signing."

I perused my paperwork, confirming that I had in fact ordered pink ranunculus. "I will be right down, Calvin. Thank you."

It's going to be a three cup of coffee kind of morning.

Needing a change of venue, I found myself sitting at a table in the executive conference room after lunch. As it would seem, my office was lacking inspiration for the Valentine's installation. On the flipside it could be due to the fact that I was missing my own personal inspiration and a decent orgasm. Along with an orgasm I was chasing a decent night's sleep. I should be sleeping soundly at night due to my recent inheritance. Thanks to Gran I was going to be able to pay off my car, pay off my student loans, and still have enough left over for savings. But, before I made any major moves, I wanted Jax to look over my spreadsheet calculations. I trusted his financial savvy.

"You have a perfectly nice office with a door, Miss Brockman," Carol said as she strolled in with an armload of file folders.

"I could say the same thing to you, Miss Edgerton, and your office has a large window overlooking the ocean."

"Right, right, well, if you don't mind my department has a human resources training session scheduled for two p.m. I'm going to need you to clear out." Carol hefted the binders out of the filing cabinet.

Knock. Knock.

"Miss Edgerton," Beth said from the doorway. "Mister Biesemeyer is on line two."

"Thank you, Beth. I'll take the call in here."

I closed my iPad and gathered my belongings. Curiosity had me lingering in the conference room.

"Hello, Stan, this is Carol, how can I help you?"

"Hey, Carol, Jackson has me looking into commercial spaces, I've got a lead on a five thousand square foot space, but as of right now, there's nothing in between. The next best location is twenty thousand square feet, which seems rather large for his needs."

What are his needs that are between five thousand and twenty thousand square feet? Not a hotel.

"I'd send him everything you have. At this point, he will want to evaluate all the options. The planning stage is going to be fun."

"Don't I know that?" his voice was light with laughter. "All right, thank you, Carol."

The call ended and Carol scurried out of the room. I hauled my bag onto my shoulder and stared at the phone for a few minutes. I wandered down the hallway in a sort of daze. The last place I thought I end up was standing in Carol's office.

"Why is Jackson looking for commercial property in Montana?"

"Campaign headquarters." She looked up from her desk, sliding her jet black hair over her shoulder. "He's considering running for Governor of Montana."

My brows pinched together in confusion, the obvious shock written all over my face. Carol looked at me as if she actually enjoyed delivering this news, like she was happy to have the information before me.

"So, he didn't tell you." She folded her arms a top her desk.

"He hasn't told me, *yet*." My voice was calm despite the emotion hammering through my veins.

"And why do you think that is?"

"Because he's been hard to reach and I've been busy. Or here's a thought, he respects me enough to tell me in person." It was the only thing that I could think of that made any kind of sense.

She rolled her eyes. "Do you really think that you're first lady material?"

I stood there like an idiot dumbfounded by her question. *Say something.*

"You know my sister fell in love with him," she said, eyeing me up and down. "All it took was a few conversations and a couple of society events. Toss in an afternoon on his yacht and Trina was hooked. I'm sure you've experienced the same thing. He's very charming that way, a true gentleman."

Still I said nothing. Jax told me it was nothing serious between the two of them and I chose to believe him.

"When it comes to selecting a wife, a partner . . . someone to be by his side, do you really think that Jackson will choose you?"

Her words cut me, the pang in my chest sharpening. *Don't cry. Don't break.*

She stood and yanked the top drawer of her desk open. Carol tossed a stack of magazines onto her desk and her dark eyes met mine. "You're no different than any of these ladies."

I winced staring down at the glossy covers. "What are you saying that Jackson is a 'use them and lose them' kind of guy?"

"No, I'm saying it won't be *his* choice. Once the press finds out about your background they won't stop digging. Jackson won't choose you—to protect you."

I blinked back the hot tears that welled. "Stop talking in circles, Carol." I spat, my voice taking on a harsher tone than I intended. "Fucking spit it out. All of it."

She scowled at me. "What do you think will happen when some reporter starts digging up your past? I'll tell you, the first thing printed will be about your affair with Cord Robinson. That story could go a few different ways. My guess is they will choose to paint you as a gold-digger or fame whore."

"But, that's not true!" I shouted.

"Doesn't matter. Your relationship with Cord will segue to your hometown. They'll go after your family, spilling everything about your middle-class upbringing and your father's blue-collar business. When some young and hungry reporter needs a breakthrough story, they'll write about your father's alcoholism. They'll drag your mother's broken hip into it painting a story of abuse and how you targeted Jackson hoping he'd pay the bills. And if you have anything remotely scandalous on your social media, they'll find it."

I held up my hand. "Stop. I've heard enough."

"You asked," she reminded.

"How do you know all of this, Carol? I never told you about my father's drinking."

"No, you didn't but Cord is a talker and when I called the

country club for references. It was easy to get information. Being from a small town people like to gossip whether they know that they are doing it or not—sweet Stevie Brockman, we're so happy she made her way out of Kennesaw. That father of hers is a real piece of work. The drinking and gambling."

I rolled my eyes. "You can't believe everything you hear, Carol. Surely you know not to fall for petty gossip."

Carol stared at me for a beat, her expression grew hard. "A few weeks after Trina and Jackson were spotted together, a reporter called threatening to break a story about my sister." She came around to stand in front of her desk. "In college, Trina had an abortion. She was raped by the professor that she was assisting. An ex-friend of hers was looking for a payout and told the reporter that she could give him any dirt he wanted for a price."

I wasn't even sure what to say to that.

"Jackson was sick about the whole thing and managed to kill the story. It cost him a pretty penny, but he wouldn't allow Trina to relive that nightmare. Then, the press found out about our mother."

I shook my head. "I don't understand."

"Our mother is in a sanatorium. She's a schizophrenic."

"Oh, I'm sorry to hear that."

She waved it off, her dark eyes piercing me. "You see there's always something from our past that we don't want dragged out into the light. Trina's philanthropic work has done a lot of good for mental health issues. She hasn't needed to bring our mother's condition into it in order to raise money. When and if she does decide to do that, it will be on her terms not when the press dictates it convenient to sell papers. Jackson was built for a life in the spotlight. He's prepped for it his entire professional life. He knows what he's getting into, but for people like you and the rest of the lot, it can end up being miserable."

Carol paused glancing at her watch. "No matter what you think that you're working towards," she continued. "It won't happen. End it now, *before* you fall in love with him."

Too late. I didn't utter a word. I just watched her walk toward the door.

"Oh, Jackson's plane lands at six eighteen p.m. tonight." She flipped her glossy strands over her shoulders and walked away.

CHAPTER
thirty-eight

Jackson

STEPPING OFF THE PLANE, I REALIZED THAT STEVIE never responded to any of my text messages or my last email. Sliding into the driver's seat of my Range Rover, I tried calling her again. Still no answer.

My fingers tapped along the steering wheel as I navigated through the heavy flow of traffic. A line of cars slowly drove over the bridge to Salissa Island. Friday night, and the Island was hopping with pre-New Year's celebrations.

Instead of going home first, I dropped by the hotel. Stevie's office was my first stop. The lights were off and the door was closed. I trekked back down the hallway to my office to find a bottle of Ardbeg Single Malt Scotch on my desk with a card. Using my letter opener I pried back the seal.

Jax,

I've been good all year. Bring this bottle back to your place and let's be naughty together.

Merry Christmas!

—Stevie xx

"Minx, I'm on my way," I murmured, tucking the card back into the envelope. When I left the hotel, a downpour of heavy rain unleashed over the city making visibility low. It was after eight by the time I arrived home. Stevie's car wasn't in the garage, but she could have taken the car service.

"Stevie, I'm back, *finally*," I called out, slipping my shoes off in the mudroom. With my luggage in tow, I walked up to my bedroom and deposited my suitcase into the closet. Stevie was nowhere to be found.

Now, I'm worried.

Braving the rain I sped out of my driveway and down the streets of Salissa Island heading towards Stevie's place. Halsey's "Now or Never" pumped through the speakers. The light for The Golden Dragon's awning was out and a large sign with the words: SOLD covered the front windows. The alley was dark and there was one street light. The city should have more lights along these streets.

I climbed up the wooden stairs and knocked on the warped wooden door. Nothing. Her car was not in the parking lot. That should have been my first fucking clue.

Trekking back down the stairs, I tried texting her again. There was only one other place I could think to look for Stevie before I called Archie and launched a statewide search—Quench.

I slid my Range Rover into a parking space and then jogged towards the front door. The place was packed, but I saw Stevie right away. Still in her work attire, she sat at the bar wearing a grey sweater and black pants. Her blonde hair pinned up showing off the slope of her neck. I desperately wanted to kiss that neck.

The lights from the bar glinted off her gold starburst necklace. Stevie and I were two tiny stars in a constellation in the same galaxy, connected. I stared at her for a long moment, studying her beauty. I moved through the crowd zig zagging through the throng of people to get to her, to touch her and hold her in my arms.

"Stevie."

Her blue eyes met mine instead of the usual beam they held a cold vacancy void of emotion. Distant. Far away from me.

"Oh, hello, Mister Hart."

Stevie

I sipped my beverage and stared at the text messages on my screen. Ten unanswered messages that I desperately wanted to type a response. I wanted to tell him about how much I missed him. I wanted to share the story about my gran helping Mr. Lin when he thought he was going to lose his business. Mostly, I wanted to hold him. I needed him.

Krystle cleared her throat. "Hey, isn't that your guy, looking all broody and wet in the doorway."

Following her gaze, my heart thumped out of sync. Jax stood bathed in the lights of the entryway wearing a white t-shirt that clung to his muscles and pair of dark denim jeans. He looked undeniably handsome with his hair slicked back. Was it possible that he'd become even more gorgeous than the last time I saw him? Panic etched visibly on his face and his smoldering blue eyes scanning the crowd, looking for me.

My eyes flicked to his and I steeled my spine. Jax maneuvered his way towards me, sidestepping patrons with effortless precision. My name rolled off his tongue and that familiar feeling took hold, tugging my need for him. Adrenaline coursed through my veins slamming into my heart.

I can do this, I can be cold.

Oh, hello, Mister Hart. I delivered his name in that proper way as if I we hadn't spent the last months running our tongues all over each other's bodies.

His eyes widened, looking surprised. "What's going on?"

"Well, I hear congratulations are in order." I snapped my fingers. "Krystle, I'm buying the next Governor of Montana a drink. Give the man whatever he wants, on me. Let's celebrate."

He planted his arms on either side of the barstool I was sitting on, caging me. The smell of spearmint and cold rain twirled up my nose. "How do you know about that?"

"Carol filled me in on your new journey and I am so happy for you. I hear that you are already looking for commercial space and with the newly acquired residential land it is such an exciting time."

His face fell, the hurt in his eyes evident. I took a sip of my wine, feeling the pressure from the tears that threatened and worried the dam would burst any second.

"Carol," he huffed. "Meddling again."

Krystle's gaze pinged between the two of us. "What can I get you there, soon to be Governor?"

Jax's eyes never left mine. "Scotch neat. House is fine."

Seconds felt like minutes. Krystle slid the glass in front of me and I handed it to Jax. "It seems that everything is falling into place for you, Jackson. Here's to you." His fingers grazed mine, and my heart beat at a bruising rhythm against my ribs.

"I was hoping to share the news with you in person."

I slammed back the rest of my wine—liquid courage. Abandoning all my previously rehearsed speeches I went for the jugular. "And I hope that you find the person who ticks all the boxes—the perfect first lady."

He pulled back, immediately straightening his posture. "Is that so?"

I nodded, forcing myself to meet his eyes. "It is."

The pain on his face disappeared, his expression turning to stone. "Fair enough. I'll be seeing you around the office, Miss Brockman." He swallowed his drink and then placed the glass in front of me. "Enjoy your evening."

This is goodbye.

Without another word, Jax turned and walked out. I was on my feet before I could formulate a thought.

Wait. I love you.

I stopped myself from running after him and planted my ass back onto the barstool. I loved him enough to let him go.

"You sure about this?" I heard from behind me, registering Krystle's voice. "He's one of the good ones."

No. I'm not sure.

"Yeah, he is one of the good guys. I'm just not the one he needs."

CHAPTER
thirty-nine

Stevie

I SPENT THE ENTIRE WEEKEND CURLED UP ON MY NEW SOFA watching Netflix and eating junk food. On the morning of New Year's Eve, I showered and then ventured out to the market. The island was alive with happy families trekking to the beach for a day of play. I stopped off at the coffee shop on my way back home.

"Any New Year's Eve plans," the barista asked.

"I have a hot date with Ryan Seacrest and my couch," I replied, handing her the cash.

As I left the coffee shop, my phone vibrated in my pocket. My heart stopped, Jax? It was my mom. Swallowing all my sadness, I answered the call with a smile on my face.

"Hey, Mom."

"Hi, sugar. Happy New Year's Eve."

"Same to you." I settled into the driver's seat. "How are you?"

"I'm good, just wanted to check in."

Switching to speaker phone, I balanced my phone on my thigh. "And by good, do you mean that things have gone smoothly with Dad?"

She let out a breath. "Yes, he moved out yesterday. Surprisingly, he seemed to be rather overjoyed to be leaving."

Not surprised, I rolled my eyes. "That sounds about right. Sorry, Mom."

"Nothing to be sorry about, this was years in the making. The good news is that he is not contesting the divorce and he's agreed to give me the house and fifty percent of the earnings from the business, but we'll let our lawyers hash it out."

"Well, you did help him build that business, it's only fair." I flicked my turn signal and drove down the alley. "And how are things between you and Darlene?"

"Rocky at best. Roger kicked her out and she tried to guilt me into letting her stay here."

"I hope that you slammed the door in her face."

She laughed. "No, but I did give her a piece of my mind."

"Good for you, mom."

This was the happiest I'd heard her sound in a very long time. She had a lot of new opportunities giving her a ton to look forward to in the new year. As for me, I had some decisions to make about how I wanted the next year to go. The end of our conversation was a blur and I barely remembered putting away the groceries.

Flopping back onto couch, I tore open a bag of chips. My gaze shifted to Megyn's room, which now sat completely empty. This was what totally alone felt like.

Tears dripped onto my grey cotton t-shirt. I didn't want to be like this. I was in love with Jax, but I made my choice. *It will only hurt for a little while.*

I will not be the girl who sits around and cries for the guy. No, I needed to figure out how to face him on Wednesday morning. Instead, I dried my eyes and decided no more.

I changed into my black running shorts and purple Nike tank. My feet hit the pavement, sweat poured down my back on the last mile. "Feel it Still" blasted through my earbuds charging my muscles urging me to keep going.

My mood had improved slightly, shifting from totally wrecked to overwhelmingly sad. At least, I think that was how I felt. I wondered what Jax was doing? Pain radiated in my chest thinking of him sitting alone at the hotel eating by himself.

I thought back to our conversation on Thanksgiving, which felt like a lifetime ago. *"And normally holidays are just another day for me."*

The pull to go to Jax was strong, but I reminded myself it had to be this way. Carol was right, which left a bitter taste on my tongue. By the time I made it back to my apartment my stomach was rumbling. After a quick shower, I made a large Caesar salad.

I pulled a fork from the drawer just as my front door flew open with Krystle breezing through like she owned the place. "Happy New Year," she yelled out, blowing a noise maker.

"Whoo hoo." I twirled my fork in the air.

"I'm not letting you sit around here being all sad."

I took in my surroundings. "Does it look like, I'm moping around?" I asked, gesturing around the space.

Krystle walked back onto the porch and returned carrying four shopping bags. "I've got all the makings for a non-mopey evening."

I stabbed at the chicken on my salad. "Well, at least you're not going to make me go out to a bar."

"No way in hell, it's my first New Year's Eve off in two years." She tightened her ponytail and then unpacked the bags. "I am not spending this night anywhere near a bar. My college education begins Wednesday. I'd rather not spend tomorrow hungover."

"At least we can both agree on that."

Krystle busied herself with the task of setting up a makeshift bar, cutting up lemons and limes while I rinsed out my bowl placing it into the dishwasher along with my fork. Krystle added some vodka to a mixture of cranberry and orange juice.

"I know you, Stevie, you love him."

"I do love him. My heart is splitting into a thousand fragments, and I'm trying hard to keep it from breaking completely."

She handed me the pretty pink drink. "You know, a broken heart is a heart that's been loved."

"Bartender therapy or general words of wisdom?" I swiped away the tears sliding down my cheeks.

"Maybe both," she winked, tossing back a sip. "After a few of these, we'll stuff our faces with pizza. And if you decide you want to chat about the guy, we will. It's okay."

"Okay, but I get to choose the toppings. Can't trust you and your sweet tooth, you're liable to put pineapples or banana peppers on the pizza."

CHAPTER
forty

Jackson

"**J**ackson," Carol's voice drifted through my office. "Did you sleep here?"

Sitting up from my leather couch, I pressed my palms to my eyes. "Yeah, I guess I did."

She began picking up the mess that I had made. Empty bottles lined my desk and dirty plates stacked on top of my coffee table. "You look like hell."

Ignoring her comment, I reached for the glass of whiskey in front of me, swallowing it down and relishing the burn.

"Hello, Maria, this is Carol, could you send a cleaning crew up to Mister Hart's office. Discretion is advised. Thank you."

"What time is it?" My head throbbed with a dull ache.

Her hands fell to her hips. "It's seventeen minutes past seven. Honestly, Jackson, get your ass into your shower before someone sees you like this."

Carol was the only person I allowed to speak to me as if I

wasn't the man who signed her paychecks. I guess I had allowed that from Stevie, but she no longer played a dual role in my life.

Convinced that she would show up at my house, I stayed in one place all weekend—camped in front of my television watching every college bowl game. By Sunday afternoon, I was climbing the walls. I picked up my phone at least a thousand times, my fingers hovering over her name. When I didn't hear from her on New Year's Eve, I climbed into my Range Rover vacillating between to rehearsed apologies and a grand speech as I drove to her place. As I turned down the street to her apartment I realized that showing up at her place wasn't going to get me the end result I wanted. And I wanted her. So I'd respect that she needed her space.

Housekeeping arrived, avoiding eye contact with me and tidying up the mess. My tongue was fuzzy and my mind a blur and I finally remembered why I came here. I couldn't sleep so I thought I'd work.

Carol snapped her fingers and pointed to my bathroom. "Jackson. Shower. Now."

Tossing a scowl in her direction, I shuffled towards the shower locking the door behind me. Stripping out of my clothes, I then shoved them into my laundry bag. Steam filled the room and I stepped under the hot spray hoping to scrub away a fraction of the pain—physically and emotionally.

Freshly showered and changed, I stepped into executive conference room and Ingrid handed me a cup of coffee. I froze when I saw Stevie sitting between Kenzie and Eric. Laughing at something Eric had mentioned, she didn't bat an eye in my direction. Her skin was sun-kissed and her blonde hair somehow lighter. Stevie must have spent the last four days at the beach. Irritation shot through me as I sank into my chair wondering if she spent it with another man. The room was too small, too hot. Part of me wanted to cancel this meeting and find a way to get Stevie to hear me out.

Carol kicked things off. "It's great to see everyone back from the short holiday break. With a new year and the end of the quarter come staff changes. We have a new head caddy, Jake Collins. There have been some changes made to the employee dress code. You will receive a memo regarding those changes today."

"Can we finally wear jeans?" Kenzie asked.

Stevie laughed and for a moment our eyes met. The conversation shifted and I barely registered Eric recapping the end of year figures. Her brows bent and her eyes dropped to the report in front of her. As the meeting trudged on, exhaustion crept over me. I rubbed at my temples and then sent a text to Ingrid asking if she could please bring me another cup of coffee.

Stevie cleared her throat bringing me out of my zombie like stage. "The Chicago property's interior design phase is nearly complete. I've been working very closely with Roseman Designs over the last few months and," her voice trailed off.

"You were saying about the Chicago property," Carol reminded.

"Lost my train of thought, sorry. The Azore Spa is going to be beautiful. I am working on the Valentine's installation. I should have it completed with a full report to you, Mister Hart, by next week."

I nodded. "Thank you, Miss Brockman." It was the first thing I'd said the entire meeting and it left me with an odd sense of relief. I heard Carol speaking, but my eyes stayed locked on Stevie.

"Is there anything else, Mister Hart?" Carol asked.

I felt their stares and my eyes darted around the table. "No, thank you everyone." When the room cleared out, I slumped further into the chair staring into space and drowning in my own misery.

My feet had a mind of their own and somehow I ended up going in the exact opposite direction of my office. *Leave her alone. Don't go to her.* Stopping outside Stevie's office, I watched her as she stood at her desk with her head bent over the laptop. She moved to her drafting table, opening a binder and flipping through color swatches. Whirling around, she sucked in a sharp breath. "Mister Hart, what can I do for you?"

Pain stabbed at my heart, her tone cold and formal. Her sweater fell low on her shoulder exposing the black lace of her bra reminding me of how her body looked in lingerie. I wanted to take her in my arms and feel her skin against mine.

"I want to talk to you. I want to tell you about what happened in Montana."

Her expression turned emotionless. "What is there to tell?" she asked, stiffly.

"Stevie, you have to listen to me."

"Is this about my job?"

I sighed. "No."

"Does it have anything to do with any of the projects that I am currently working on?"

I shook my head. "Can we just talk? Stevie, have dinner

with me. Give me that much, please."

She walked around to the front of her desk and turned to face me, straightening her shoulders. Needing to feel something, I reached for her, sliding my hand down her arm. When she didn't push me away I took that as a positive sign.

"I'm trying to say goodbye to you, Jax."

"Yeah, I gathered that the other night with your first lady jab. Let's put politics aside for the moment. Why don't you tell me why you are so upset?"

"I'm not upset, I just realized that you and I want different things in life and it's best if we part ways now before things become serious."

"Bullshit," I snapped. "You think what we *have* isn't already serious?"

I watched her, waiting for her to give me something of substance. Something in her eyes said something that words just couldn't. And then I reached out taking my opening. My thumb brushed down her cheek. "Tell me you miss me." One step was all I needed to close the gap between us.

She turned away, but I wrapped my arms around her waist. "Stevie, say that you miss me." Breathing deeply, she relaxed into me. A small victory, her warm body against mine somehow thawing the ice between us.

My lips ghosted over the skin beneath her ear. "Sweetheart, please."

Hearing her breath shake she twisted out of my arms and turned to face me. "You need to find someone whose past won't damage your future."

My brows pinched together. "What are you talking about?" *Knock. Knock.*

"Oh, I'm sorry, Miss Brockman, am I interrupting?" Maria

asked from the doorway.

"Not all, Mister Hart and I are finished."

"For now," I whispered. "We'll be continuing this conversation."

I turned and walked out of her office, but there was no way in hell I was letting Stevie walk out of my life.

CHAPTER
forty-one

Stevie

R ACKED WITH EMOTION, I PUSHED THROUGH MY MEETING with Maria and managed not to crumble into pieces. I told myself I could do this, I could get through the rest of the workday without falling apart but that didn't happen. My brain was mush and I couldn't focus on anything. Jax was doors down from me and I wanted to rush to him, but I needed to stay away.

Pushing Ingrid's extension, I told her I would be working from home for the rest of the afternoon. When three o'clock rolled around, I made a quick and silent exit out of the building. I'd known from a glance at the shared executive calendar that was when Jax would be off the property in a meeting across town.

I collected the mail and walked up the stairs to my apartment.

"Hey, do you live here?" A gruff voice called out. Looking

down, the voice belonged to a guy with sandy blond hair carrying a large five gallon bucket.

"Hi, yeah."

"I'm Joe, we're doing demo in the restaurant. We had to shut off the water. We'll have it turned back on by five."

"Thanks for letting me know."

With the door to my apartment locked, I slid to the floor bringing my knees to my chest. Tears carved paths down my cheeks. This was becoming a depressing habit.

I pushed myself up off the floor. Plodding towards my bedroom, I deposited my handbag onto the couch. My eyes squinted against the blinding yellow spilling across my wall. *Stupid sun.*

I fell onto my bed, exhaustion taking hold. Gripping my pillow tightly, my eyes closed.

My head was pounding. Nope the pounding wasn't my head, it was my door. Blinking, I swung my legs over the side of the bed. The time on the microwave read six forty-five.

The knocking continued. "You can stop with the noise, I'm coming."

As I unlocked the door someone pushed through sending me flying back against the island.

"Where's the money?" my father snarled.

"Not this again." Shaking the cobwebs, I straightened my back and rounded the island. "I burned the money. Now leave."

Prowling towards me, his face was etched in anger. A cold chill settled in in my spine with every step as his brown boots chewed up the space between us.

"Stop!" I eyed him, warning him not to come any closer.

"Tell me where the money is or I will tear this place apart." His hand gripped a barstool sending it crashing to the floor.

My gaze swung to my purse on the couch. I needed my phone. "Do it and I'll call the cops."

He lunged at me, his hand curling around my wrist. "Don't make me ask you again."

I twisted from his grasp. "Tell me why you need it."

"Like I said, it's none of your business," he gritted out.

"Tell me and I will think about giving it to you," I lied.

A single brow rose as his thumb scratched along his jaw. "I have a debt that I need to repay."

"Keep talking. If you're getting *my* money, you're going to have to give me more than that."

"So the old bitty did have a stash." He rolled his shoulders back. "I owe some really bad people a lot of money. If they don't get it, they'll come after me."

I laughed. "Get out. Go peddle your lies somewhere else."

He glared at me. "How do you think that your mom broke her hip?"

My heart jumped in my chest. With Mom, it was an accident. He *was* lying. I felt it. Mom would have told me if someone had hurt her. "Was that like a warning to you or something?"

He nodded stepping towards me. My back hit the refrigerator.

"And now this is me warning you. Give me that fucking money."

Holding up my hands, I shoved past him. "Listen, Dad, thanks for dropping by, there's the door. Don't let it hit you on your way out. If you were in real trouble you would have asked nicely, but it's been nothing but threats—empty threats and lies.

Get the hell out of my home."

He grabbed my biceps heaving me into the chair in the living room. "I'm not leaving without that money. So tell me where it is or you will live to regret it."

"Fuck you."

He slapped me across the face and my head snapped back. Fire blazed across my cheek and everything went fuzzy. He tramped across the hardwood towards the kitchen yanking out the drawers and dumping the contents onto the counter. Next he flung open my new cabinets, pulling out my new plates and mugs smashing them to the floor.

Rage curled my fingers into the palms of my hands. "Stop it!" I shot up out of the chair and raced into the kitchen. My father swung his hand out grabbing a fistful of my hair. My hands flew to his and I dug my nails into his skin drawing blood. Moving backwards I knocked over another barstool.

"You little *bitch!*"

I cried out in pain when he slammed my head against the pantry door. Sickness swirled inside me. Light mixed with darkness turning everything around me into a hazy shade of grey.

"Stevie!" I heard Jax calling out my name.

Jackson

"Jax, help me." Stevie's voice cracked as she fought against her father's grip. Anger coiled through my veins and my chest shook as I charged through the kitchen.

In a blur of movements, I pulled Martin off Stevie slamming him into the wall.

"You'll pay for that," he growled pushing off the wall.

Squaring up to Martin, I struck a swift blow to his stomach. On shaky legs, he landed a punch to my jaw. My hand shot out and I hurled Martin's body to the floor. Cursing, he pushed up to his knees. I kicked him in the ribs, and he groaned in pain clutching his side.

"Stay down, old man," I warned. "Don't make me fucking hit you again."

Stevie's eyes met mine. My hands framed her face, and I swept my thumb across her cheek. "Are you okay?" My heart throbbed in pain, at the sight of her reddened cheek. Cocksucker manhandled her pretty good.

"My head hurts, but I'll be okay." She winced, swallowing thickly. "What are you doing here?"

"I tried calling your cell, but my instincts told me that you'd see me if I came by," I said. "I told you that I wasn't done with our earlier conversation." I kissed her forehead, rubbing my hands up and down her arms.

She broke out into a smile and tears welled in her blue eyes. "I'm glad that you trusted your instincts."

"What do you want to do about him?" he asked, jutting his chin towards her father.

"Call the police. I don't care what they do with him."

CHAPTER
forty-two

Jackson

ONCE THE POLICE LEFT, I CLOSED THE DOOR TO STEVIE'S apartment. I lifted one of her barstools and then pushed it back in place. Busying herself in the kitchen, she made quick work of putting things back in order.

"This drawer will need replaced," she commented, setting it on top of the island. "All my beautiful mugs and plates smashed to pieces." Her hands shook as she held the pieces.

"They're just things that you can replace. *You* can't be replaced." My eyes lifted to hers and she broke. Tears cascaded down her cheeks. I wrapped my arms around, holding her tight. "What do you need?"

"You," she breathed. "Don't let go, ever."

My heart throbbed with pain. "I can do that." Quiet fell over us. I am not sure how long we stayed like that but all I knew was that it felt good. It felt so right. "I'm sorry I wasn't here for you sooner. Your dad never should have entered the state without me knowing."

She pulled back from our embrace. "It's okay, you can't keep tabs on him twenty-four seven."

"Well, actually I can, but I stopped. What was he even doing here?"

She breathed deeply. "He wanted money and I need to tell you about that recent development."

Taking a seat at the breakfast bar, Stevie launched into a story about how her Gran had helped Mr. Lin when he was about to lose his business. She asked me to advise her on what do with her money and I happily agreed. I would do anything for her, which meant that I needed to tell her about what I knew about her father.

"I need to tell you something I found out about your father."

Her soft fingers drifted over my cheek. "He hit you."

"Doesn't hurt a bit," I assured her. "According to my father, back when he was running drugs, on occasion your dad let the Miami crew stash the cars and drugs in empty wash bays for a small fee."

Her eyes widened. "Are you serious?"

"That's what my dad said. I have no idea if there's any truth in it. I'm sorry I didn't tell you sooner."

"That's very interesting, because tonight my dad said he needed the money because he owed some very bad people."

"Do you believe him?"

Stevie took a deep breath, letting it out slowly. "I don't know. He mentioned something about them hurting my mom a few months ago. Oh my God—Mom!" She hopped down off the barstool and skirted across the room grabbing her phone. "Sorry, Jax, I need to call her."

"I understand." I realized I'd left my own phone in the car. Giving Stevie some privacy, I trekked out to my car. Swiping the screen to life, I dialed Archie.

He picked up on the first ring. "What can I do for you, boss?"

"How quickly can you get someone stationed outside Danielle Brockman's place?"

"Got one of my best guys up in Athens, should be a few hours. Is there an imminent threat?"

"No, my gut tells me this is simply precaution. Martin Brockman was arrested tonight here, he attacked Stevie. Says he needs money to pay off a debt. Look into that for me would you?"

"Right away and I'll let you know when we have eyes on the house in Kennesaw."

Stevie's mom was safe and sound in Kennesaw. Apparently she had a security system installed after Martin moved out and she changed all the locks. Smart woman. I finished helping Stevie put her apartment back together and then convinced her to spend the night at my place.

We lay facing each other in my bed. Too afraid to close my eyes for fear she might not be here, I stared at her, drinking her in with every breath. Stevie's hair fanned out over the pillow and she looked like an angel in white lace.

"I'm sorry I tried to push you away," she whispered.

My fingers stroked the tears from her cheeks. "Yeah, what was that about, anyway?"

"Temporary insanity?"

"I would almost buy that, but I think there's something else."

She sighed. "I know the real reason you called things off with Trina."

I shrugged. "I told you that our relationship was meaningless."

"Not for her apparently. According to Carol she fell in love with you."

"What else did Carol say?"

"She told me that I needed to let you go and explained to me that you wouldn't choose me to protect me. A life in the spotlight would be damming for the both of us." Her bottom lip quivered, and she swallowed hard. "But, I was wrong. Maybe this moment in time is all we have, Jax. But I don't want to live with any regrets. Past, present, future. You can't control any of that and when you love someone you fight for them."

A slow smile spread across my face. "You love me?"

Her blue eyes went wide with fear, and her fingers flew to her lips.

My fingers teased under the thin strap of her lace tank. "You love me," I whispered.

Stevie searched my face, worry still apparent. *"Fuck me. Shit."*

"I love you like crazy," I breathed out. "I've never had what I have with you, with anyone else. I love you."

"Jackson."

"I'd rather face a firing squad than live without you." My fingers drifted along her ribcage, and I brushed my lips to hers. "And I'll gladly take you up on your offer, but we need to have a discussion."

"Are you moving to Montana? Are you selling the hotel?"

she rushed out.

"Okay, first I need you to breathe. I know at Thanksgiving, I blindsided you with a lot, including my political aspirations. Honestly, I never dreamed that I'd be considering it so soon. I thought I'd at least be thirty-five, when the time came to make a decision. Those few days in Montana gave me a lot of time to think. I know what I want. I'm not selling Hart Hotels, it's mine and I will run things daily until it becomes something that I can't do."

"Carol painted a very vivid picture about what the press might dig up about my past. My life."

I'm going to have to deal with Carol. Meddling in my personal life and screwing with Stevie's emotions was not okay. Part of me wanted to fire her on the spot. The other part of me didn't care what Carol's motives were now that I had Stevie back—for good.

"Now, my dad is in jail. It's embarrassing."

"And my brother is in prison," I reminded.

"Yeah, but no one knows that he's your brother."

"If the press looks hard enough they'll find out. There was a student journalist at the FIU gala who pressed me about my last name and my past. She's probably close to cracking the case."

"But still, I can't possibly do the job of governor's girlfriend," she protested.

I pressed my finger to her lips. "Let me win the race first and then we can talk about your role. And if I can point out, the way you handled yourself at FIU when I gave my speech, in my book that is definitely 'first girlfriend' material."

"That was different. Are you willing, really willing to take that chance?"

"I am. I'll take a thousand chances on you. Say you'll take a chance on me."

She snaked her arms around my neck. "Okay, I'm in. I'll stuff envelopes and hand out buttons. I'm going to have to trade in my bikinis for winter coats."

"Keep the bikinis," I told her. "Our house will have an indoor pool."

"Our house?"

"Yeah." I tilted my mouth to hers. "Move in with me." I pinned her beneath me, layering my lips to hers. "Say yes, Stevie."

"Yes, I'll move in with you."

"Yes." I repeated.

She kissed me slowly, nodding. "Here's to another new beginning."

CHAPTER
forty-three

Stevie

Summer

I WAS CERTAIN THAT THE FATES ABOVE WERE HAVING A GOOD LAUGH. It had to be the hottest day on record. Lucky for all of us, the breeze coming off Lake Michigan offered some relief. The sun shone bright in a cloudless sky drenching every inch of Masson's Rooftop Bar at the Hart Hotels and Spa.

I stood sipping my champagne admiring the design of the outdoor seating area. It was a proud moment, I watched as the staff from *Chicago Magazine* photographed the design concept that I crafted right down to the candle holders and topiary trees.

I caught Jackson's stare from across the terrace. Wearing an impeccably tailored, ink black suit in only a way that he could, his blue eyes dazzled as he spoke—every powerful inch of him was captivating. Jackson Hart, so perfect. So handsome. So sexy and all mine. Once the hoopla ended, I planned to take him up to our suite and christen every flat surface and then some.

"Your dress is a little short, Miss Brockman," Carol interrupted my scandalous thoughts.

"Dressed like nun per usual, I see, Carol," I chided taking in her beautiful navy, Dior jumpsuit. "Or do you call this Olsen twin chic?"

She bumped my arm with hers. "Well, some of us need to leave something to the imagination for our suitors."

As it turned out, Carol actually liked me. All her bitchiness was her way of testing me. On some level, I was the Andy Sachs to her Miranda Priestly. Over the last months, we'd become quite good friends.

February

On a Tuesday afternoon, I find myself sitting in Jax's office along with Carol. Carol is sitting on the edge of the couch looking impatient as shit. I have a million things to do and this impromptu meeting has curiosity clawing at every inch of my brain.

Jax steps inside closing the door behind him. "Sorry I'm late. I appreciate you both meeting me on short notice." Unbuttoning his jacket, he takes a seat across from us. "I've called you both in my office today because, Carol, I'd like to transfer some of your responsibilities to Stevie."

"You cannot be serious." Carol narrows her gaze and stands. "I'm being demoted so that you can give your girlfriend more responsibility?"

"Great here we go," I say tossing a glare at Carol.

Carol's head snaps in my direction. "I started working for this company well before this hotel even opened." She shifts towards Jax. "I've been your right hand and your left hand, Jackson, and now you expect me to step aside just because your girlfriend's temporary position will be up in a few months?"

"Carol, hold on a moment," he says, waving a hand through the air.

Keeping her focus on Jax, she points to me. "Miss Brockman is completely underqualified and this is extremely unprofessional."

Eyes wide, I stood in a rush. "Now wait a minute. We don't know what responsibilities Jax has in mind."

She cuts me a sharp glare. "Oh please, like I'm to believe the two of you didn't already discuss this during pillow talk."

"Maybe they're the duties that you hate doing," I countered.

Carol scowls at me. "I don't dislike any part of my job, probably because I earned it by standing upright."

Anger funnels through my veins. "Wow, really? Are you that threatened by me? No, you just like messing with people's personal lives. I'm sick of you treating me like I'm an incompetent twit. I am very good at what I do, and this 'created job' is perfect for me. You and I both know it—so I suggest you suck it up, Miss Edgerton, and realize that I am not your competition, but I am here to stay."

Jax clears his throat. "Are the two of you finished?"

Crap. My heart jumps in my throat at the sound of Jax's voice. Slowly I turn to face him. "I'm finished if she is," I nod towards, Carol.

Carol crosses her arms. "Yes, I'm finished."

"Good, now sit back down and listen to what I have to say."- Jax leans forward. "Carol, I'd like you to shadow me for the next few months. Stevie and Beth will be splitting your responsibilities. I have big plans for Hart Hotels and you will be a key player. Furthermore, Stevie is right—she is here to stay. And Carol, I don't know why you saw fit to meddle in our relationship, but it ends now. You will treat each other with respect, and if I so much as hear a snide comment or a degrading remark, I'll fire you on the spot. Do we have an understanding?"

Nodding, my response comes out in a full boom. "Yes."

"Yes, Jackson, and thank you for the opportunity," Carol says, clasping her hands in her lap. "May I say something?"

Jax nods and leans back into the chair.

"It was wrong to meddle, and for that I am sorry." Carol shifts to look at me. "However, I am not sorry that I pressed you, Stevie. You show great promise as a woman in business, but as a woman in the spotlight, I had my doubts. I didn't want people to assume you only earned your position because you were the boss's girlfriend."

My brows crinkle. "Yet you see fit to remind me of that every chance you get."

Her lips twist into a small smile. "And the more you heard it, it pissed you off. You never went off on me, well, until today, but I deserved it. You always show grace and poise. Never let them see you sweat." She pushes to her feet and smooths her sleek ponytail.

"Wait, what?" I ask and stand. "This was all a lesson?"

Carol places both hands on my shoulders. "Yes, and you pass with flying colors."

I look at Jax who shakes his head and closes his eyes. She brushes past me and walks to the door.

"Carol, you told me to break up with Jax. I could have let him go forever."

"But you didn't," she shot back. "Jackson, let me know when you'd like to start this transition. Stevie, let's have cocktails tonight after work. We'll discuss everything."

She walks out the door and I am again left stunned. "What just happened?"

Jax stands. "I think you're having drinks with Carol. You two are going to be besties."

I cut him a sideways glance. "Besties, you're funny."

I turned to face her. "Are you excited about moving to Chicago?"

"Hell yes," she squeaked. "I am ready for the change of seasons."

"Cheers to that," I replied, clicking my glass to hers. "Okay now scoot, Madam President, you have a speech to deliver."

Those big plans that Jax mentioned to Carol and me was the transition of the corporate offices for Hart Hotels from Salissa Island to Chicago. Nearly everyone on the executive team relocated to this location. Those that couldn't leave were offered a different position or a substantial severance check. Carol was promoted, and rightly so. Aside from Jax, she knew the day to day operations of Hart Hotels better than anyone. Jax never had to worry or micro-manage with her in charge, he was solely focused on announcing his candidacy. Environmental issues, education, and jobs were his top platform agendas.

I watched as Carol took her place at the front of the crowd. Several eyes swung in my direction when my phone buzzed. I thought I had turned off the ringer. Carol tossed me a scowl. Some things never change.

"Sorry," I whispered and urged the crowd to turn around.

It was my mom. She'd sent a photo—smiling with fruity cocktail in hand and having the time of her life on cruise for singles in the Caribbean. It was a birthday gift from me and Jax.

For my own birthday, Jax surprised me with a trip to Bermuda. We stayed at the Hamilton Princess Hotel. We explored caves and coves looking for buried treasures on the beaches of sea glass. And the pink sands matched the exterior of our hotel. It was just the escape we needed once the news of our relationship became public knowledge.

It was surreal. I never thought my love life would be splashed all over the internet. Of course, there were stirrings that I'd only been promoted because I was the boss's girlfriend, but Jax shut the gossip down. Even, Carol came to my defense. Women *should* have each other's backs.

There was no defending my father's actions for what he did to me and Jax. He spent three months in jail for assault and had pay a thousand dollar fine. He returned to Kennesaw and according to Mom, he spent his days at the car wash and his nights alone drinking at whatever watering hole didn't cut him off before nine.

As for James Dennison, his wife sent a letter to Jax informing him that he passed away at the end of February. After hearing the news, Jax went to his study and I heard the sound of Billy Joel piping through the speakers. At some point he managed to make it to bed. He's never spoken to me about what happened and I've never asked. When he wanted to talk to me about it he would.

"You are distracting the hell out of me in this sexy-ass dress," Jax whispered standing beside me. "Your legs look fantastic."

"They'll look even better over your shoulders."

His hand landed on the small of my back. "I think we

need to leave this party. *Now.*"

"So this is where the party is," said a deep voice from behind us.

My eyes lifted to Matthew Barber standing to my right wearing a navy suit. "Holy shit." I was standing inches from a movie star.

"Matt, thanks for coming out," Jax said, shaking his hand.

"Sure thing, man," Matthew said, directing his gaze towards me. "And who is this pretty lady?"

Jackson wrapped his arm around my shoulder. "Matt, I'd like you to meet Stevie Brockman."

"Stevie Brockman, good to meet you," he said in his distinct Texas drawl extending his hand to mine.

I nodded, shaking his hand. "Yeah, you too."

I don't really remember what happened next, but somehow Matthew Barber floated up to the front of the crowd. I heard Jax's name on repeat like a record.

"Ladies and gentlemen, not only would I like to congratulate my friend, Jackson Hart, on this magnificent grand-opening, but I'd officially like to throw my endorsement to him for Governor of Montana."

Cheers erupted and confetti rained down, floating around us like snow and covering everything in blue and silver. Congratulations and best wishes stirred from the crowd as Jax shook hands and smiled for the cameras.

"Mister Hart, could you stand right here," the photographer instructed, before disappearing behind the lens. "Yes. Perfect. This one is going on the cover."

"Tours of the hotel will begin in thirty minutes," Carol announced.

As dusk faded into evening, I found myself walking down

the hallway of the mezzanine level. This was my favorite part of the property. Beautiful paintings from local artists hung on the walls. I stood in front of a large window overlooking the city.

"I thought I'd find you here." Jax said, just above a whisper as he wrapped his arms around me.

My body shook with a little laugh as I twined my arms around his torso. "Couldn't have been that hard, I think I've mentioned this is my favorite spot like a hundred times."

I soaked up the sensation of his hard body pressed to mine.

"I'll always find you," he murmured, kissing the soft spot under my ear.

"You promise?"

"Always."

My stomach growled and Jax tipped my chin forcing me to look up at him. "Did you eat anything tonight?"

"I had a little bit of bread and cheese," I admitted.

Saying nothing, he took my hand and walked me down the stairs passing through the lobby. The sound of my heels clacking against the marble echoed all around us.

Jax pushed through the glass doors. "Where do you want to eat?" He turned to face me, smiling at me with more joy than I knew what to do with in that moment.

"Why are you looking at me like that?"

"Because *I* can." He laid his hands gently on my jaw and he kissed me. The noise of the city pumped with electricity around us. I was lost to all of it but him. "I'm so in love with every little thing about you."

"I love you, Jackson Hart." My heart skipped in my ribs as our lips collided once more.

"Now, about dinner, where do you want to go? I'll take you anywhere you want."

"Anywhere, hmmm. How about pizza in bed?" I mused, smiling against his lips.

He smiled at me with that slow heart-stopping smile. "Anything the lady wants, she gets."

epilogue

Stevie

Two Years Later—Election Night

"**W**ELL, WE HAVE ALL THE MAKINGS FOR A HELL OF A party," Jax remarked, turning his gaze towards me. He wore his ink-black tuxedo as if he'd been born in designer threads. His broad shoulders and narrow hips filled every inch of the tailored lines to perfection.

"Friends, family, cake, champagne, even a band." I nodded towards the guys from Rebel Desire on stage rocking out to "New York Minute" as they warmed up the crowd. A fitting song since our whole lives changed in the blink of an eye.

"So what do you say? Marry me tonight?" he asked, rubbing the pad of his thumb over the three carat, cushion cut diamond on my left hand. My pulse raced, tripping in my chest skipping up my throat. The room filled with people faded away, the candles vanished, and the music ceased to exist. My eyes darted to our union, my hand in his as I took in the rose-gold setting.

I let out a shaky breath. "Your ring is at the jeweler, I don't have it with me."

Jax's hands framed my face. "Sweetheart, do you trust me?" His blue eyes smoldered with promise. It was hard not to smile.

I looked up at him and the word rolled off my tongue with ease, like taking a breath. "Yes."

"Give me thirty minutes and I will make this the most amazing night to remember—at least one that we want to remember."

"So this is your way of masking what happened here tonight?"

Sharpening his gaze on me, a shiver twirled up my spine. "No, not at all. In life you take the bad with the good. When we met you were having a bad day and I was having a great day—and then there you were and my day, my life somehow became more amazing that day. So marry me, right here, and right now, and let's make this day one to remember."

"Well, with an offer like that how can I say, no?"

Around midnight, we arrived home, Jax insisted on carrying me up to our bedroom. I didn't mind though my feet were aching from the long day and then there was the dancing. I placed my sparkling Louboutin heels onto the rack in our walk-in closet. "That was bad."

"So bad," Jax said, loosening his white tie.

"Epic fail."

"Will I even be able to show my face around town?"

I laughed. "I still can't believe that you lost the election. I mean, those early polling numbers, how could it have ended in a landslide?"

Jax shrugged out of his jacket. "The biggest political upset in Montana's history and I was on the losing side."

"On the bright side, you're probably going to be a *Jeopardy* answer one day."

"That's your silver lining," he cocked his head in my direction.

"Nope," I smiled, dropping my eyes to the sparkling wedding band on my left hand. "Becoming your wife tonight is definitely the silver-lining."

"Guess that I'm not such a loser after all."

"I think we're both winners tonight," I answered, rolling up to my tip toes and fusing my lips to his.

"Definitely a checkmark in the win column."

About a year ago, Jax had asked me for my travel bucket list. He promised to take me around the world. In between touring factories, wildlife preserves, and schools along the campaign trail, there wasn't a weekend that went unplanned. Jax proposed while we were on a weekend getaway in Napa Valley. I don't even know how I got so lucky. With my answer, there was no hesitation, just like our first kiss.

All my firsts were with him. The first time I stepped foot on the cobblestone streets of Rome. The first time I laid my eyes on the on the turquoise waters and pristine pale sand of the Ionian Islands. He even made good on his promise and took me to New Haven. Our life was a series of adventures and now we were taking the biggest journey of our life—husband and wife.

My husband's fingers tugged the zipper at the back of my ivory dress. "Do I really need to take this dress off so soon? It's beautiful, so beautiful it should hang in a museum." My hands smoothed down the bodice.

"You can leave it on. I'll fuck you where you stand, because we *are* sealing the deal on this marriage tonight, Missus Hart."

Mrs. Hart. I loved the sound of that. Jackson pressed his mouth against mine. Kissing me hard and reckless, my dress fell to the floor pooling at my feet. He hoisted me up and my legs locked around his waist.

"I'll look into having that dress preserved in a museum for you."

Jax set me onto the edge of the bed and my fingers brushed against the buttons of his dress shirt. "What do you want to do now that you're not moving into the governor's office?"

"Right now, I want you to take off your bra." He unbuckled his belt and tossed it aside. "What do you want to do?"

"Besides you right now," I teased, running my hands along the muscles of his stomach. "There's that shipwreck in Turks and Caicos I want to visit . . . and the museum."

"Panties need to go to, sweetheart," he ordered, his blue eyes sparkling.

"We can take a jet ski out to Dellis Cay, that tiny private island," I pointed out, discarding the fabric to the floor. "I hear it's a bit spooky, but we can explore the hotels that were abandoned mid-construction during the 2008 financial crisis."

Naked, my gorgeous husband climbed onto the bed and settled between my legs. "Turks and Caicos, huh?" A smirk tugged at the corners of his mouth.

"Mmmm," I moaned, at the feel of his erection sliding against me. I loved him so much. I touched Jax everywhere I could reach.

He rolled his hips, and his hands palmed my ass. "Tell me you love me."

"I love you, Mister Hart," I said, closing my eyes and relishing the feel of him moving inside me.

Wins. Losses. Good times. Bad times. No matter the situation. The two of us were family now and forever. *Family.* I realized that Jax and I hadn't really touched on the subject.

"Do you want kids, Jax?"

Stilling his hips, his eyes snapped up to look at me. "I'd like to have you all to myself for a little while longer, but yes, if it's with you, I definitely want them. Do you?"

A thousand emotions flickered inside me feeling like the luckiest woman in the world. "Yes, I want that too."

He searched my face looking at me with a lazy smile. "I want you to have everything you need in life, Stevie. Everything."

"Well, right now, I need an orgasm, and make it a good one."

He laughed, his lips brushing over mine. "Yes, that is something I can definitely give you right now." His lips pressed to my throat and pumped into me with exquisite strokes, pushing me closer to the edge.

I would gladly go over the edge with Jax every day. With him I was never afraid to fall. I would never be afraid to take risks, because even if I didn't need him to catch me—he would always spot me.

"When do you want to go to Turks and Caicos?"

"The sooner the better," I moaned. "It's so cold up here."

My nose, my toes, and my lips everything tingled. All of my body trembling as the epic spasms jolted through me.

He came with a quiet roar, his fingers digging into my skin. "How was that orgasm?"

"It was fine," I teased.

Jax's brow furrowed. "Fine," he murmured. "We can do

better than fine."

"I don't know, hubby. Maybe this is your best. You're getting up there in your years. Should we be thinking about getting you some medical help?"

He shook his head. "Remember what happens when you doubt my abilities?"

"I'm counting on you to prove me wrong."

"You're a wicked woman, Stevie Hart."

I looked up at him, my lips curling into a small smile. "Yes, I am."

THE END

books by
CHRISTY PASTORE

The Scripted Series
unScripted
Perfectly Scripted

The Harbour Series
Bound to Me
Healed by You
Return to Us

Stand Alone Titles
Fifteen Weekends
Wicked Gentleman

Be sure to sign up for my newsletter at
christypastore-author.com for the latest news on
releases, sales, and other updates.

acknowledgements

Jackson and Stevie—these two, I cannot believe I started plotting this book two summers ago on the way to an author signing. As I started writing these characters and this story it became something deeper than I originally anticipated. I know that you have many choices when it comes to your one-click decisions. From the bottom of my heart, I cannot thank you enough for picking up Wicked Gentleman.

None of this is possible without my husband, Kevin. Thank you for reading through scenes when I ask for an opinion and for spending an entire Saturday afternoon with me talking over that one tricky plot line.

Missy Borucki, thank you for your editing skills, your guidance on everything from content to details in sentence structure, but mostly your time. I appreciate you more than you know.

Rach & Fabi, we're still on this journey together. Can you believe all that we have survived? Thank you both for your friendship and never-ending support. No one hustles harder than the two of you—and you both do it with such grace. Grateful to have you both in my life, your friendship means the world to me. #SoapyThighs4Life #CrazySauceDeflectors

"Morning, ho bag!" Cary Motha-F*ckin Hart, thank you for your constant stream of motivation and for helping me deconstruct and then reconstruct this storyline. Also, thank goodness for "Dynasty," and in the words of Fallon . . . "Never get between a Carrington and her Cabernet!"

Linda Russell, thank you for promoting Wicked Gentleman as if it were your own book baby. I adore you and I love our chats. I appreciate your time and endless passion for this industry.

Christina, you are absolute magic. Whenever I need you, you are there for me, I cannot thank you enough.

To the book community, for the bloggers, promo companies, authors, and readers who've shared my books, embraced these characters, and introduced them to new readers. So I raise a glass of wine to all of you, many thanks and believe me when I say that your hard work does not go unnoticed.

Whiskey, you get me. Thank you.

Please connect with me in my private reading group, Christy's Classy Lit Chicks, where we chat about everything from pop culture to books and everything in between. Casual Conversation for the #ClassyAF Reader. Don't let FOMO happen to you.

about the author

Christy Pastore lives in the Midwest with her husband, their loveable springer spaniel, Bailey, and their crazy cool cat, Boomer. She has a Bachelor's Degree in Textiles, Apparel and Merchandising and Marketing. Writing has always been a part of her life. Her first writing gig was for a celebrity entertainment website. Later she went on to create her own blogazine and media company combining her love of writing with fashion and marketing.

When's she not writing flirty and dirty books or updating her celebrity fashion blog, she loves shopping online, binge watching her favorite shows and daydreaming.

She believes books, especially love stories are an escape from the real world.

A few of Christy's favorite things:

Bold Heroine's – Swoony Hero's with a Naughty Side—Guilty Pleasure Reads and TV Shows – Designer Handbags – Men In Suits – Black and White Photos—Sexy Accents—Snow—Pinterest – Twitter – Instagram—Wine—Champagne—Soy Latte's – Gummi Bears—Gourmet Grilled Cheese Sandwiches – Pickles—Popcorn—Sparkling Water—Eye Cream—Pedicures—Traveling—80's Music—Musicals—Movie Trailers – Celebrity Red Carpet Interviews – Award Shows – Making Lists.

Please connect with me on:

www.christypastore-author.com

Facebook: www.facebook.com/ChristyPastoreAuthor

Twitter: twitter.com/christypastore

CPSIA information can be obtained
at www.ICGtesting.com
Printed in the USA
LVHW041514131121
703241LV00023B/335